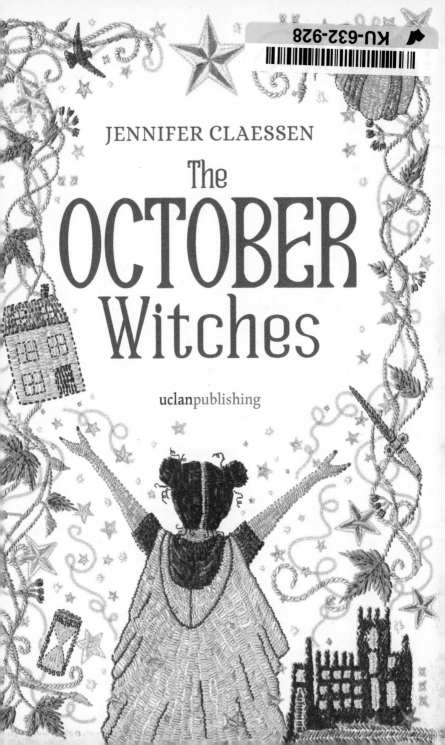

JENNIFER CLAESSEN

The
OCTOBER
Witches

uclanpublishing

The October Witches is a uclanpublishing book

First published in Great Britain in 2022 by
uclanpublishing
University of Central Lancashire
Preston, PR1 2HE, UK

First published in the UK 2022

Text copyright © Jennifer Claessen 2022
Cover artwork © Heidi Olivia Cannon 2022

978-1-912979-90-5

1 3 5 7 9 10 8 6 4 2

Set in 11.5/18pt Kingfisher by Amy Cooper

A CIP catalogue record for this book is available from the British Library.

Printed and bound in Great Britain by Clays Ltd, Elcograf S.p.A.

For Matilde Claessen,
without whom I would not
have been awake at 4.30 a.m.,
thinking about magic

CHAPTER 1

It is beginning. Or it will do as soon as I can persuade Mirabelle to get up.

She's face-planted into her bed so I'm talking to the back of her head, which is wedged deep in her pillow.

'They sent me to come and get you, you know that, right? Aunt Connie is counting every second.'

'Twenty-nine minutes!' Aunt Connie shouts up the stairs, as if to prove my point.

I glance out the window between our two beds. The moon is high and it's well past my bedtime.

'And the aunts are excited – they think it could be my year.'

My cousin, Mirabelle, groans into her pillow. 'You're too young, Clem. It's not your year,' she says in a muffled voice.

In twenty-nine minutes – at midnight – September will end, October will begin, and, if Aunt Connie's right, magic will descend on me for the first time. She's convinced this is the year.

I've seen twelve Octobers now and never fully been a part of it. So now, even though I don't live for October like my family do, a small nervous tingly thrill is hovering at the base of my spine.

I sit at the edge of my bed and kick my feet. Mirabelle and I have shared a room for as long as I can remember. And while we've both grown, the room has not. There's just about enough space for our two beds, and that's it. So, my side of our bedroom is covered in art and bits taped up on the wall, but Mirabelle's wall is blank. My clothes are half on the floor, half in a mound at the end of my bed, and Mirabelle's are neatly folded away underneath hers.

'Twenty-eight minutes!' Aunt Connie hollers up the stairs. 'Chop, chop, young hags!'

'Cannot be late! Stars don't wait!' another voice adds. That's Aunt Prudie. Our family is a lot sometimes.

Finally, Mirabelle rolls over in her bed. She's already frowning, but when she catches sight of me, it turns into a full-on glower.

I reach up and pat my hair self-consciously. I've spent most of the evening fiddling with hair ties and pins to get my hair up into two buns on either side of my head, like Mirabelle, but I couldn't manage to colour it.

Mirabelle has purple streaks, which she always wraps into double top-knots.

Mirabelle is almost fourteen now, so she thinks she's loads older than me, even though it's not actually quite a year's difference. Her First October was last year and, since then, she doesn't listen to anyone, especially me. She doesn't seem to have time for me anymore.

I tell myself that things might, just might, be different if I get my magic this year.

'Urgh,' Mirabelle says, and sits up to pull out her own buns, shaking her big curls loose. She'd almost rather choke on her own hair than share the same style with me. Mirabelle tosses her curls forward so that they cover as much of her face as possible, then her frown moves from my hair to my clothes.

'You're not going in those, are you?' she says, disgusted.

I look down at my pyjamas. They have a pattern of dancing penguins on them. 'Why not?'

Mirabelle pauses for a moment, clearly keeping everything she might say on a leash. Then she sighs and says, 'You'll get cold. Come on then, let's get this over with.'

I'm leading us down the stairs when there's a knock at the door. I hop the bottom step and look down the corridor where my family are all lined up, ready to go; Aunt Connie at the front, clutching her egg-timer.

'Twenty-five minutes!' she announces.

I glance back at the door. 'But Aunt Connie, who is that?'

'None of humankind!' Aunt Prudie howls, already waving a long, bony finger about.

In October, we witches are hidden deep under layers of magic that muffle us to ordinary humans.

'Maybe we shouldn't answer it, love—' my mum says but it's too late, I've already swung the door open.

'Delivery for you,' the postman says, with a grin.

'Psssht!' Aunt Prudie hisses at the postman, swatting the air as if he was a stray cat roaming around.

'Aunt Prudie!' I exclaim, then whisper over my shoulder, 'You can't hiss at him! It's just the post.' Nevertheless, I frown at the postman. I don't know why anything is being delivered this late.

'We're late!' Aunt Connie says, peeking around me, her white hair puffy with outrage. 'We're meant to be there in . . . twenty-two minutes!'

Aunt Flissie, right at the back, doesn't say anything, she just adjusts the straps on her huge backpack.

'Um, sorry, it can't be for us,' I tell the postman.

We don't really get much delivered, as four out of the six people in the house never use the internet and the other two of us don't have our own bank cards.

'Sorry about that,' the postman says. 'Must be for next door. Can you sign for it anyway?'

'Yeah,' I say, though I can't see the neighbours getting their parcel 'til at least November.

The postman, who has been delivering our mail for as long as I can remember, peers around me down the corridor, where my whole family is fidgeting, impatient to leave.

'Family ... party?' he asks.

Aunt Prudie glowers from behind Aunt Connie. Aunt Prudie is, as always, in her green gardening overalls and Aunt Connie is in her favourite apron, *still* clutching the egg timer.

'Yeah, something like that,' I say. 'Where do I sign?'

'Right there, ta.' The postman holds out a small digital tablet for me to scrawl my initials on to.

I scrawl a quick "CM" with my index finger and pull away instantly. No tingles, no sparks – yet.

'Thank you! Enjoy your . . . party!' He hands me the parcel: a long rectangle.

'Get rid of him!' Aunt Connie hisses down the

corridor behind me but, luckily, the postman has already turned to go. At the garden gate, he lifts his hand as if to wave, but then drops it instead and shakes his head.

I hurriedly prop the parcel in the corner by the door with all the other junk and clutter my family accumulate and follow them out of the house.

If Aunt Connie could, she would round us all up like ducklings and have us march in a line. She tries to do a head count but Mirabelle has slunk right to the back and Aunt Flissie has marched on ahead.

Mirabelle clicks the door shut, lingering by the house for just one more moment, then joins us in the street.

Our quick procession into the night is quiet, both by my family and the city's standards. We silently make our way past row after row of terraced houses. Even Aunt Connie doesn't say anything, she's so tense with focusing on what is about to happen. As always, the preparations for October started months ago, so my aunts are, by now, extremely highly strung and manic with nervous energy. Even my mum stares into the darkness intensely, squeezing my hand.

As the tightly packed houses of the city streets start to open up and the low buzz of traffic fades, Mum sniffs, taking in the air. Then Prudie and Connie sniff. My aunt Flissie and cousin Mirabelle do not sniff.

I can't smell it yet, but magic must be in the air.

'Soon! The autumn gift! The lawless month! Freedom!' Aunt Prudie shouts, hobbling forward more quickly. Even in her usual half-sentences, she can be a bit of a poet when the mood takes her.

As we pass through the gates into the deeper dark of the park, I join in with the sniffing. The night air is damp, earthy, like fallen leaves.

The park is silent and gloomy, but in its quiet stillness and under the faint moonlight, I spy a cluster of figures moving.

'Mum, the Morgans are already here!' I whisper.

'The Morgans are already here,' she passes back.

I hear Aunt Connie take up the message. 'Prudie, Flissie, the Morgans are here!'

'Typical!' Aunt Prudie shouts, but she doesn't mean it. For tonight at least, the feud between our two families is on pause.

Our family tree is one of those old, knobbly ones with two main branches that grow in completely different directions and only a few fresh, green shoots. The branches are the Morgans and the Merlyns – us.

My aunts, Prudence and Constance, are our elders. They are definitely not always prudent or constant, though. And they're not sure who's actually oldest. If it's the one with the whitest hair, then it's Constance, and if it's the one with the most wrinkles, it's Prudence. They're both selectively deaf and shout most of the time.

Then there's Aunt Felicity, my cousin Mirabelle's mum, who always takes the October opportunity to go as far away from us all as she can. There's something bothering my Aunt Flissie which we don't talk about, but in October she can't get far enough away from the rest of us. Every year, my aunts try to keep her at home, but they never can.

And then there's my mum: Patience. She lives up to her name most days. We all live together in our definitely too-small, nondescript terraced house and for eleven months of every year, my aunts are miserable; and for one month, they are mad. I don't know how my mum puts up with it, but I do know that witch sisters are no ordinary sisters. My aunts call her Pattie, and I call her Mum.

Aunt Temmie – Temperance Merlyn – is the one I'm kind of named after. She would have made up the fifth and final point of the Merlyn witches' star. But Temmie died one October and we don't talk about that either.

There is nothing *spooky* or *ooky* about my aunts but if you wanted to use the word *kooky*, you probably could.

The Morgans are the other branch of the family. At best, they're plain rude. At worst, super creepy. There are more of them than us – thirteen, to be precise, which Aunt Connie is secretly very jealous of. I don't know much about the Morgans, but my aunts decidedly dislike them. Mum of course manages to be polite to them; Aunt Prudie, not so much.

We set off across the grass towards the Morgans, Aunt Prudie stomping determinedly forward in her big gardening boots.

'Merlyns. The stars don't wait!' A great voice booms across the dark lawns of the park to us.

'I know, I know, three minutes!' mutters Aunt Connie then she raises her voice to reply. 'Morgans, welcome.' Our two families never say hello to each other like normal people.

The Morgans all share matching expressions of distaste as we approach. They don't want to be here, and they definitely don't want to be here with us. I get the shiver I always get when I see the Morgans. They're waiting, stone-still, but somehow obviously impatient.

'Hm,' the owner of the voice says, out of the dark. 'Your little park will suffice. Though of course we keep and protect the place where greater power resides.'

The October magic only comes when we're all together, so the Morgan family and the Merlyn family have to tolerate each other for just one night. The two covens must meet on neutral ground. Centuries ago, they used to meet on clifftops, or out on the moors or at midnight under bridges and that kind of thing. Now we meet in this 'little park' because we Merlyns are not welcome at theirs.

'You hope for a First October?' the voice remarks. It means me.

Mum had her First October when she was eleven. Aunt Prudie had hers when she was nine. It comes to every witch at the time which is right for them, apparently. Aunt Connie has wanted me to join the circle for the last couple of years, but it's like the magic has been staying away on purpose, just to frustrate her.

I attend this midnight gathering every year but the Morgans have never even noticed me before, just another young hag, lurking behind her coven elders. Aunt Connie pushes me forward a bit. I now see all thirteen Morgans. They are all a lot taller than us.

The shortest of them, still a head taller than me, is a girl about my age who has her mouth open as if she is about to speak to the witch who is obviously their leader. I look up at the witch with the booming voice.

'Hello,' I say. 'Um, Ms ... Morgan?'

The witch is silent for a moment, inspecting me from her great height with a slight sneer and cold eyes. She looks like someone who'd accept 'Your Majesty' as a title. She has an impossibly straight back, and is standing like a headmistress. Like most of her coven, she has thin, twitchy lips and a high forehead with floating, unimpressed eyebrows. She is still staring into my eyes with laser focus. Under her scrutiny, I am suddenly nervous.

'You may call me Aunt Morgan,' she says eventually. Her face is dark with disdain.

Aunt Connie elbows me and I dutifully reply, 'I hope it will be my great honour to join the coven officially.'

Aunt Connie checks her egg-timer, squints up at the stars and nods. It is time for the two branches of our family to come together.

As if following an invisible order, the Morgans begin to approach us.

The group of witches shifts, and all of us – Merlyns

and Morgans – stick in an arm as if we're going to stack our hands like a team about to enter a competitive sport. In front of me, Mirabelle puts in her arm with a loud sigh which makes Aunt Morgan raise her disdainful eyebrows even higher. Behind me, Mum nudges me so that my hand, with hers, meets all the others.

'Sorry,' I murmur as I stub someone else's fingers with my own. Someone swats my hand away. I glance around the circle, looking for whoever has tried to push me out of it.

The Morgan girl who was going to interrupt earlier, taller but no older than me, raises her eyebrows then smugly lays her hand right on top of everyone else's. She has two stubby braids with a little halo of flyaway hairs and an extremely condescending nose. I'm still staring at her as she smirks at me then tilts her chin upwards and starts to watch the sky, earnestly.

The circle tightens. There's a moment of silence, then, as one, all our hands are hoisted into the air.

I look up. Above us, the trees are already a bit skeletal, their fingery branches black against the dark sky. At this time of year, when the leaves come down, something else does too . . . magic.

'The stars know,' Aunt Morgan says.

'The stars know,' everyone echoes back to her and for the first time, I sense it too. Then I see it.

'They're coming!' I say, and Mum shushes me. 'Oh my . . . stars!' I breathe.

There are actual stars, seemingly coming straight from the dark sky, shrinking smaller and smaller as they descend in a funnel of light towards where our outstretched hands meet.

The magic comes as streaming light. I feel a prickle I've never felt before. Tiny beads of light are beginning to descend down our arms and cluster around us. It's like being walked on by hundreds of gentle, wispy feet. I shift as if to brush them off but, behind me, Mum puts a gentle hand on my shoulder.

The magic settles like confetti across the heads and shoulders of the gathered witches. It sparkles strange, glittery dandruff onto each of us. Across the circle from me, partly visible behind the pyramid of arms, Aunt Morgan is glowing all over. The lights are the iron filings and she is the magnet. The magic is finding its home in her; it appears to cluster most densely in her head and her heart. The lights look like they're winking out but really, they're sinking into her, slowly.

Then I look down at myself. My chest is lit up, tiny stars sparking and then flaring and vanishing . . . inside me.

I don't know how long we stand there, absorbing the magic as it flows down into us. But when the circle sighs collectively and our arms drop, my hand is thick with tingles and my shoulder is sore.

'Ah, old friend, we missed you,' Aunt Connie says, standing straight with a crickety-crack of each knobble of her spine for the first time in a full year.

Around the circle, the witches are taking a moment in their own way, each shivering or stretching into her power as it suits her.

'Are we done here?' Mirabelle asks, shaking her head so that her purple-streaked hair falls forward, hiding her.

'Always a bit rusty to start with,' trills Aunt Connie, swiping left and right and up and down with her finger, though nothing happens.

'After eleven months off . . . we should start slowly and carefully, right?' I whisper to Mirabelle.

'You would if you wanted to live,' she says, darkly, to me.

As my family all crick and crack their hands, a pale wave falls across the Morgan witches. There's a long white cloak unfurling around each of their shoulders, reaching all the way down to their ankles, making them look grander and taller. I look for the smirking Morgan girl my age but when I find her, the smirk has disappeared.

Aunt Morgan, even more menacing in her cloak, crooks a finger at her, the youngest of her coven, and the now smirkless girl steps forward. She takes the girl's chin in her hands and tilts her head this way and that. With a tutting noise, Aunt Morgan looks away. Something flickers in her eyes.

In fact, all the Morgans have something glinting in their eyes.

The young witch bows her head as she's released, as if with shame, and I realise: the magic didn't descend on her this year.

Summoned by Aunt Morgan, another young hag with elegant long braids rushes forward. 'We don't need her, Mother, your plan can still proceed,' she says eagerly.

I'm instantly curious: about their plan and the two girls, the one who has failed to gain magic this year and the one who fails to care about her.

'Come away, Morgans – we are not witches who *hide* in such a human place,' Aunt Morgan announces to her entire coven and her face is somehow wrong. The way she says 'human' with a twist of disgust is ... disgusting.

Their youngest young hag looks like she wants to stay, stick her hand back into the middle, demand we all try again.

But the rest of the Morgans move in haste; they must be in a rush to begin their 'plan'. The feeling of dread that I have doesn't seem to bother any of the rest of my coven and my mum lifts one glowing hand in a farewell wave.

''Til All Hallows',' Mum says, but the Morgans aren't the waving kind.

None of their coven reply. Instead, all eyes turn to Aunt Morgan, who raises her chin high and, as she closes her eyes, they all disappear.

CHAPTER 2

The park is suddenly much emptier without the Morgans.

'Did the magic descend on you?' Aunt Connie asks me urgently, her hair as white and round as a cauliflower. 'Show me your hands!'

I hold up both hands, as if in surrender.

'How do you feel?' she asks, quickly taking both of my hands in her own and turning them this way and that, like a doctor.

'Terrible,' I say, but my mind is still on the Morgans and whatever they were racing off to do.

'I knew it!' she trills. 'This year is the year!'

My hands do feel heavy and strange. I clutch them to my chest.

'Starry gift!' Aunt Prudie crows, lifting both of her own hands in celebration.

'Come on, young hag, you should be delighted,' Aunt Connie urges.

I look at Mirabelle, but her eyes are fixed on

her mum, my Aunt Flissie, who is not waving her hands around. In fact, she's already put on a pair of gloves.

'Be safe. Stay home,' she says quietly to Mirabelle, before hoisting her large backpack onto her shoulders.

'Flissie, we need your help!' Aunt Connie calls after her.

'Fruition!' Aunt Prudie adds.

'This could be the year! We have so much to do; we can finally—' Aunt Connie says, always translating for Aunt Prudie.

Aunt Flissie flinches away. There's a stiff silence between the sisters.

'Have you at least got clothes, Flissie love?' Mum asks.

'And food?' Aunt Connie asks.

'Must dress! Must eat!' Aunt Prudie adds.

'Sisters, you know I can't stay,' Aunt Flissie says. 'I'll be fine.'

With a tent rolled on top of her backpack and big walking boots, Aunt Flissie looks as if she's going to lead an expedition. But it's an expedition for one. Mirabelle is staring at her.

'Mirabelle, you know I have to—'

'Yeah, yeah, every year, you "have to",' Mirabelle says, all her sarcasm on the 'have to', and she starts stalking back through the park in the direction of home.

'Mirabelle! Wait – I can't stop you from using your magic. But if you must, please take this with you.' Aunt Flissie pushes a piece of paper into Mirabelle's hands and says, even more quietly, 'We can't have a repeat of last year.' And off she strides, into the night.

Even though Aunt Flissie lives with the rest of us, in October, without explanation, she checks out completely. She always heads somewhere remote. So there are five of us left – four now, because Mirabelle is already stomping back to the house.

I know where she'll go when she gets there. She'll retreat straight to her room. We share it, but she always calls it *her* room.

I trail after my family, twisting my fingers together because they feel really, really strange and glancing back behind me at where the Morgans were – and then were not.

As we walk, I notice the streetlights flicking off. At first I think it's a coincidence, but when a bulb pops directly above us and my hands suddenly start stinging, I know it's our fault.

'Mum . . . what are the Morgans out there doing?' I ask quietly.

Mum shrugs, a happy ostrich ignoring what the rest of the world is doing because only we matter to her. 'I'm sure it's better if we don't know,' she says. 'And better to see what we are going to do.' And she beams as if, in disappearing from the park, the Morgans have also vanished from her mind too.

My aunts have a sense of excitement as we make our way back to Pendragon Road, like they're carrying home a favourite takeaway that they can't wait to get stuck into.

The gleams of the morning light of the first of October are appearing by the time we reach home. Mirabelle has already let herself in; I can see light in her – our – bedroom at the front of the house.

Once we're back in the living room, Aunt Connie turns to the window and says, 'I have hated those curtains for eleven solid months,' and waves her finger with a flourish. 'Yellow is not a living-room colour.'

A fire starts at the bottom of the curtains and licks up them fast.

'Con,' my mum says with mild reproach, waving her own finger to stop the flames.

'Red,' Aunt Connie mutters, flexing her finger. 'I meant a nice, burgundy colour.'

'Gently, witches, gently,' my mum reminds both of my remaining aunts, who are poised with a finger already outstretched, ready to use their October magic. 'Remember, it always takes us a couple of days to ease into.'

I doubt the Morgans are back at theirs, fixing the curtains.

'Start small. Minor magic,' she tells us all, and whirls her own finger in a little loop. Nothing happens. She shakes her finger, like you would a pen when no ink comes out the end. It starts to glow. She gently twirls it round and round in small circles, her clothes transforming slightly on each rotation.

Mum is still wearing her uniform from the dry cleaners where she works: a polo shirt, pressed trousers and a pair of sturdy shoes. It isn't too bad but it isn't very Mum.

Now, a mass of stars gathers around her and as the stars individually spark out, her trousers shorten, then billow and become a skirt. The skirt grows in volume, petticoats layering over each other, until it sits like a triangle outward from her waist. Her polo shirt with the dry cleaner's logo on it sprouts a lavish collar and becomes the silky bodice of a dress. The sleeves lengthen and shoot out and, finally, the logo disappears.

The thick rubbery-soled shoes peel backwards until they become little flat ballerina slippers and her thick, curly, dark hair tucks itself neatly into a bun.

'Much better,' Mum says with satisfaction, and gives a pleased little wriggle. Then she flicks a final spark and the entire ensemble turns from dry cleaner's beige to a vibrant mustard yellow.

It is impressive. Like seeing a Christmas tree when the lights turn on. Something you only see once a year and it gives you a tingle of anticipation.

When I was little, October was the best thing ever. I used to wait for it all year.

We don't really have a garden, only a small patch of patio. But one year, Mum used her October magic to make the garden huge, with a stable, complete with a small sandy-coloured pony with a white mane who lived there. I called the pony Bobby and I loved her so much. We trotted around everywhere, and she loved to eat with big snuffles directly from my hand.

But – and it's a big 'but' – nothing we make in October can last past Halloween. The very next day, it's all gone. Everything is back to normal. Aunt Flissie returns as if she never went away, Mum's beautiful yellow wardrobe disappears and anything my aunts have gifted themselves vanishes too. My First October with Bobby had been my best one yet, but when Bobby the pony went away, magic lost its magic for me. I was too young to understand at first, stood staring at an empty patio on the first of November, clutching a carrot pathetically.

Ever since then, I stopped believing in the joy of October. I got magic-month fatigue. As soon as September began and my aunts' excitement started building, I would sigh, thinking of all the temporary nonsense that would descend for October. I've had my fair share of October tantrums. Nothing frustrates me like it.

I used to feel sorry for my aunts, wasting almost an entire year to have one month of fleeting fun. However, now there's finally *actual* magic under my own skin . . . I glance at the ceiling, wondering what Mirabelle is doing upstairs. I have so many questions.

'Only one month and so much to do,' Aunt Connie says, and Aunt Prudie nods fervently. 'This is going to be the year. Let's get cracking.'

'No cracking, please,' my mum says, mild but firm.

Aunt Connie now reaches inside the large frilly front pocket of her apron and pulls out her egg timer.

'No cracking,' she says with a smile at my mum, and taps the egg timer with one finger.

The egg timer is shaped exactly like an egg and it's made of white plastic (worn white plastic; Aunt Connie uses it in the kitchen every day) but as tiny stars stream around it, it begins to grow. It seems to turn molten and stretches, becoming see-through at both ends.

When Aunt Connie uses her magic to hold it in mid-air and slowly rotate it, I can see it has become a giant hourglass.

'Thirty-one days,' she says reverently. She flexes her fingers, flicking them out one at a time, like she's warming them up for some hand gymnastics.

My own hands feel itchy.

As the sparkling sand begins to trickle through the hourglass, Aunt Connie turns her glinting spectacles on me. 'Clemency, your assistance, please?'

'It's *Clemmie*,' I say. 'And . . . Aunt Connie, I've got . . . um . . . homework.'

'Really?' She adjusts her spectacles to see if I mean it. And I do mean it, kind of. 'But it's your First October.'

'And I've got exams before Christmas,' I say.

She shudders at the C-word. I love Christmas. All the October nonsense is done and dusted and any presents I get are one hundred per cent real.

My family might be able to magically enhance my

grades this month, or even speak every language in the world, but at the beginning of November, it will all go away and nothing they can do will help me with those December exams. Mum magicked me great at maths one year but once October expired, all I had left was a vague memory of knowing how to do long division.

'Connie wants to ask you—' Mum starts, but Aunt Connie sweeps in front of her and takes my hand, which feels especially thick and tingly. She tucks my hand tightly through her arm and leads me through to the living room where she parks me on the sofa.

'You know the story, Clemency. Our great ancestor, Merlyn herself, was the very first witch.' Aunt Connie gestures at the ancient, slightly moth-eaten throw that lies draped over the back of our sofa, where the image of a woman with big hair and a pointy chin is embroidered.

Mum sits down next to me, running her fingers over the rough weave of the throw.

'I wonder . . . where did this come from?' she mutters, though in our chaotic house of junk and clutter, I don't know where a single thing comes from.

'You didn't make it?' I ask.

'If I'd made it, it would be much prettier,' she says with a grin, as Aunt Connie taps her hourglass already drizzling away our limited time with magic, and sets it down.

It's true – anything my mum made would be more colourful. This ugly, old, bobbly blanket is mostly grey and the woman, who might be the first Merlyn, is gazing miserably upwards, looking like she might be crying.

'If I'd sewn dear Merlyn, she would have a lot more stars. And hands to do magic with,' Mum says, eyeing the rug-like thing with distaste, and I realise the throw cuts our ancestor off at the wrist.

'In all the books and films, he's called Merlin and he's a man: a wizard,' I say to Aunt Connie, out of stubborn argumentativeness more than anything. I sound like Mirabelle.

'Wizards? Human nonsense,' Aunt Connie says in disgust, and Aunt Prudie spits on the floor.

'Prudie!' Mum admonishes gently, and flicks her finger to make the sticky puddle disappear in a spark.

'You know magic descends down the female line. We witches are rare; there are only nineteen of us now! And it doesn't matter how you spell it. I sometimes like to think of her as Merle for short,' Aunt Connie says, looking like she's daydreaming about hanging out with our ancient ancestor.

If you tried to map our family tree, it would be a magical mess. We got asked to draw it in primary school and I had too many aunties to fit on the paper. I got in trouble for putting the Morgans on the back of my page with a big question mark.

The teacher had said something like, 'You can't be related to just all of these women, surely? What about the men in—' Then she stopped herself and said, 'Families come in all shapes and forms, I suppose, and I got an all right mark.'

'Right,' I say.

'She was the very first enchanter. Then came her sister Morgan. Merlyn *then* Morgan. The two branches of the family we take our names from.'

The Morgans naturally disagree, they claim it was their ancestor who was the first. But the truth is that our Merlyn was a hero. And their Morgan was a villain.

'Our great ancestor was the very first witch to be blessed by the stars. Ah, but the world was young then. What did folk think of the odd gryphon or a cyclops?' Aunt Connie smiles ruefully.

'Seas full of sirens!' Aunt Prudie adds, looking pleased by the thought. 'Dragons in the skies! Forests full of fiends! Rampaging witches!'

'And that's why humans call them the Dark Ages?' I say quietly, just to Mum.

She flashes me a conspiratorial grin. 'Well, it might have been a bit dark for humans,' Mum replies in a low voice. 'They hadn't come up with electricity yet.'

Aunt Connie puckers up her mouth in sour-berry distaste. 'But that Morgan,' she says. This is a rant I've heard before. 'She could not bear to be the less powerful witch. She persecuted our poor ancestor.'

Not much can ruffle Mum but she sucks her teeth sharply.

'Morgans! Pfft,' Aunt Prudie interrupts, and spits on the floor again before glancing guiltily at her sisters.

'Mighty Merlyn gave as good as she got – the battles were legendary! They lit up the very sky!'

'Um,' I say, 'that doesn't sound very secret.'

'No, secrecy came later,' Aunt Connie says, which is technically her agreeing with me but she manages to make it sound like it isn't.

Mum draws the gold thread of her magic through the air and illustrates as Aunt Connie talks: a gold outline-sketch in the air of Morgan turning Merlyn into a mouse, then herself into a hawk; an epic chase. Then Merlyn transforming into a spider, and a huge Morgan trying to stomp and squash her.

As Aunt Connie recounts the bedtime stories I've heard my whole life about the first Merlyn and first Morgan, I look away from the pictures in the air and down at my hands. I splay my fingers out in front of me. My nails look pearly at the edges and catch the light, almost as if I've dipped the tips of them in sugar. They look longer than usual, and they're sparking slightly, almost fizzing.

'Before long, lands were swarming with Morgan's trolls and ogres. Battling Merlyn's dragons. Volcanoes erupting out of nowhere, hurricanes larger than you can imagine. Merlyn always had the upper hand, until—'

'Betrayal,' interrupts Aunt Prudie. 'Wicked betrayal.'

'Until,' Aunt Connie persists, 'Morgan stole Merlyn's magic!'

'Now, Connie, we don't truly know that,' Mum says, always trying to add moderation when there isn't any, the two figures of Merlyn and Morgan frozen in the air in front of her.

'You know as well as I do, Pattie! It's how the legend goes. Morgan was jealous of Merlyn's greater power and so she tried to limit it. But she failed and, in her wickedness, she cursed us all,' Aunt Connie says.

'The Morgans are cursed too, then?' I ask, thinking that they didn't look very cursed, apart from maybe that one young hag.

'Yes, it rebounded on her line too. The two branches of the family, though at war for centuries, must come together to receive the same measly month of magic. Our families are equally miserable and miserably equal in having just a month when we can wield our powers.'

'Wicked! Wicked, wicked witch!' Aunt Prudie shouts. She is very serious and very loud – and that is probably good because it covers my snort.

'Forget Morgans!' Aunt Prudie squawks directly at me. 'Only Merlyns!'

'Yes – what does matter is that now that you are with us, now that you have the power too, we can share our life's work with you,' Aunt Connie says.

'I didn't know your life had a work. Or any work, really,' I say, sounding bitter as Mum makes the pictures in the air dissolve again. Storytime is over and now they want me to get to it. But not school work; magic work.

'Enough, young hag,' Aunt Connie scolds. 'Now, we have been trying—'

'For decades!' Aunt Prudie interrupts.

I look down at my tingling hands, still sparking

slightly, and up at Mum, whose eyes are asking me to stay, just for a bit, so her witchy sisters can explain whatever it is they're trying to explain to me.

'Yes, yes, it is our constant quest. We've been trying for a long time to harness the October power.'

'Right,' I say, when really I should say, 'Right?'

'To harness the power so that we can keep it all year. Four seasons, twelve months, five points of the star. Because we need a full star to be at full power – and you are the final fifth point.'

I knew something was coming. Aunt Connie has been waiting my entire life for me to be old enough to finally make up the fifth point of the coven's star. With Aunt Temmie permanently gone and Aunt Flissie temporarily gone during the magical month, their generation is two witches short of the five they want or need.

'We must find a way to store the October power.'

'Stretch it!' Aunt Prudie shouts. 'House it! Grow it! Keep it!'

'Yes, yes,' Aunt Connie says, flapping a hand at her sister. 'All of those.'

'But aunts, I haven't even used it yet!' I wriggle my hands at them. My fingers feel strange.

'You're a fledging, it's true, but the fledgling we've been waiting for.'

'What about . . .' I start, thinking hard, '. . . any of the Morgan witches?'

Aunt Prudie blows out through her lips, making them vibrate with disgust. Her frown lines are deep and abiding but mention of the Morgans can make them even deeper. She is tree bar: sharp and prickly. An angry bush of a human being.

'Yes – Prudie is correct. Including Morgans would be far too risky. It must be Merlyns only.'

'Study hard! Learn fast! Work hard!' Aunt Prudie shouts.

But not for my exams. I sigh deeply and resign myself to not being able to revise.

'I really don't think I'm the right—'

'You may not be the "right", but you are the only. Consider yourself chosen, nominated, elected – however you like to think of it. You are a Merlyn and now is the time to act. We've been waiting for you to take Temmie's place!' Aunt Connie announces.

When I was born, Aunt Connie demanded that I be named after dead-and-disappeared Temperance, and for once in her life my mum was not patient about her instructions. Aunt Connie had then demanded that at the very least I be called Clemency and she's still trying to make that stick.

However, Mum went with Clementine. 'Less loaded with coven history,' she said. But Clemmie still sounds like Temmie and that's the compromise.

'I'm not just a Temmie replacement,' I mutter but really, my brain is haltingly putting everything my aunts have said together.

My whole life, my aunts and my mum have been pursuing permanent magical power, twelve months of the year.

They want us to be more than just October witches.

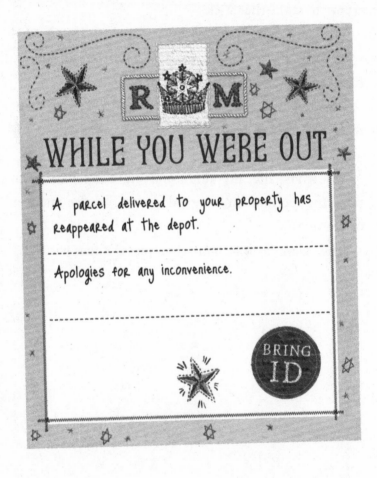

R M

WHILE YOU WERE OUT

A parcel delivered to your property has reappeared at the depot.

Apologies for any inconvenience.

BRING ID

CHAPTER 3

'Now,' Aunt Connie says. 'It is very important that you listen to me, young hag. It is your first year with your magic – you're expected to be clueless.'

'Oh, thanks.'

'But you do not—'

'Absolutely not!' Aunt Prudie squawks for emphasis.

'You do *not* practise by yourself outside of the coven's star.'

Oh, I think. It's like being given a gift and told you can't open it.

'We don't want to wrap you up in cotton wool,' Mum adds. 'But we do need you to be safe.'

'There are so few of us witches,' Aunt Connie adds. 'Every young hag counts.'

I'm torn between frowning and rolling my eyes at her. It's a numbers game – and I'm only a filler witch.

'First Octobers are always a little . . . unpredictable,' Mum says softly. 'And we can risk no witch.'

'But now,' Aunt Connie says triumphantly, 'we find out what kind of witch you are!'

Aunt Prudie launches herself at me and seizes my stinging hands. She traces all the lines on my palms then holds them up to show her sisters with a 'huh'.

'Impossible hands,' she mutters, giving the centre of my palm a good poke.

My mum turns her hands over so I can see that all the main creases of her palms glitter. Mine do not.

Aunt Prudie squints at me. 'Green-fingered young hag!' she announces decisively, as if she'd just read it in my eyes.

'No, she has a fiery heart!' Aunt Connie argues. 'Come, young hag – let's see you aflame!'

'Young hag must *grow*!' Aunt Prudie insists.

They're clashing . . . over me. But I don't think I take after either of my aunts. Or my mum.

I wish Mirabelle would come downstairs, join in the row and tell my aunts that I'm going to be a witch like her instead.

'Transform! Create! Conjure!' Aunt Prudie adds, sounding a bit maniacal and jabbing the air with her magic fingers.

'There is nothing that witches cannot do,' Aunt

Connie translates. 'It's time to light the flame of our craft!'

'Gentle,' Mum advises. 'Be soft with your magic. It's warm, you can shape it.'

'No, fast is better,' Aunt Connie contradicts, lacing her hands together to crack all of her fingers. 'Magic is a fire and you have to stoke it properly. But set boundaries. Magic likes boundaries.'

'No! Nurture it!' Aunt Prudie shouts. 'No boundaries! Grow wild!'

I don't know what to do with all this conflicting advice.

Magic isn't like school – there are no handy online guides and there's no homework to catch up on.

'Start by trying . . . a simple stitch,' Mum says, raising a hand which gently bobs through the air.

As bookcases grow gracefully up the walls, replacing the piles and piles of dusty odds and ends, and our paper lampshades become fringed and pretty, Mum looks like she is carefully sewing, her hand both the glimmering needle and the thread.

'No, no!' Aunt Prudie shouts. 'Grow green!' she jabs at the kitchen and, with an explosion of stars which quickly turn green, the floor is mud and grass.

In her olive overalls, Aunt Prudie is the only one of us who looks at home in the mossily overgrown kitchen.

Aunt Connie, unsurprisingly, is bossing the magic around. Her fingers twizzle and spark as she shows off, and a huge new fire roars in the middle of the room. It's the kind of bonfire you might toast marshmallows on – not safe and indoorsy, but crackling and wild. She also sweeps a hand through the air and the entire wall between our living room and kitchen disappears, both rooms stretching into one.

I fidget, despite how amazing this magic is to watch. They each want me to be a witch like them, but there's no space for young hags to do anything in this house.

Aunt Prudie won't be outdone, though. Messy, muddy snarls of foliage burst across every surface and she makes an *aie!* noise in triumph as a sinkhole appears.

With a smile, Mum steps forward and runs both hands repeatedly through the air, as if soothing a giant, invisible beast with kind, gentle magic. The muddy floor twinkles as it turns into golden flagstones.

Mum keeps Aunt Prudie's foliage but pots it around the room. She keeps Aunt Connie's fire too, but houses it in a grand fireplace, pinching the air so that the bricks of our kitchen wall pull themselves into shape.

Mum flicks her fingers and sparks turn into golden cutlery which lays itself out on a new dining table.

'Fine!' Aunt Prudie grumbles, which is as close as she gets to admitting defeat.

'Nice touches,' Aunt Connie murmurs appreciatively, touching the new counters that run along the sides of the kitchen before she turns to me. 'To achieve these results, you have to be extremely detail-orientated. And you must have . . . patience.'

She exchanges a smile with my mum.

Sometimes I forget that Mum is just as much of a witch as my aunts are. My mum and her sisters love each other and they all love magic – they sparkle with it.

Mum nods contentedly at a job well done. For the rest of the year, our kitchen is a bit beige and quite old, and though Aunt Connie can rustle something up in it most days, now she could feed kings and queens.

Aunt Prudie *pffts* this away. 'Minor magic! Finger tingles!' she says dismissively and returns to me, still standing useless with my heavy hands limp.

She tugs on my fingers one at a time, as if trying to crack them into magical shape.

'Not witch hands,' she mutters.

'Flissie would say you were a stuck compass,'

Mum says with a smile. 'It's OK, there's time to work out your witchery.'

'Practise inside the star! You have the star and the star has you.' Aunt Connie says, unreassuringly.

They're basically saying that I'm useless by myself but could still be useful to them in the star . . .

Aunt Connie crosses into the kitchen and hovers over a towering pile of odd crockery. She splays all five fingers over the clutter and one especially old, battered-looking tin pot rises into the centre of the room. The pot begins to grow, rotating it in the air as it grows a large belly and a thick rim.

Aunt Connie would definitely deny being messy, but she is. There are trinkets and ornaments and bits and bobs everywhere. Our whole house is full of junk, though Aunt Connie would say 'magical artefacts'.

By the time the pot is a fully-fledged cauldron, it is spurting and sending jags of tiny stars in all directions.

The cauldron is vast. In fact, the whole kitchen is now vast. Inside, the house is about four or five times as big as it looks on the outside.

Mum, Aunt Connie and Aunt Prudie gather, looking like they might be about to chant. Instead, they stare at the round belly of the cauldron admiringly.

Mum dings it with one nail. It makes a deeply resonant noise. 'You kept her cauldron,' she says.

'And the memories,' Aunt Connie says, and she lovingly buffs up the cauldron with the edge of her apron. 'I look after them both.'

Now, she clicks a spark of flame into life with two fingers and sends it under the cauldron.

'Cosy,' Aunt Connie says as the fire roars dangerously close and her spectacles steam up. She frowns and peers over them instead.

'Whose cauldron is it?' I ask, peering over the lip into the deep, dark well. 'And what's going in it?'

'Soup!' Aunt Prudie shouts, giving me a long glower.

'Soup?' I say. 'Of course.'

'It was your Aunt Temmie's cauldron,' Mum says. 'And it's October – so there must be soup.' She smiles at me again, which does make the tingle of my hands feel better. 'That's not exactly a witch rule. But it is a wise one.'

'Necessity means we must rein in our more fantastical ideas – but witches need to eat,' Aunty Connie admits, looking extremely disgruntled about it. 'But imagine what you could do with those hands, young hag! Populate the sea with merfolk, fill the skies with unicorns and fairies and—'

'Or make some soup,' I say, pointing at where the cauldron has started to bubble and hiss. The cauldron smells spicy.

Aunt Connie levels a hard stare at me over her spectacles.

'Hearth witches have heat!' Aunt Prudie cackles delightedly, and Aunt Connie seems to glow red in answer.

'And, the stars know, if we are lucky, then it will not matter how long it takes you to grow into your powers, because we will have them year-round,' Aunt Connie says, eyes on her hourglass, 'Instead of for just one poor month.'

'What would we even do with year-round power?' I ask. 'And how would we do it? Does Mirabelle know about this? Do you already have her involved in this too?'

'*Involved* . . .' Aunt Connie tuts, making it sound like I've accused her of something. 'Yes, your cousin is already well aware of these excellent plans,' she says, her raisin eyes peering at me over her spectacles. 'Fetch her please. We must begin.'

CHAPTER 4

I open our bedroom door and see that where there used to be two beds, there's now only one – mine. I sigh, the sight of my bed making me realise we full-on skipped a night's sleep. If it wasn't for the jiggly feeling of the stars inside me, I would burrow straight under my duvet and stay there. I look down at the penguin pyjamas that Mirabelle hates and slide on my matching penguin slippers before going further down the (now unusually long) landing until I find another door. Mirabelle has wasted no time using her own magic to divide our one bedroom into two. My half looks like exactly the same as it does in non-October times, just half the size, which somehow makes the mess even messier. But Mirabelle's has become a vast suite in a moody shade of purple.

Normally our house has a kitchen and a living room downstairs, two bedrooms and a bathroom upstairs.

It can be a bit of squeeze with all six of us living here so one of the only useful October gifts is a bit more space.

'Hey,' I say, slowly opening the door.

'What do you want?' asks Mirabelle from the bed. Her single bed has mushroomed into a gigantic four-poster, with huge drapes flowing all the way down to the floor and mounds of differently textured blankets. It's purple, to match the rest of the room.

'Do your hands hurt?' I ask her, still stretching my fingers. They feel like they need to crack at every joint. They're . . . fizzy. I remember the feeling of the stars sinking into my skin in the park.

'A whole month,' Mirabelle says, ignoring me. 'Stuck with you lot.'

Last year was Mirabelle's First October and it was agreed by everyone that it was a disaster. She tried to send herself to join her mum, Aunt Flissie, who was maybe in Aberdeen at the time. No one ever found out where she actually was because Mirabelle's first magic came in strong and muddled and she ended up somewhere in the Arctic. It took my mum and the aunts a long time to work out what had happened and find Mirabelle and bring her back.

If Mirabelle had happily rolled with the witchery in our household, then I probably would have too. But she spectacularly didn't and only just made it back for Halloween. She was stroppy before, but when she got back from her accidental diversion to the Arctic, she was *so over* everything. Over me, over her mum, over magic.

And I know that could happen to me. One or two spells gone wrong and, at best, I could have a truly terrible October; at worst, I might end up so traumatised that, like Mirabelle, I will hate my whole family and everything else in our lives together.

I look at my cousin on her enormous new bed, complete with luxuriously soft and furry purple throws, hugging her knees. However grumpy she's being with me, I need to try to be as kind to her as Mum would be.

'Now that I have magic too, maybe we could . . . do something together? Make something?' I suggest, but the word 'magic' sticks in my mouth. It sounds silly when I say it. Mirabelle ignores me.

'The thing is, Aunt Connie is downstairs making plans,' I add. 'And she says you know all about them.'

'Oh. That.' Mirabelle sighs heavily, making me

feel like I'm pestering her. 'The glorious pursuit of eternal magic?'

'Yeah.' I rub my hands together and my palms spark.

'Come back when it's Halloween,' Mirabelle mutters, reaching for a blanket to drag around herself.

Halloween is a full thirty-one days away.

The Merlyn Halloween parties at the end of October are legendary. It was Mirabelle who started them.

Everyone gets to be a little bit wild and magical on Halloween – it's what makes it the best night of the year. It's the only day, ever, when witches and humans are the same. We all have the tiniest little tingle of magic.

I hate October but love Halloween because it's the day the magic spreads out across everyone. It's the day the magic leaves.

Before her own magic came in, Mirabelle used to spend ages planning the party. One year there was bunting across the ceiling that squeaked at you. They weren't actually live bats strung together by the wings, but it looked like they were. Another year, the pumpkins up the front steps all sang as the guests arrived. And another time, there were human-sized cobwebs spun in every corner.

There have been many gentle hauntings, ghosts that appear and tell jokes or you catch them out the corner of your eye, striding from room to room straight through the walls. One year, Mum grew a forest of twisting trees down the hallway and guests had to pass under their branches to reach Aunt Connie's epic buffet.

So, I love Halloween because of Mirabelle's parties. One day a year, our house is the main attraction instead of a complete liability. I have Mirabelle and her party to thank for everyone at school automatically thinking I'm cool too. I don't want anyone to forget us this month but the official line is that we're 'taking time out of formal education for personal reasons'. Mum wrote a letter and everything.

It's a late party – it has to be so that humans can come too. As soon as the magic starts to slowly fade away, we're no longer hidden from them, and by the first of November, we're back to normal, and Aunt Flissie is back home too.

Last year didn't quite work out the same way. The party did – everyone had the best time. But Mirabelle wasn't the same. Coming back from the Arctic had changed her.

'Go then!' Mirabelle says, pulling a massive, new,

down-filled duvet up to her ears until all I can see is her purple hair. 'At least you've got a mum who wants you for something.'

I don't know what to say to this.

'Maybe you could help me – you know – like, do something?' I say, all in a rush.

'Slow down, Clem. Can't you just hold on 'til life goes back to normal? We just have to make it to Halloween.' Mirabelle mutters that last bit, I think more for herself.

So, defeated, I add, 'They've sent me to come get you, too.'

'Fine,' Mirabelle drawls slowly, 'I've been got. Let's go.'

Aunt Connie and Mum are waiting for us at the bottom of the stairs, as Mirabelle thunks heavily down each step.

Aunt Connie has her hands on her hips. 'Ah, young hags! We're all here – we may begin!'

Except, we aren't all here.

'Where's Aunt Prudie?' I ask. She was here just a moment ago. 'Why does no one ever know where anyone else is in this house?'

'Oh, you know Prudie,' Mum says gently. 'She's probably—'

'At the allotment, yes, right,' I say with a sigh. All the women in my family (so, my whole family) have a problem with vanishing.

And I wouldn't even be needed for their five-pointed star if my disappearing Aunt Flissie would just stay at home with her sisters one October.

'At least Aunt Prudie says where she's going, unlike my mum,' Mirabelle says bitterly.

'You must be—' Aunt Connie starts.

'— kind to Flissie,' Mum finishes.

'What happened to Temmie has made it impossible for Flissie to be part of the coven,' Mum says to Mirabelle, gently.

'But Mum – what *did* happen to Aunt Temmie?' I ask, but we're interrupted by the loud clang of metal on metal. I jump, almost expecting to see a sword fight, but it's Aunt Prudie, clanking three huge pitchforks.

'Allotment time!' she announces, holding out a fork to Mirabelle.

'She's going to the allotment,' Aunt Connie translates unnecessarily. 'And you're going too.'

'Do you need help, Aunt Prudie?' I ask.

'Prudie? Help? Not for a single day in her life.

No, young hag, she wishes to teach you,' Aunt Connie says, speaking for Aunt Prudie again.

'Can't she teach us here?' Mirabelle asks, reluctantly taking the giant pitchfork, her shoulders sagging under its weight.

Aunt Connie points at the tiny flakes of sand in her precious hourglass. 'Chop, chop, young hags. October waits for no witch.'

Clocks stop in October for witches. I don't know if magic makes the mechanisms explode or disappear, but if there's any machinery or technology involved, we witches will end it. We don't need watches, though – we have Aunt Connie to count every minute for us.

'Shall I . . . change?' I ask lamely.

Aunt Prudie squints at my penguin pyjamas. 'Why?' she asks, and I shrug.

'Boots, at least!' Mum protests, and my slippers grow up my legs and toughen into wellies.

'Soup, at least!' Aunt Connie corrects, shoving flasks into our hands.

Armed with the giant pitchforks, we follow Aunt Prudie's bobbing grey head to her allotment, which is round the back of the park.

'Home. Coven. Star,' Aunt Prudie says firmly. 'No messing!'

If this is what she wanted to teach us, she definitely could have done it at home.

'Disaster,' Aunt Prudie says seriously and sagely, pointing directly at Mirabelle.

'Yeah, Aunt Prudie, it was,' Mirabelle says, sagging against her pitchfork. 'Now, what are we doing here?'

Gardening isn't interesting to me, but Aunt Prudie looks the most content I've ever seen her as she stomps down the rows between the lines of fruit, vegetables and flowers.

The allotment smells earthy but fresh; it's Aunt Prudie's smell.

There's the odd older person in their own allotment. But as we pass by, they move away. October magic means regular humans can't get anywhere near us. I've never had to deal with the full effect before, but for the rest of this month I am stuck with the four remaining residents of 15 Pendragon Road. Humankind, and human-made things, are off the table. We frazzle our phones and repel our friends.

'I think,' I say to Mirabelle, 'that Aunt Prudie is queen of the allotment.'

'And I can see why,' Mirabelle says, pointing.

The field is split into lots of miniature gardens with sprouting rows. Some have a little shed built on their land or have netting or sheets over their fruit, I guess to protect them from birds.

But right at the end is what appears to be a giant's vegetable patch. Everything is massive, unnecessarily massive. None of the produce there could ever fit in an oven and cutting any of it into chunks would take hours. You could feed hundreds with such enormous vegetables, each anchored by massive green tendrils. Everything in Aunt Prudie's allotment is leafy and vast. But there's one vegetable which towers over all the others.

'Pumpkin!' Aunt Prudie says, pointing at, what is obviously, a ginormous pumpkin.

'You're kidding,' I say, staring at it.

The pumpkin is huge. It is taller than me and far wider. If hollowed out, a group of people could stand inside it. I hope that's not part of the plan though. It's a perfect cartoon of a giant pumpkin: a true solid orange, ridged with thick curved lines leading up to a gigantic green stalk with hulking leaves.

'Don't kid,' Aunt Prudie growls. 'Perfect receptacle!'

'A perfect what?'

'Hold the magic! Release the magic! Share the magic!' Aunt Prudie trills.

To one side, Mirabelle mirrors my feelings by rolling her eyes dramatically.

'Is it . . . real?' I check.

Aunt Prudie tsks. 'Nature-made! Not man-made! Organic matter! Sturdier! Better!' she shouts. 'Harvest season! Useful gourd! Tastes good! Real!'

I shrug. If those are her reasons, then I'm not sure I can persuade her that a witch growing a giant pumpkin is too much of a cliché.

'From seed!' Aunt Prudie shouts happily, giving her pumpkin a hearty smack. 'Thirteen years!'

'That pumpkin is thirteen years old?' I ask. We're almost the same age, me and this giant beast.

Aunt Prudie has probably spent more time with the pumpkin than she has with me. She must have spent hours in silence, alone, feeding this monster.

'Blankets in winter!' Aunt Prudie shouts, crinkling in joy. She has a well-worn gardener's face with countless creases and now, as the crow's feet at the corners of her eyes deepen, I realise this is the most gleeful I've ever seen her.

'You wrap it in blankets?' I ask.

'You baby that thing?' Mirabelle says, sounding disgusted.

'Pumpkin home,' Aunt Prudie says, gesturing with her fork, which now makes sense because it's almost big enough to contend with the giant pumpkin. 'Hard skin,' she adds, rapping on the outside of the pumpkin. 'Soft inside!'

I wonder if Cinderella's fairy godmother chose a pumpkin for her mode of transport for the same reasons – plush, comfy interior and solid carriage walls.

'Thick-skinned!' Aunt Prudie boasts. 'Bred for strength! Bred for magic!'

I want to ask Prudie more about this, the history of pumpkins made for magic, but I don't have time because she has produced a giant knife from nowhere at all and is ready to cut.

'Cannot be harmed by hand,' Aunt Prudie says boastfully.

I can see that. If it was the pumpkin versus a person, the pumpkin would win, especially if there was a slight hill involved. It would roll and squash anyone in its path. It's a serious heavyweight.

Aunt Prudie boosts herself up to where the pumpkin

has a thick green stem, and she must be using magic because, though she is rickety for eleven months of the year, she is now glowing with strength. She beams and then begins to saw into the pumpkin's stem.

'Here we go again,' Mirabelle says, but I've never seen my aunt do anything like this before.

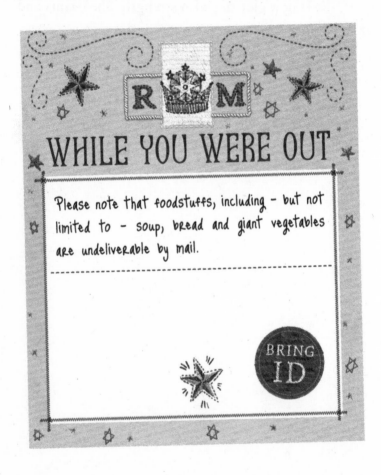

WHILE YOU WERE OUT

Please note that foodstuffs, including - but not limited to - soup, bread and giant vegetables are undeliverable by mail.

BRING ID

CHAPTER 5

With a grunt and a yank, the pumpkin is free from its green foliage.

'Now, young hags, dig!' Aunt Prudie commands, waving her huge pitchfork at us.

'Yeah, but Aunt Prudie, you can get this done in one October click,' Mirabelle says.

'Young hag work!' Aunt Prudie insists and grunts. 'Magic! Or dig.'

I stomp round to the other side of the pumpkin to wriggle my hand in private and try to make something – anything – magical come out. When nothing does, I sigh and pick up a pitchfork.

'Dig, young hags!' Aunt Prudie shouts, sticking her pitchfork joyfully into the soil. 'Till the earth!'

'Till the earth we must,' Mirabelle says to me in a squeaky, high-pitched voice. 'Work for mad aunt we must.'

I snort downwards at the soil.

'Till the earth! We must!' Aunt Prudie agrees with two quick shouts over her shoulder.

'Not mad aunt,' Aunt Prudie corrects us. 'Aunt Prudie.'

'Uh-oh,' I say quietly. We dig in silence after that, down along the edge where the orange pumpkin meets the sticky brown mud, pushing it back and scraping it away. This pumpkin has sat on this patch for thirteen years, so it is wedged deep into the soil.

I don't see Mirabelle use her magic but her pitchfork is smaller and she's definitely making faster progress than I am.

'Now!' Aunt Prudie commands after we've gone all the way round with our pitchforks, easing the mud away like you might run a knife around the inside of a tray that you've baked something in, but much dirtier and less delicious.

Aunt Prudie raises one finger and, with a huge, groaning lift, the pumpkin comes free from the ground and hovers in place. Clods of mud are still attached to it and, underneath, all kinds of scuttling creatures are running for cover.

'Homeward!' Aunt Prudie commands Mirabelle and I, sweaty, dirty and still confused, simply stand

and stare at her. 'March!' Aunt Prudie prompts us.

'Your grandchildren?' one of the gardeners calls from a distance as we mock-stagger, pretending to be carrying the pumpkin. She tries to walk in our direction, but instead of getting closer to us, it's as if she keeps bouncing off a giant invisible blob of jelly. Our magic masks us from humankind – and befuddles people.

'Nieces!' Aunt Prudie shouts back. 'Trouble.'

'How lovely. You must be so proud!' the allotment lady says, walking on the spot.

'Proud of pumpkin!' Aunt Prudie shouts. 'Come, young hags!'

The nice allotment lady falls forward a step as we move away from her. She half-watches us leave with the pumpkin, a bewildered look on her face. I don't know what she's seeing and I don't think she does either.

All the way home, Aunt Prudie lists things that she's happy to be called, 'Aunt Gardener. Aunt Horticulture. Aunt Greenfingers. Aunt Harvest. Aunt Planter,' she says, and then has to stop so she can laugh. The pumpkin, Mirabelle and I hover awkwardly on the pavement as Aunt Prudie enjoys her own joke.

'Aunt Plant! Ha! Ha!'

It takes something quite dramatic to stop her being entertained by the rhyme.

A large bird cruises down past us, less than a wingspan above our heads.

It's a crow. No, a raven. It's definitely not a pigeon. It doesn't even matter. It's a big dark bird is what it is.

Above us, more of them gather, forming a dark circle.

'Away!' Aunt Prudie shouts at them.

The birds hover lower.

'Away, away!' Aunt Prudie shouts again, throwing an arm towards the birds. I can feel the magic in her gesture, but the birds are still coming lower. Pigeons are a normal thing to see around here and I'm sure no gardener wants their produce pecked but these birds are bigger, glossy and with dark brown wings. There are so many of them now the sky above us turns completely black.

I'd seen the netting protecting the vegetables, but it hadn't really occurred to me to be *worried* about birds.

'Oh no,' Mirabelle says as the slow drift of the birds stops, and they turn, arrow-like, on their target and head down in a funnel of yellow-beaked dots.

Mirabelle and I duck out as the birds zoom down, one after another, fearlessly stupid as they try to get their little beaks around the mighty pumpkin. Mirabelle grabs my pyjama top and pulls me backwards as, for a moment, the birds engulf the pumpkin in a tornado of dark wings.

Aunt Prudie rolls up her sleeves, lifts one bony hand as high as she can in the air and then brings it down against the other with a reverberating clap, which makes a small explosion of stars spurt out between her palms. The birds are whisked away, leaving the vast orange pumpkin alone. Aunt Prudie raises a hand again and the birds scatter in different directions before she has a chance to channel more of her magic at them.

The pumpkin's thick, orange hide doesn't have a single mark but Aunt Prudie squeaks, then leans her entire body against it and croons to it, patting it as if to make it feel better.

We make our way back to Pendragon Road in much more of a hurry after that.

'Aunt Prudie, those birds—' I start to ask.

'Flying pests,' Aunt Prudie squawks. 'Forever bothering me!'

We stop outside the gate of our house, having largely given up even pretending to hold the ginormous pumpkin. Mum and Aunt Connie appear, punctually, to stretch the gate so as to allow Aunt Prudie to levitate her pumpkin up the path.

'The doorframe, Con,' Mum says and quickly, she and Aunt Connie both have their hands up. They move so they are shoulder to shoulder and the entire front of our house glows then folds back; the stars moving bricks, wood and plastic window frames out of the way like curtains.

Mum peers out into the street, then up at the sky. The neighbours' houses on both sides are silent, even in the middle of the day, as if no one lives there at all.

We proceed slowly into the living room where the pumpkin floats sedately to the floor. Mum raises her hands to about shoulder height, and her fingers orchestrate the clutter of our living room, scooting the sofas out of the way.

Then, with a bright, almost blinding rush, all my family's bric-a-brac whips away, clearing more floor space for the giant pumpkin.

'It is marvellous,' Aunt Connie says, and gives a real-life cackle. Sometimes we witches don't help ourselves.

I look around our reworked house. The pumpkin, looming in the middle of everything, manages to look even stranger than it did out in the allotment.

'Marvellous,' Aunt Connie repeats.

'If you're into large legumes then . . . yeah,' Mirabelle says.

'Revolutionary pumpkin!' Aunt Prudie shouts directly at Mirabelle. 'Perennial, not seasonal!'

'But what do we do with it now?' I ask.

'Maybe a nice glass carriage?'

I think Mirabelle is joking but I'm not 100% sure.

'Magic in! Now!' Aunt Prudie commands, raising her finger to swipe as if testing the air for dust. It forms a glittering gold line in front of her, about a hand-span across. Aunt Prudie keeps drawing.

I back away from the luminous lines beginning to form in the air, my own hands beginning to spark. A shimmering outline of a massive five-pointed star now floats above the pumpkin. Slowly, majestically, Aunt Prudie brings her hands down and the star obeys, settling itself on the floor around the pumpkin.

'Gather round, hags old and young, time to get into formation!' says Aunt Connie as she steps towards one of the five points of the star.

CHAPTER 6

'To work, witches!'

Aunt Connie steps into the star, which is shimmering on the floor around the pumpkin.

Mirabelle gives the most epic eyeroll and throws her mass of curls backwards.

Mum leans forward to lightly touch Mirabelle's shoulder. 'I like the purple,' she says.

'Thanks,' Mirabelle mutters, twining one of her thick curls around her finger. I swear her hair has slowly but surely got more purple since October began.

Aunt Connie hustles everyone into place – each of us to one of the remaining points of the star. Mirabelle has to be manoeuvred onto her point.

'Now. You have to picture it with all your senses, as deeply as possible, and will it into existence. You there, you there, you there, you there and I will stand . . . over there, on the other side of the pumpkin.'

I have to 'picture . . . *it*'. But I don't know what '*it*' is yet.

Aunt Connie coughs pointedly, interrupting my thoughts.

They're waiting for me.

I glance at Mirabelle to my left but her head is tilted back, staring at the ceiling with her arms crossed. I step into the star, lining up my muddy boots so that I'm exactly within its triangular point. I should feel something, I think, the magic inside me clicking into place. But I just feel nervous.

'The star is complete,' Aunt Connie says, and she sounds so gratified I feel like I've already done a good job, even though we haven't started yet.

'Hold the magic! Release the magic! Share the magic!' Aunt Prudie shouts, repeating what she told us at the allotment.

It's obviously not clear enough for Aunt Connie. 'We will pour our October magic into the vessel. It will slowly seep out over the course of the year, releasing a steady stream of magic into the house – and us, all year-round.'

A rotting pumpkin. This is their grand plan.

'This pumpkin?'

'Yes. Having the correct vessel to put our magic into is everything.'

I eye the pumpkin dubiously.

'And we believe that to create our own vessel is the best solution.'

I stare at the orange monster. 'And you've been planning this since I was born?'

'We don't want to put any pressure on you,' Mum chips in.

Aunt Connie ignores her. 'Yes. You are the fifth point of our star, and we've been waiting for this October for a long time now.'

'You've got my mother to thank for that,' Mirabelle says, back to her hard-shelled self.

Aunt Connie doesn't respond.

'You've tried this before, right? You've tried to keep your power in past Octobers?' I'm trying to understand what has led us into giant pumpkin territory.

'Everything! We have tried everything!'

I am certain that can't be true.

'We thought we'd come close to a solution several times. Our tried and tested methodology is to store our October power in a vessel, such as a book of power, a statue or a cauldron. Pattie even tried to sew it into fabric. Why do you think we have all of these things?' Aunt Connie asks, gesturing around the room.

I look again at the clutter and strange objects scattered all around us. 'You tried to store your magic in all of this?'

'We have failed many times,' Mum says, quite brightly. 'Temmie's cauldron was the first receptacle we tried to store our magic in. But it was sadly too . . . unpredictable. A natural receptacle will be better.'

I look around at my aunts. They might be slightly mad, but they are not stupid.

'Young hag, pay attention!' says Aunt Connie. 'At midnight on the first of October each year, the stars are absorbed into us. If they can be absorbed into our bodies, they can be absorbed into something else. We simply hadn't found the right vessel but now, we believe we have. We shall have great, great power!'

'With great power comes great responsibility,' Mirabelle says with a smirk.

Aunt Connie whirls around to my cousin. 'Yes, you are so right! We do, we have great responsibility. And we will soon have the greatest of all powers, all year round.'

She gives Mirabelle an affectionate pat on the hand. Mirabelle grins at me. I feel stupidly grateful.

Aunt Connie takes up her place on the star. I can't see her around the pumpkin anymore.

'Now what?' I shout over the top of it.

'Well, we don't exactly know,' Aunt Connie says, reappearing.

'So, you've got a giant pumpkin and you want to put our magic in it and you don't know how?'

'I am not, I repeat *not*, getting in that pumpkin,' Mirabelle says, even though, from the size of it, she could definitely fit – we all could.

'No, no, we'll start simply. Hands up. And point.'

I follow my mum's lead and raise my hand and point at the pumpkin. I feel very, very silly.

Just at that moment there's a glassy knock as a bird smacks against the front window. I see its dark wings as it wheels away. These birds must really like pumpkins. Or more than I do, at least.

'I can't believe I got out of bed for this,' Mirabelle says, both hands on her forehead.

'We must all have the vision,' Aunt Con says. 'Prudie – take us away.'

'Year-round power! In our hands! Malleable power! Strong women! Powerful family! Maintain magic! Magic is kind! Magic for good! Powerful hands! Use it well!'

But I can't imagine it. And maybe I don't want to.

I glance sideways at Mum and then at Mirabelle.

Their eyes are shut tight. Mum is smiling, a vivid, rich smile, as warm as the world she is probably envisaging.

My arm is very heavy.

'Focus, witches, focus!' Aunt Connie's voice comes around the pumpkin, urging us on. But I don't really know what she's urging us on to do.

I imagine writing one of those reports we used to have to do in school. *What I did at the weekend: my family and I stood and pointed at a pumpkin for hours at a time. Sometimes someone grunted.*

Time passes, my mind wanders. It won't even matter that I won't see any humans ever again if the aunts are successful because I won't have any friends anyway – I'll be completely left behind by the rest of the human world.

'This isn't necessarily fast magic,' Aunt Connie reassures us all, but if anything is happening, it's so slow I haven't noticed it yet.

'Are we done?' Mirabelle asks, shaking tingles out of her arm.

I drop my own arm, exhausted. Thinking about things is more tiring than I could have imagined.

'No, young hags!' Aunt Connie commands. 'We must maintain focus, we only have thirty days to get this right.'

Thirty more days of pointing at a pumpkin. My shoulders slump.

Mirabelle looks as dismal as I do about our October prospects.

'We'll try again tomorrow; we've been up all night. I prescribe soup, then a good night's sleep,' Mum advises gently.

I take a step backwards from the pumpkin and look at my family again. If a human – a non-witch – was to see us now, I wonder what they'd think. Individually, I don't think we look that strange but together, especially standing like this in the formation of the star, we probably look very odd indeed. That's without even taking the giant pumpkin into consideration.

Mirabelle slopes away and I trot after her. 'A pumpkin!' I say to her back. 'It's so . . .'

'Round?' she offers over one shoulder.

'Yeah!'

'And orange?'

'Yeah,' I agree but more reluctantly.

'Quite like a clementine then,' Mirabelle says and takes the stairs, away from me, three steps at a time.

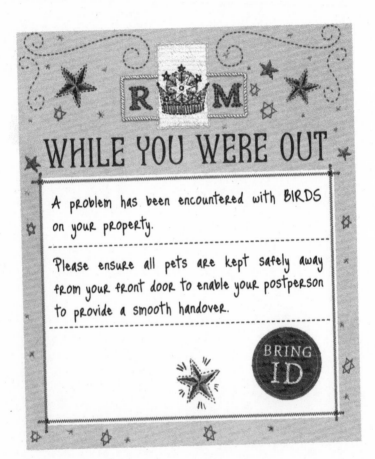

WHILE YOU WERE OUT

A problem has been encountered with BIRDS on your property.

Please ensure all pets are kept safely away from your front door to enable your postperson to provide a smooth handover.

BRING ID

CHAPTER 7

My aunts' grand pumpkin-plan experiment does not happen quickly. I've spent eight whole days trying to put magic into the pumpkin, not to mention seven uncomfortable, disturbed nights' sleep, trying to work out where to put my hands in the bed so that they don't throb.

Aunt Connie's hourglass on the mantelpiece has never been so loaded with meaning and I watch it sometimes as she moves around us, adjusting the hold of our hands, repositioning us, trying us in different constellations around the pumpkin. She barks at us so much that, at one point, she loses her voice and my mum forces a break for restorative soup.

However, unlike me and Mirabelle, Aunt Connie has an endless stamina for pumpkin experiments. Her round apple cheeks push up her glasses, which are slightly steamed, as she huffs, and reorganises us witches, and huffs again.

One day, Aunt Connie thinks we're close to a breakthrough, which is then interrupted by Aunt Prudie needing to monitor the pumpkin, adjusting the light and moisture in the room as if the pumpkin is Goldilocks' and it must all be "just right".

The next day she thinks we're close to a breakthrough again, but Mum can't quite decide on an appropriate outfit. She tries a flaxen, drapey, elvish-looking number with a slight train. Then Aunt Connie taps her toe while Mum magically alters it to a spangled bodice with big, poufy sleeves in a rich, butterscotch-coloured material. She looks like a princess from a fairy-tale, not the resident witch.

Every day is its own unique disaster, with Mirabelle escaping to her room at least twice a day. I have to fetch her back each time.

But mostly, I think the problem is me. Mum is polite about it, but my aunts obviously don't think I'm trying hard enough.

So here we are, eight days in. Mirabelle is flopped on the sofa, where, utterly fed up, I join her. She reaches for a folded piece of paper in her back pocket, the way that in non-October times I would reach for my phone – compulsively, privately.

I try to peer over her shoulder, but she bends the piece of paper away from me and gives me a special glower.

Aunt Connie appears from her side of the pumpkin. 'Now, young hag, you must try because—'

'Perhaps,' Mum says, neatly stepping between us. 'Perhaps I will have this conversation with Clemmie?'

I look at my mum in confusion.

Aunt Connie is already frowning but beneath her spectacles, her eyes narrow further.

'Come, love. Let me show you. Magic has a good side too,' Mum says, and leads the way into our large, magically-enhanced kitchen, leaving my aunts in close communion with their pumpkin.

I cross my arms and tuck my hands tight into my armpits, but I still follow her.

'Now,' Mum says but she doesn't put her witch fingers down. 'Let's start fresh. Can I, love?' A few wispy stars circle my head and my bad copy of Mirabelle's double topknots is gently tightened and rearranged.

'Better.' Mum smiles in satisfaction. 'Now.'

Before she can continue, her phone rings.

'Oh dear,' Mum says, rooting in the folds of her dress. 'I forgot that was still in there,' she mutters, pulling out what was once a mobile phone. It is ringing its last ever ring, the tone warping as it dies. It looks like it's been slightly melted.

Mum waggles it at me and grimaces. 'And yours?' she asks.

'Upstairs,' I say and nod at the ceiling.

'I can turn it into something witch-made if you'd like?' Mum offers. 'Otherwise, it might not make it through the month.'

I try to shrug as if this is no big deal, as if being phone-less isn't a sure-fire way to be forgotten by everyone human.

Mum opens one of the kitchen cupboard doors and drops the dead phone onto a pile. Inside are all the human-made things which over the last week haven't survived the exposure to our magic – stacks of mobile phones, the cheap kind; two laptops; dozens of exploded lightbulbs; the toaster . . .

It's not a good reminder of why magic is great.

'No human-made things,' Mum reminds me.

Our whole house is full of junk. I wonder what they'll do with the giant pumpkin if it joins the hodgepodge of other failed magical vessels. It won't be so easy to squirrel away.

Mum is a little bit nervous, I realise. I've never seen Mum nervous. She is usually completely unruffled, like a swan.

'We follow some October rules that you're experiencing for the first time. It's very simple really: "hidden and no harm". Our rules are known by all witches, both Merlyns and Morgans. Unwritten, but known. They form our truce. That is how the two families may have faith in each other.'

'Not much faith, though,' I scoff, thinking about how Aunt Morgan said, as our magic descended, that her coven wouldn't hide among humans.

'Yes,' Mum agrees. 'The truce holds, but there is tension. We stay at home, *hidden*, and use our magic kindly, so, *no harm*. The Morgans use their magic . . . differently . . .'

'Different isn't *always* bad, right?' I ask, thinking about the Morgans' 'plan' and how their young hag scurried.

'There is a lack of . . . trust between our two families,' Mum says, looking uncomfortable. 'So – about your Aunt Connie's endeavour . . . you must continue to join us in the star, love.' Mum's warm brown eyes are crinkled in worry.

'I must?'

'Yes, love.'

There aren't many 'musts' with my mum.

Mum puts out one of her hands to calm my twiddling ones. October has got me antsier than usual. 'You know we are not ambitious witches,' she says with a smile. 'You asked what we would do with more power, and in truth, Aunt Prudie would be delighted not to have to see humans ever again. And Aunt Connie feels that it is our right and we are owed that power. But, truly, it is so that we can be who we are meant to be, all the time. And to do that, we must have our magic back first.'

'First?' I ask, feeling my own crinkle of worry begin.

'Before the Morgans. To ensure we are safe. If they achieve year-round magic before us, our truce may no longer hold.'

'I didn't know we were in a race to reclaim our magic,' I say wonderingly.

'I wouldn't call it "a race",' Mum says. 'We still wouldn't turn our power against each other – but their ancestor did and we fear the Morgans will again.'

'And do what?' I ask, fishing for consequences.

'The stars know,' Mum says simply.

I frown up at the ceiling. All-knowing stars. Right.

I understand Mum's worry crinkle. It doesn't sound like the stars would stop power-hungry Morgans.

'And there is, of course, banishment. If a witch turns their power on another witch, they have to leave their coven,' Mum adds, as if this is the small print. 'But don't worry about that. Think of how happy it would make your aunts to have the limit of time removed,' she says, her smile turning to full beam. 'I think it might even make Mirabelle happy.'

'It would?' I ask.

'With October alone, there isn't much time for fun – but as long as Connie doesn't hear us, there is time for . . .' Mum takes a step forward so I'm not within range of her arms. She's left-handed like me so she swings up her left hand until it's in front of her face.

Mum normally has calluses from sewing and ironing and all the hundreds of jobs she does when it isn't October but, now, her hands are smooth, elegant, long.

It's the hands that make a witch. You can always tell. Mum's are long-fingered, long-nailed, tapered with magic in the tips. The pattern of lines in her palm is very clear as she swishes her index finger up above her head, three times in a spiral, then down across the opposite shoulder as if throwing on a scarf.

'Mum,' I say wearily.

She's so good. If it was the first time I saw her do this, I'd applaud. But to live like queens for one month a year makes a mockery of the other eleven.

Then I hear the whinny.

'Bobby,' I say.

'She's waiting for you,' Mum says, and a tiny pony trots out from behind our kitchen bin. Bobby is much smaller than I remember, but that could be either just how Mum thought of her this time or I've just grown.

My tiny childhood pony noses at my thigh, and Mum cups her elegant hands together, grain pouring into them from nowhere, and then tilts her hands to me so that I can feed my pony.

'Oh, Bobs,' I say as she nuzzles into my hands and happily crunches away.

Bobby the pony has a tufty blonde fringe that flops forward over her thick-lashed eyes and the rest of her mane is quite quiffy. And, the bit that made me fall in love with her that First October, she has a white star on her forehead. She's fluffy all over but she also has the daintiest little beard and tufts of hair falling over her fetlocks too, as if she has feathered feet.

'I always thought it was strange you didn't want

something more extravagant,' Mum says with a smile. 'I spent most of my childhood Octobers on a beautiful, winged unicorn.'

Bobby has a very round belly. I wouldn't want to mention it because I wouldn't want to hurt her pony feelings, but if you look at her head on, she bulges on both sides like a barrel. Both Bobby and I are 'stocky', though proper horse people who know about these things in a non-magical way would also say that Bobby has a thick neck and thick coat, and I don't necessarily have those bits too.

'You might feel that when the October magic descends, you lose many things. But you gain so many more.' Mum is earnest and honestly believes that magic is the best thing anyone can ever have, even if it's only for a month.

I swallow. It's not about the pony. The pony is cute. It's about my family's secret plans. I can't believe I'm letting myself be bribed by the consolation prize of a small horse.

'Do you remember the movements I taught you?' Mum asks with a hopeful smile.

I don't. And last year, with Mirabelle coming of magical age, Mum didn't show me any magic.

She didn't have time, with Mirabelle's Arctic Crisis.

'Kind of,' I say, giving my finger a tiny whirl in the air.

Mum's smile slips a little. 'Be careful, love.'

I wish we had detachable magic. Magic you could carefully put away in a drawer or only get out when you need it. Whoever came up with wands was on to something. The idea that the magic is in my hands is alarming.

I hold them out in front of me.

'These are the tools,' Mum says, doing the same. 'But it is your vision which matters. You have to see it exactly how you wish it to be, in your mind's eye.'

I know this, but it doesn't help. I'm starting to think my mind doesn't have an eye.

'Just think of it as a glowing, gold thread,' Mum says.

But I don't have a gold thread inside me. I maybe have jumping jacks.

'I feel silly,' I say.

'Yes, love, but that's OK.' Mum puts a hand on either side of my shoulders and wriggles a bit as if trying to loosen me up. 'I bet you haven't even tried it yet. Of course you're going to feel silly until you put the power into it. The power that kicks. Then you'll feel much better,

I promise. Now, I kind of stitch with my magic, like this. Maybe for you . . . it'll be like drawing? Try – up, down, across, swish, swish, swish.'

They are like ballet movements, but with my feet sturdily rooted on the floor.

I look, and feel, like an idiot.

'Just remember: the stars know. You find the stars inside you, tell them what you wish to make and then send them out into the world. Your brain and heart are doing most of the work – maybe ninety eight per cent – the rest is your hand directing it,' Mum says.

My hand is shaking. I take a deep breath and try to bring the tremors under control, but my hand is too heavy to sweep gracefully with.

I feel like a piece of equipment, badly flawed in design, not functioning properly. None of my body feels right, it's all too much. I need to release the magic in my hands, but I'm not sure how to do it.

I focus my mind instead of my hand, like Mum said, and swish my finger. Absolutely nothing happens. I'm not even sure what I'm meant to be making with my mind and magic.

Bobby trots over and sniffs with a whiffle, then whinnies up at me.

Mum peers over my shoulder and laughs. 'Oh, don't worry, love, it'll come together,' she says, giving me a one-armed squeeze. 'You're just a little blocked, there's nothing more natural.'

'Are you sure? Because it doesn't feel natural,' I say, a touch bitterly.

I know there's something in here, I just don't know how to get it out. I smack one fist against the other as if one is a ketchup bottle and I might be able to squirt the starry power out.

'You need time to get used to it. Receiving all those stars is a big thing to happen to a body. But your mind is getting in the way.' There is no disappointment in her voice – which somehow makes it worse.

Bobby snorts and backs into the kitchen cupboards, knocking over a bowl of fruit and the bread bin.

'The stars know that you'll find your way in your own time. You didn't want to ride a bike for a while either. Or your lovely, little pony. You always said you felt silly.' Mum's eyes always stay big and sincere when she smiles so I try and smile back.

'Bobby isn't going to help me feel less silly now,' I say, 'and Aunt Connie isn't going to be into . . . an October pet.'

Mum raises a finger and one tiny gold star alights on Bobby's nose. Bobby whiffs at it, sneezes and shrinks. 'Now you can take her with you.' Mum smiles, picking up Bobby gently and presenting me with the pony on her palm.

I give my newly miniature pony a dubious look. She's like all Merlyns, short and thick of leg. Bobby rears up and whinnies, her tiny hooves striking Mum's hand.

'I'm not going to carry Bobby around with me, Mum,' I say scathingly, but bad moods bounce straight off my mum.

Weird stuff happens in October. I know that, all my family know that. And I'm not making a great start by carrying a tiny pony around with me.

'She's just a little reminder. That magic can be . . . magical.'

I sigh and hold out my hand for Bobby to trot on to my palm. I wonder what it would be like to have her there all year. She's not a good enough replacement for everything else I'd lose.

'Young hags!' Aunt Connie bellows, and she sounds very close. She isn't, though, she's still stuck tight to the pumpkin. But I can see a few sparks fizzle around her as she calls again. 'Mirabelle and Clemency!'

Mum gives me a glowing thumbs-up which, instead of just encouraging me, reminds me of my own unsparkling hands.

'Pumpkin!' Aunt Prudie commands.

'Let the young hagging commence,' I say.

CHAPTER 8

'So! Now!' Aunt Prudie chirps.

'All of our Octobers have been leading here,' Aunt Connie says reverently. 'And your First October will be a mighty one!'

It hasn't been yet, though I don't say that.

She is circling the pumpkin like it's her opponent and she's about to try to take it down.

'Join us, Mirabelle!' Aunt Connie says, but with her back to us, so Mirabelle simply pulls the old throw with the picture of our ancestor, Merlyn, on it down over herself, hunching deep under it.

She has that same piece of paper, folded even smaller so I can't see what's on it, propped upright against her knees. Mirabelle is giving it her full attention and a full scowl.

'Year of Octobers!' Aunt Prudie hollers at me. 'Replenish! Lifetime of Octobers!' She buffs up a patch of the giant pumpkin at roughly shoulder height, then gestures me forward with a jerk of her head.

I glance at Mum. She said I must. Now she nods and smiles at me, doing the encouraging parent thing really well. Then I glance back at Mirabelle, but she's ignoring us all.

I am in a witch's hot seat and it's not just the pressure of this October that I feel, but the pressure of all my family's Octobers.

Aunt Connie has pressed one ear right up against the pumpkin, listening keenly, but now she frowns over her glasses at me. 'Palms up,' she instructs and demonstrates, her palms already glowing, against the surface of the pumpkin.

I copy her, my palms tingling then stinging on contact with the cool, hard surface. In front of me there is only orange.

'Now – focus on the stars inside you and send them into the pumpkin. It should be easy, as we're not asking you to create, only—'

'Transfer!' Aunt Prudie interrupts Aunt Connie loudly, startling me, and pulling my hands back. I readjust them and try to look like I'm focusing, witchily.

Dotted around the pumpkin, all three witches' heads swing expectantly in my direction. Mirabelle is now less witch and more blanket pile.

After a moment of nothingness, I ask, 'Does it have to be my hands? Because I don't think they're—'

'Mother Nature's own instruments!' Aunt Prudie shouts, gesticulating wildly. 'Magic raw! Uncooked!'

Aunt Connie looks askance at Aunt Prudie.

'Merlyns use hands!' Aunt Prudie adds in a bright shout, then her tone darkens. 'Morgan way – pfft.'

I use this as an out to drop my hands from the pumpkin's surface and give them a rub to try and stop the tingling.

Aunt Connie doesn't immediately notice as she is tap-tap-tapping all the way along the pumpkin, like a carpenter tapping on a wall.

'Perfect level of porous interior,' she mutters to herself. 'Still unknown how it will respond to further probing—'

'Resonance?' Aunt Prudie asks, and then both of them have their ears up against the pumpkin, earnestly listening to the inside of the vegetable like it has secrets to offer up.

'Mum – about the Morgans?' I ask, sidling away

from my aunts. 'They've never really bothered us, right?' They usually come swishing in on the first of October, claim their power and go away again. I only ever see them twice a year, and I know they're arrogant and self-important – but not necessarily evil.

But Aunt Prudie's hearing is excellent. 'Morgans? Not hidden! *Do* harm!' she growls.

'Bother us! Bother us! They have bothered generations of us!' Aunt Connie says, her indignation making her stiff curls wobble.

'We don't know that . . .' Mum interjects and there's a hectic moment where all three of them are trying to explain to me at once. Aunt Connie wins by having the longest explanation.

'There are always strange October happenings,' she says grimly. 'Even the humans know there is something strange about this month. We hear the rumours trickle through and we believe the Morgans are behind them.'

'Monsters! Yetis! Pixies!' Aunt Prudie shouts. 'Uffos!'

'That's *U – F – Os*,' a muffled voice spells out behind us. The sofa can't let Aunt Prudie get that wrong.

Aunt Connie carries on regardless. 'There was an incident at a lake in Scotland which sounded Morganesque. No one was killed but several boats went down, tangled in a giant sea snake. One October, on the full moon, we heard of werewolves! We never know their plans – and last year was . . . we were busy.' Aunt Connie coughs. 'The point is: if the Morgans don't stay properly hidden, we cannot guarantee they do no harm either. We must have our own magic to protect ourselves.'

I raise my eyebrows. October has a spooky reputation for a reason and it might be the Morgans taking things too far.

'And when we are safely tucked into eternal Octobers, we can use the craft to craft! I will cook all the time. Infinite magic, infinite recipes.' Aunt Connie's voice sounds dreamy for a moment, then she coughs herself back into the present.

I glance back at Mirabelle but after her U.F.O. correction, she's all but submerged under the sofa's throw, only tufts of curls visible.

Aunt Connie has gone into teacher-mode now, though, as she lectures me, she keeps one hand on the pumpkin. 'After First Morgan's attempt to steal our ancestor's magic failed and cursed them both with limited powers, Merlyn concealed them both. Their witch battles had been vast – and public. The humans wanted to—'

'Witch-hunt!' Aunt Prudie half-shouts, half-mutters.

'So you have the Morgans to blame for only one month of magic, but Merlyn to thank for keeping you safe during that month,' Aunt Connie says and turns back to surveying the pumpkin.

I don't really want to thank either of those first two witches, but I think about the current Morgans in their white cloaks, a creepy colony of pale bats. The young hag that smacked my hand away left me annoyed – but she wasn't necessarily wicked.

I wonder if the Morgans also have a house full of junk. I wonder if that young hag is currently standing in front of a giant vegetable, feeling like she might as well bang her head against it for all the good it would do.

'The Morgans are less . . . hampered . . . with secrecy,' Aunt Connie says as stars form into a ladder under her feet, propelling her up the pumpkin where she presses her ear up against it again.

'A little jealous, perhaps, Con?' Mum asks with a kind smile.

'You know witches are a joke out there, with cats and brooms and stuff?' I say. 'Humans think we're into toads, candles, pointy hats, warts – it's a whole thing.' I tell my coven elders because this 'hidden and no harm' stuff is all well and good, but they know nothing about what the rest of the world is actually like. I still go to school; I still know that witches are in the same category as aliens in spaceships – imaginary and very silly.

'Warts?' Aunt Prudie shrieks.

'The indignity!' Aunt Connie says sniffily from the top of her ladder. 'The inaccuracy.'

'As so?' Aunt Prudie asks, shoving a hand towards me – and she does indeed have a wart right at the base of her thumb, like a knot in the bark of her skin.

There might be the tiniest little snicker of a laugh from the depths of the sofa where Mirabelle is still doing her best to hibernate, but I'm not sure.

'Humans fear us. As they should. We are hidden from humankind and their human-made things for our protection, Clemency. Witch-hunters have been seeking us out and killing us for generations,' Aunt Connie instructs me as she straightens up the ruffles of her apron.

'I'm sorry about . . . humanity?' I offer weakly. 'Humans say—'

'Humans say! Humans say!' Aunt Prudie exclaims, as if she's outraged by the very idea of humans saying anything.

'We don't have time for this. Precious October days are slipping away from us,' Aunt Connie says, her ladder dissolving away in a puff of stars. She hefts her hourglass up to show the slipping sand and eyes the sofa for the first time. 'Chop, chop, young hags.'

Aunt Connie lays her hand flat on the pumpkin, Mum puts hers on top, and Aunt Prudie adds her crinkly hand as the top layer of their magical hand-sandwich. This is how we stack our hands to receive our power and I can see stars around their fingers, but as time passes, a series of looks pass between my coven elders.

'Well,' Aunt Connie coughs, pulling her hand away first, 'perhaps there might be other issues with transferring our power to this pumpkin. But, we won't know for certain until these disrespectful young hags obey their elders!'

Aunt Connie raises a single finger and the mound of blankets concealing Mirabelle lifts in the air. Mirabelle leaps up as if thrown into an ice bath, dropping her piece of folded paper on the floor.

She snatches it back, glaring at us all as if we might take it, and holds it tight, both arms wrapped around herself.

The Merlyn throw separates from the others, leaving mangy quilts and splodgy tartans behind. Aunt Connie conducts a shower of stars to unfurl it, showing the woman, her big hair and pointy chin definitely making her one of us. Her sad face, shown in profile, looking upwards, is stitched in dull grey fabric, her arms reaching out to nothing. Stars twinkle at the edge of the ancient-looking throw, pinning it against the wall, like a propaganda poster for our great ancestor. Except, she doesn't look like someone worth following; she looks exhausted and defeated.

'We must work for the honour of ancient Merlyn!' Aunt Connie declares, but Mirabelle doesn't wait. She doesn't disappear instantly but she's gone up the stairs really quickly.

'Fetch your cousin, please, young hag,' Aunt Connie instructs me while she turns away and distractedly sparks another fire in the chimney, scorching the ceiling. She jumps back. She smells a bit singed, like a firework.

I sigh. Mirabelle never wants to be fetched.

I start up the stairs, watching behind me as my mum and my aunts take their places in the star around the pumpkin.

CHAPTER 9

Mirabelle might not be allowed to use her powers on me but that doesn't mean she can't make my life very difficult. Our staircase has turned into a spiral that just keeps going up and up and up.

When it comes to avoiding me, Mirabelle is so excellent she could win prizes, I think as the corkscrew turns make me dizzy. She is going big on privacy this year and I don't think she would fear banishment. Her room seems to have grown into a turret. My whole family must think they are the most brilliant magical architects. I lose count of the steps but I'm panting before I reach the top.

The landing also seems to have got even longer, her room even further away. When I finally reach it, I'm completely out of breath.

I knock on Mirabelle's door, which is now made of thick dark wood and has no handle. I get no answer so I peer into my own room.

'Go on,' I tell the heap of clothes, half on the end of my bed, half on the floor. 'Sort yourself out, then.' I flex my fingers.

The mess doesn't move at all, of course. I catch a glimpse of my revision homework, mostly finished but half-submerged in my bed. I always start my homework, but I'm not as great at finishing it. I don't know when I'll hand it in, now that I'm magical and so isolated.

I knock on the wall that separates me from my cousin.

'Mirabelle?'

There's a quiet noise inside. Then I hear the door open the narrowest crack. 'Can't a witch just get a bit of alone time?' she says, throwing both arms up in despair.

Through the crack, Mirabelle looks like she's wearing a huge furry coat with a collar up to her ears. I think it's a blanket slung around her shoulders. Her room is glowing warmly under the lights of a new chandelier.

'Aunt Connie is on fire,' I tell her.

Mirabelle doesn't even smile.

Sisters and cousins are meant to be like in-built best friends, according to my mum, but not in my case.

And I'm not going to magically transform into

someone Mirabelle wants to hang out with when I turn thirteen. Older doesn't necessarily mean cooler – just look at Aunt Prudie and Aunt Connie.

It's difficult to admit, but my cousin just doesn't like me.

Mirabelle has already retreated back to her bed, which has moved into a fairy-light-covered nook, the walls reshaped to hug the bed close. All the windows have disappeared, replaced by thick, purple wall hangings with pretty, embroidered patterns.

'And she says she needs us back at the pumpkin . . .' I say, and then confess in a burst, 'but I *can't*.' I hold up my hands to show her their un-Octoberness.

'Don't wave those hands at me,' Mirabelle says from a majestic pile of pillows. Her room is really, really warm.

'But I can't get the stuff in here to come out there!' I gesture a bit more, pointing from my heart to my waggly fingers.

Mirabelle sighs too. 'I don't have the answer. But you don't need to make a huge fire or a big fancy dress or a massive sinkhole to be a real witch. Our aunts, including your mum, are random. They conjure big and do weird stuff because they love it.'

'I don't know how I can join the star,' I say, trying to keep the whinge out of my voice. 'My hands tingle all the time.' Right now, it's more like burning. 'What do I do with it all?' I ask, meaning my magic hands. 'They're so . . . annoying. And it feels weird. Like magical shortcuts are *cheating*.'

'You're talking to the wrong witch,' Mirabelle says. 'Big magic never worked for me.'

Last year, Mirabelle was gone for three weeks in the end. And when she came back, she went straight to her bed.

As I try and think of something to say back, there's a faint whinny. Deep inside my jacket pocket, Bobby snorts.

'Clem,' Mirabelle says, her voice as sharp as her chin – which is jutting towards me. 'Is that you?'

'Um,' I say, clamping a hand over my pocket. 'No, not me exactly. But, yeah.'

Bobby is still in my pocket. I'm not sure about real ponies, but it can't be good for her. Bobby snorts again.

'Oh,' I say, lifting Bobby out and placing her as gently as I can on Mirabelle's thick purple carpet.

Bobby whiffs out a big breath and tosses her head,

probably feeling quite grand, not realising she's smaller than an apple. She parades around, so sassy for such a small thing.

'A magical pony. A tiny, magical pony,' Mirabelle says. Bobby is cute but also cringe, in front of her.

'Yeah, I know. But it's embarrassing, it's not a normal thing to have.'

'I'm sure your mum told you that you could have *anything*, right? A troll! Or a goblin! And you've got a pony, Clem.'

I stash Bobby in my pocket again and gently pat the little lump she makes there.

'I like ponies,' I say defensively. 'Or, I used to when I was little. And I don't think I'm a troll kind of person.'

'Good for you,' Mirabelle says. I check her face to see if she's being snarky. She is.

I turn my attention to the folded piece of paper Mirabelle has been clutching tightly. Now that it is open on the floor, I can see the lines and squiggles of a map; a small mark drawn on to a small box on a small grid.

I pick it up and slide it onto the edge of the bed then stand there, letting Mirabelle be silent. She stares at the map then turns her eyes away.

I carry on talking to fill up Mirabelle's silence.

'I know they want five of us to form a star – but there are six, if you count Aunt Flissie.'

'No one ever counts her,' Mirabelle says, and she's right. I have no idea where Flissie is right now, or what she might be doing.

'Last year was my first with magic,' she says, 'and all I wanted was to be with my mum.'

'But Aunt Flissie — I mean, your mum—'

'She doesn't care about me at all,' Mirabelle says, matter-of-factly, sitting up in the giant bed which makes her look like a fairy-tale princess, but a stroppy one. 'There isn't enough of her left to care. She is using up all her caring on Temmie, all the time. Mum's absent even when she's here.' She sighs again. 'It was the first spell I ever tried to cast. I pictured my mum and willed myself to be where she was. And you know where I ended up, right?'

I shift uncomfortably. 'My mum said . . . you got stuck in the Arctic.'

Mirabelle laughs an unfunny laugh. 'I thought of my mum and I ended up in the middle of the ice – nothing, forever, in every direction. Cold and empty. Like her.'

I tentatively sit down on the edge of her queenly

bed, next to the map and stay quiet. I try to think what my mum would do – she would give Mirabelle space to talk if she wants to talk.

'When you touch ice with your bare skin, it'll take the skin off. My fingers . . .' she says, holding her own hands. 'I thought it was the magic at first, but it was the ice.'

I've never seen Mirabelle cry and I don't know what I'll do if she starts now.

'All the magic in the world couldn't have helped me, surrounded by ice and cold. I just . . . couldn't make the stars work for me.'

I stay silent, waiting to see if more will follow.

'It's just a map,' she says, shrugging at the piece of paper next to her.

'A magical one?'

'No. Just a regular map. Made out of paper. Useless.'

'Where of?'

My cousin rotates the map so she can glare at it. 'Here! It's a map of here, our city. Our house is even marked, even though I know exactly where we are. So useless.'

Mirabelle sits up straighter. She takes a moment to sniff any lurking tears back in and blink a bit. Then she stares at me from under her hair, as if daring me to notice that she might have been about to cry. 'No one is happy in our family.'

She's right. From January to September, the aunts are waiting, anticipating. Then from November to Christmas, they're in mourning for their loss. My family are bored and fractious during spring, impatient during summer and completely miserable during winter.

'Mum only gave me this map so I won't try and follow her and get lost again. It's not a gift, it's a warning.'

I remember last October with a tightening guilt-headache. I missed Mirabelle, but I couldn't help her.

'I wanted to have an extraordinary life,' Mirabelle says, looking at the canopy of her bed instead of me. 'And extraordinary doesn't have to mean magical. I wanted to go places and see things. But now . . . I don't think I can go anywhere anymore. I'm too scared.'

I can see the tears in her eyes as she stares at the ceiling.

'It's all right for you, you're ordinary. You're ordinary without your powers, you'll probably still be ordinary with them,' Mirabelle says dismissively.

I glare back at her. She really should be Mirabelle the Miserable. But Aunt Prudie added 'Miracle' to her name after she survived in the Arctic.

'You can be the extra and I'll be the ordinary,' I tell her, as generously as I can.

Mirabelle smiles and for a moment it seems almost OK that her mum is gone and there's a giant pumpkin downstairs. A single tear rolls down one cheek and she wipes it quickly away.

I pretend I haven't seen.

'There's nothing you want badly enough, Clem. All you have to do for your magic to work is to really want something. You're lucky, being ordinary and wanting for nothing.'

Mirabelle slides off her bed and stalks away. I thought she would just go, but she comes back and hands me something warm.

'Unbelievable cramping, right?' she says with a small smile. It's a hot water bottle in a purple fluffy knit case.

I take it and hold it close, curling my hands around it. It takes a moment, but when the relief comes, tingly and cosy, I could almost cry.

'Heat helps,' Mirabelle says briskly and turns away.

'Hags!' Aunt Connie shouts up the stairs. 'Young hags!'

'Let's get this over with qui—' Mirabelle starts to say, but she is interrupted by a loud clunk downstairs.

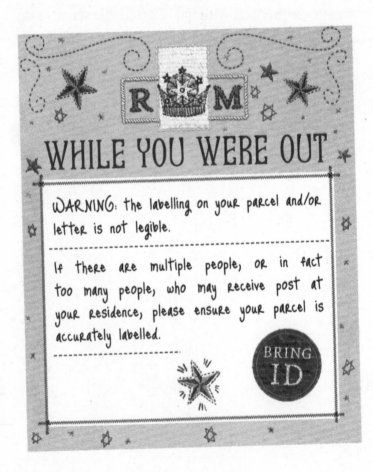

R♛M

WHILE YOU WERE OUT

WARNING: the labelling on your parcel and/or letter is not legible.

If there are multiple people, or in fact too many people, who may receive post at your residence, please ensure your parcel is accurately labelled.

BRING ID

CHAPTER 10

The clunk is not his usual polite rat-a-tat-tat on the door, but still, through the glass panel in the door, I can see the postman is standing at the end of our garden path, one hand on our gate, looking confused.

I hop the last couple of steps and open the door to him, also confused. Humans shouldn't be anywhere near here.

He has a job to do but no way of doing it. He has post to deliver to a household of witches – something his brain won't even let him acknowledge. We are hidden from him by the presence of our magic, but he's trying hard.

At the garden gate he seems to be trying to move forward, but it's like he's headbutting an invisible forcefield.

'Delivery for you!' he says with an automatic wave which should be cheery but looks strange. He's staring slightly above my head.

Then, like a malfunctioning robot, he moves forward and kind of bumps off our gate.

'Hi!' I shout, keen to stop him coming any closer. I'm careful not to wave at him in case something magic happens. 'Just throw the parcel down there.'

'I think I've got a headache,' he says, a bit woozily.

'It is October,' Mum tells the postman seriously over my shoulder, though she and the rest of my coven are as far back from the door as they can get.

'The ninth of October,' Aunt Connie shouts, emphasising 'ninth' as if it is a ghastly thing. 'Time is slipping away!'

It's like we haven't spoken for a moment and then he responds slowly, as if from underwater. 'I'll just leave this here,' he says and props the long parcel up against the gate.

Poor thing, I think. Given that no human can come near us, he's made an impressive effort.

I watch him bumble away. He gently zig-zags for a bit then stops, shakes his head as if to reset, then walks briskly on, reaching into his bag for the next stack of mail.

As soon as he disappears from sight, I trot out and pick up the long, rectangular parcel. It's heavy in a familiar way and I fumble it with my numb hands but I want to open it – who is it even addressed to? As I carry it inside, I notice another large bird perched on the front windowsill looking in, almost as if it is watching us.

'We are thirty per cent through the month, young hags! Chop chop!' Aunt Connie says, tapping her hourglass and scowling through her spectacles at the descending sparkles of sand, which do indeed look a third gone.

Then, Aunt Connie's eyes crinkle into suspicious lines beneath her glasses and, with a crook of her finger, the parcel is firmly pried out of my hands and set aside.

My family are so annoying.

'No distractions! Now, remember, young hag – see it in your mind; the stars lift inside you, travel down your arm and you send them into the pumpkin.'

'See it! Dream it! Make it!' Aunt Prudie shouts.

'With great power comes great vision,' Mirabelle says with a big, fake grin.

'Why, yes, Mirabelle, exactly. Exactly!' Aunt Connie looks moved by Mirabelle's fake wisdom, which she's borrowed from somewhere. 'The future is in the hands of the young. This eternal power will belong to you young witches and you will lead. We won't be around forever – but you are our legacy.'

Mirabelle looks embarrassed and I feel awkward too. It has never occurred to me that Aunt Connie might want more power for us, not just for herself. I worry that I am holding them back – I might be the fifth point, but I am a weak one and nothing seems to spark for me or with me.

'Work, witches!' Aunt Prudie shouts.

I lose track of time. At some point, I see tiny flakes of golden stars rise around Aunt Prudie, giving her a halo around her head and shoulders. But, after we've been stood in our star pointing our power at the pumpkin for so long my arm feels like it might drop off, Mirabelle gives up again.

She turns to go and I turn after her.

'Mirabelle, wait!' I say and reach for her hand.

'No, young hags!'

In the exact same moment that Aunt Connie's fingers brush against my left hand, Mirabelle's grazes my right hand.

As our hands make contact, a spark passes – somewhere.

Aunt Connie freezes, looking down her own arm

towards me, and then beyond me to Mirabelle. I'm a link in a chain between them, the unwitting net in the middle of a tennis match, and my head whisks from Mirabelle to Aunt Connie and back again.

I didn't feel the magic in my palms, I felt it right in my chest.

'What was that?' I ask.

'We've been thinking about this the wrong way!' Aunt Connie says in triumph, spectacles jiggling. 'The power of the star – we can't pass our magic directly into the vessel as individuals – we must channel it as a collective! Then you, young hags – you're simply the links in the chain!'

'We witches will soon have our full birth-right! Eternal power!' Aunt Connie breathes. 'This must be it! Witches! In formation!'

She excitedly rearranges us so we form a human chain leading towards the pumpkin: Mum, then me, then Mirabelle, then Connie and finally Prudie. We're stretched out like a row of paper dolls leading to Aunt Prudie, who has one hand in Aunt Connie's and the other firmly braced against the solid, curved orange wall of her pumpkin. One hand is stretched out in front of me in Mirabelle's hand, one behind in Mum's.

The one in Mirabelle's feels like a normal hand; a hand that after a while is slightly clammy with sweat.

Aunt Connie, usually so happy to let Mirabelle and I trail behind, has now sandwiched us between the more experienced witches and peers round us to look at Mum.

'Ready, Pattie?'

'Ready,' Mum confirms.

'Send your magic through,' Aunt Connie instructs. 'Clear your minds, young hags.'

'Flow! Flow!' Aunt Prudie shouts.

There's a huge shove from Mum behind me. I turn round to see if she's moved but of course she hasn't. The shove is magical – her magic pushing through my hand, into me. I suddenly feel twice as big as I did before. I must be twice as strong. It's like a collision on the motorway, cars backing into each other. There's a pile up of magic inside me and I can't contain it all, so it has to go somewhere.

CHAPTER 11

I focus, close my eyes and try to move the magic towards Mirabelle. I see her jump and almost drop my hand, but I squeeze hers tighter and think *shove – push – pass on*.

I can only hope she's doing the same thing. I know I couldn't handle keeping my mum's magic inside me, on top of my own . . . I don't know what might happen to Mirabelle with three people's magic in one body. The magic has to move on, up the chain and into the pumpkin.

Mum keeps going; her magic is strong and I stop thinking shove and start thinking flow. I imagine a gold thread of light, sparkling with stars, going up one arm, across my chest and down the other arm into Mirabelle, and immediately I stop jumping with the physical force of Mum's power.

I squeeze Mirabelle's hand again.

'That's it!' Aunt Prudie whispers. 'That's it!'

I open my eyes to look down the chain. I can see Aunt Prudie's hand, stark against the orange surface of the pumpkin, fizzing and sparking, illuminated all the way round with bright golden light.

Suddenly there are the faintest lights inside the pumpkin. Through the thick orange walls, in among the dense flesh and seeds, sparks of magic are glowing, moving. I've never seen fireflies in person, but this must be how they look.

At first, there are only one or two little sparks, but then there's a cluster, then hundreds, maybe even thousands. Soon, the entire pumpkin is glowing.

'Pull from deep within!' Aunt Connie calls back to us.

'Deep the well! Deep the power! Deep the connection!' Aunt Prudie shouts.

We're really doing it! The pumpkin is going to be full of power that we've dredged up from deep within ourselves and passed on. It's lit from the inside by thousands and thousands of tiny gleaming specks of light. We're capturing the magic. Now that it's really happening, my breath seems to have disappeared.

Apart from the gentle falling 'shush' of the hourglass, I have no idea how time passes. Sometimes, I feel the shunt of magic from Mum but it's easy to let it glide through me. It's like Mum herself: warm and light and easy to accept.

'Flow, witches, flow!' Aunt Connie urges.

Aunt Prudie leans in towards the pumpkin with the force of the magic, flattening her palm further against its surface until I can see every joint of her hand straining.

And that's when our little magic train derails.

Aunt Prudie mutters something and I don't quite hear it but it sounds like it must be really rude. There's a bird – a large, black bird with a flashing white belly – perched right on the middle of her head.

'No, pest, no!' Aunt Prudie hisses at the bird, stiff and apparently holding her breath.

The bird hops forward and leans over the front of Aunt Prudie's forehead, staring, upside-down, right into her eyes.

'Go! Away!' Aunt Prudie's voice is tight.

'Prudie!' Aunt Connie calls in a warning tone.

But it's too late. With both clawed feet still planted in Aunt Prudie's tangled grey curls, the bird stretches its whole body up, both wings beating, pulling at Aunt Prudie's thick hair. Aunt Prudie's straining against the bird, straining to keep her balance.

Aunt Connie is frozen in bewilderment.

Aunt Prudie can't take it. Like when you have an irresistible itch on your nose, she can't help but swat her hand – the hand that was holding Aunt Connie's – at the bird.

The connection is lost. Mum's hand goes rigid in mine and the thread of light disappears, both from my mind and my body. Mirabelle drops my hand. Both of my arms have gone dead, heavy.

We all break apart and I fall backwards with a thunk. I feel dizzy without the golden thread to hold me up.

Aunt Prudie yowls, reaching with both hands to grab the bird, and with our train now fully off its track, the thousands of lights inside the pumpkin start whisking back to the still glowing spot where her hand once was. The spot turns brighter and brighter until all those thousands of stars we funnelled into the pumpkin come bounding back out. For a moment, the room is filled with the brightest light as the stars find their way back to my coven. Settling back into our skin like they did at the very start of October.

The pumpkin, teeming with light just moment ago, has returned to its dull self.

There isn't time to be disappointed because, suddenly, there are more birds exploding out of the fireplace. Another flock bursts through the kitchen windows so that, in a matter of seconds, the ground floor of our house looks like a tornado of swirling, dark feathers. The bird on Aunt Prudie's head makes a *scraw scraw* noise and takes off into the flying melee.

'Under attack! Protect the pumpkin!' Aunt Prudie shouts, as the birds close in on us from all sides. Mum rushes forward. She and Aunt Prudie throw their hands up in unison, and a protective barrier of leaves and vines begins to grow up around the pumpkin.

I don't immediately feel any fear because they're, well, birds. But it's a numbers game and as a mass of flapping wings forms, I realise this isn't just a few accidental animals falling down the chimney. It doesn't help that they have hooked beaks, darting, beady eyes and thick yellow talons.

I crouch further down, covering my head with both arms. Just as they did on the way back home from the allotment, the birds dive-bomb the pumpkin, jabbing it with their sharp beaks, but now I don't mistake it for hunger. Aunt Prudie gives another thunderous clap.

The birds spiral up the corridor to the front door, which blasts open under their force. Among their twisting wings and beaks, I can see a figure.

I narrow my eyes at the outline but all I can see among the birds is a human shape. It could be the postman, but I don't recognise the silhouette.

'Mirabelle!' I call. 'Look! There!'

But Mirabelle is standing still, as if petrified.

The figure moves out of my line of sight. I glance backwards at my aunts who each have an arm extended, shielding their precious pumpkin.

'Hey!' Mirabelle calls. She's in the front doorway to our house, hesitating. Then she takes the leap and gives chase.

'Mirabelle!' I shout after her and start running too, because this October, I won't let her go.

I careen wildly down the road and, in motion, I can see the figure more clearly. It has legs and arms, both moving how human legs and arms move when you run. We're on its tail (though it doesn't have a literal tail), and I'm accelerating with that unstoppable arm-pounding, leg-piston feeling of someone who, to be honest, doesn't run that much.

But the figure ahead of us is speedier. It pulls away, shrinking as it moves faster than I ever could. Too fast. Whoever it is, they must be an athlete . . .

. . . or a witch.

Then I see the figure lift into the air.

I try one more sprint, putting a burst of speed into my limbs, imagining myself fast enough to catch up with them. If there is any magic in me that could make me faster, it fails.

I stop, gasping, and bend at the waist, hands on my knees. It was a short run but with no one to judge me, I swallow in air like I've come up from a deep-sea dive. Blood is pounding in my head, chest, calves as I squint upwards.

I straighten, one finger pointed up at the escaping figure. Nothing happens.

Mirabelle is still chasing but it's futile. The figure has almost disappeared.

She walks back to me with daggered eyebrows.

'She's gone,' Mirabelle says with a defeated, yet angry, shrug.

'She?'

'Yeah. Must be a witch. Or she couldn't have got so close. Or um – flew?' Mirabelle glances up and down our road, then scans the houses on either side. She wraps her arms tight around herself and gives a little shiver.

'Who was she?' I manage to get out.

'I thought it was Mum. My mum.' Mirabelle shrugs off her hope. 'That was stupid, though.' And before I can think of something kind to say to her, she takes off running again.

'We have to tell the aunts,' she pants over her shoulder. I haul myself upright and stagger after her, back down Pendragon Road.

Fear gives me an extra spurt of speed as I see our house, in the middle of its row. Number 15, usually so bright, so busy, looks strangely dark. The front door is open, as we left it, but inside there is a cluster of figures that most definitely wasn't there before.

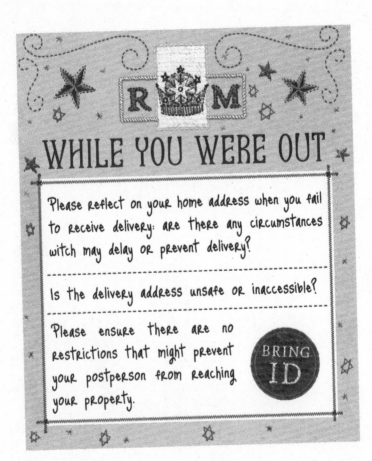

WHILE YOU WERE OUT

Please reflect on your home address when you fail to receive delivery: are there any circumstances witch may delay or prevent delivery?

Is the delivery address unsafe or inaccessible?

Please ensure there are no restrictions that might prevent your postperson from reaching your property.

BRING
ID

CHAPTER 12

At our front gate, Mirabelle turns to me with one finger to her lips.

She ducks low and pulls me down with her as we sneak across the front garden, ending up crouched together underneath the window.

'Protect! Ward! Guard!' Aunt Prudie yells from inside the house. 'Evil at the gate!'

'Someone hush that old hedge-hag,' a cold voice instructs.

Wait – I know that voice . . .

'No need to descend to name calling, Morgan,' says Aunt Connie.

Mirabelle nods at me.

'It's the Morgans? What are they doing here?' I whisper.

We see the Morgans twice a year – when our power descends from the stars and a month later, when it leaves. They have never, ever come visiting.

Aunt Prudie will be having absolutely none of it.

But here we are, hiding from them.

'Get down!' Mirabelle whispers so intensely that I can only actually hear the 'g' and 'd' of the words.

'We have to go in,' I hiss at her.

Mirabelle's hair is in my face as she gets close enough to actually whisper in my ear. 'You've heard about these witches!'

I pause for a moment and mentally dig around. What do I really know about the Morgans? I know they live somewhere they're very precious about and they think they're better than us. And they have some kind of plan – and don't necessarily care who it harms.

We huddle on the ground, aiming for silence and waiting to see what might happen inside.

'You descend on our coven, sabotage our work and destroy the safeguards on our home,' Aunt Connie continues, listing the crimes of the Morgan witches. 'But you have been practising against us for far longer than that. Morgans have long betrayed Merlyns. We are simply trying to reclaim the power which should be ours.'

'No, witch,' the cold voice says. 'Do you know your history so poorly? It was your ancestor to whom we owe our October problem and it is we Morgans who are redressing the balance.'

Underneath the window, Mirabelle and I both raise our eyebrows. There is a chilly moment of silence which, of course, Aunt Prudie has to fill. 'Crooks!'

'Be wise, Merlyn,' the cold Morgan voice warns. 'Think about what you accuse us of.'

My knee jiggles, without my permission.

'There is no sisterhood between our families,' Aunt Connie says viciously. 'And there are centuries' worth of accusations that remain unanswered.'

'Mind your falsehoods, witch!'

The tension in their voices is rising. I can feel the clench of collective anger. My fingers spark unintentionally. I have to see what's happening in there.

Mirabelle's hand on my forearm is heavy. 'Stay. Low,' she hisses.

But I have to see – I have to see what's happening to my mum. I inch myself upwards, my thighs complaining at my half-squat until my eyes are level with the windowsill.

Peering in through the open window, I can see our house has changed shape again, stretching to accommodate a full fleet of Morgan witches who stand still, their cloaks slightly moving in no breeze at all.

Our family have their hands up, on guard.

There may be no official rules about witches casting spells against other witches but it would be very bad manners. I've never seen my aunts do it, no matter how annoyed they get with each other. But this looks like it could get very dangerous, very quickly.

Aunt Prudie is crouched low and defensive. Mum has drawn herself up incredibly tall and has one arm raised straight above her, ready to swoosh it down in magical fury. She has outdone herself in her attire, even by her own standards. She's in a huge yellow ballgown, a spectacular meringue which makes everyone else look small in comparison. It's not what you might imagine someone would wear for battle, but it sure is intimidating.

Aunt Connie has one arm out across both of her sisters and one finger pointed and ready, aiming directly for the witch opposite her – Aunt Morgan. She's the witch who noticed me when the magic first descended in the park. I remember the sneer, the cold eyes, the pause in which she assessed me and then didn't give me her first name. I must not be important enough to her to receive her first name and, looking at

Aunt Morgan now, I can almost believe that she is so cold and impersonal that she doesn't actually have one.

The Morgans are now completely still, their cloaks making them limbless columns. They're in a tight triangular formation, as if they're about to break into a dance routine. Although I'm sure they wouldn't find the idea of that very funny.

Any moment now, someone is going to move a finger and there will be all-out chaos.

'The Morgans don't even have their hands up, Mirabelle, they didn't come here to fight,' I say, but she shushes me again.

'Magic works in more than one way, Clem,' she whispers through her teeth.

I feel Mirabelle slowly rise, her head bobbing up next to mine at the window. While the Morgans face away from us, as Mirabelle moves, Mum's eyes flicker over to us and widen. She shakes her head, so gently that I almost don't realise it's a warning. I don't know what I thought she would do – maybe welcome us in, introduce us – but she's telling us to keep out, turning her attention back to Aunt Morgan.

'Two branches of the same family tree, from the same soil, under the same stars,' Mum says gently.

She beams a smile across all the Morgan witches and the warmth of it reaches us too. 'The magic is always brighter in someone else's coven but . . . despite your unexpected visit today, I'm sure the October truce still stands.'

'Aunt Pattie can't stop them,' Mirabelle whispers to me urgently.

But my mum can do anything.

She is radiating positivity. The Morgans could be actual monsters and she'd probably still find a way to be nice about them.

'The Merlyns and Morgans are in this together,' Mum says. 'It's magic for all, or magic for none.'

'They're not magical musketeers,' Mirabelle whispers, even more urgently. But my mum is the best spokeswitch for our coven, and I'm sure she can make the Morgans see reason.

'Perhaps a cup of tea?' Mum continues, gracious and even a bit majestic. 'It is so difficult when we are only three and you are thirteen.' She is looking at me. 'We Merlyns are so few. Not even a full five-pointed star, as our young hags have left us.'

I open my mouth, almost rising from my crouch, and get a pointed elbow into my side.

'Stop,' Mirabelle hisses. 'She's covering for us. Protecting us.'

'We don't need protecting,' I hiss back.

'Oh, yeah? You wanna take on that lot?' Mirabelle jerks her head back inside. Thirteen witches, focused and fierce.

But Aunt Morgan's cold voice sounds almost amused. 'We Morgans don't lose witches. But they seem to bleed straight out from your broken coven. And we Morgans don't kill each other either, of course.'

A ripple of movement and quiet laughter passes across all the Morgans. Mirabelle suddenly looks like, she would like to 'take on that lot'. I put my hand out to her, feeling her rage like a radiator.

As they shift, I quickly count them. They are still as statues. I count and count again. *Thirteen.*

If this deadlock is broken, I don't rate my family's chances of winning. We – they – are severely outnumbered, and probably outwitched too. They look a mismatched and odd trio in the face of the Morgans' full coven.

'The October truce still stands,' Aunt Morgan announces and the witches behind her relax.

My family stay stiff in their poses, ready to act at any moment.

But they are still too slow as Aunt Morgan, hands motionless by her side, nods sharply. She disappears with a pop and reappears immediately next to the pumpkin, her cloak settling gently around her.

Next to me, Mirabelle's breath catches, like mine does when I run.

My mum and Aunt Connie keep their hands aimed at the remaining Morgans, but Aunt Prudie turns around sharply.

'Stay away!' she shrieks as Aunt Morgan softly settles on her feet next to the pumpkin.

'Now, answer to greater power, Merlyns. What is this monstrosity?' Aunt Morgan demands. 'We felt the vibrations, even in our stronghold.'

'No!' Aunt Prudie protests.

'You felt the magic we made?' Aunt Connie asks, seemingly dazzled.

'You didn't make anything.' Aunt Morgan sniffs. 'You moved the magic. You unbalanced everything.'

Aunt Morgan raises both hands and runs them along the outside of the pumpkin, like she is a metal detector.

Aunt Prudie hisses at her, her wrinkled face crinkling further in dismay.

'You have tried to imbue your . . . large vegetable . . .

with magic?' Aunt Morgan asks, rubbing her palms together.

'Yes,' Aunt Connie says. It's not really a compliment but, suddenly, Aunt Connie is glowing, as if with success.

'No,' Aunt Prudie chips in unnecessarily, stepping protectively between Aunt Morgan and her pumpkin.

'Well, yes, but then you sabotaged us,' Aunt Connie adds, turning to examine the pumpkin.

'We did no such thi—' Aunt Morgan starts, but something distracts her as she stares at the pumpkin.

Then I catch sight of it too.

One gleaming, tiny spark of magic, floating inside, turning the thick pumpkin walls a glowing red-orange when it bumbles against them.

Aunt Connie trills in triumph; Aunt Prudie sighs with happy contentment, like you might if you were looking at a puppy or a kitten, but Aunt Morgan gasps.

I watch the single floating spark, like a pool float bobbing around a swimming pool, knocking and rebounding easily against the sides. It is hypnotising to watch its random progress inside the pumpkin; it looks like a little lost firefly pottering around.

This could be the start of eternal magic. Not just tricky-to-navigate Octobers. I'd never go back to school;

I'd be stuck at home with just my own coven forever and ever. Unlike all my coven elders, I have friends who are humans and I've been looking forward to seeing them, at Halloween and beyond. I know there are bigger problems out there in the world, but imagining a life, where it's always October and never Christmas, fills me with dread.

'You really did it,' Aunt Morgan breathes, stepping instinctively towards the pumpkin. Aunt Prudie blocks her path and stands squarely, legs braced.

Emotions flick across Aunt Morgan's face with speed and, just for a moment, she is gleeful. Then she looks hungry and I realise – she wants that pumpkin.

'How?' Aunt Morgan asks quietly.

'Natural! Witch-made.'

'And you have managed this . . . here?' Aunt Morgan gives our house and all its clutter a special sneer. 'Do not fear, I shall not damage your vessel. This represents a breakthrough for all of witchkind. But it is only a start. One speck of magic does not a lifetime supply make.'

Every witch is still gazing at the pumpkin and the speck of magic cruising around inside it.

And I realise with dread that Aunt Morgan has much bigger plans for our pumpkin.

CHAPTER 13

Aunt Morgan turns from the pumpkin to my mum and I only catch a glimpse of her face but there is something . . . wrong with it.

'You little Merlyns and your little ways,' Aunt Morgan smiles, almost indulgently. 'Now, it is the Morgan way to reconcile magic with modern advancements. So, only we Morgans have the resources to develop this . . . fledgling research. We do, after all, have a shared goal – whether Morgan or Merlyn, we seek to extend the reach of our power,' Aunt Morgan says.

'We do indeed,' I hear Aunt Connie agree.

Aunt Morgan's tone is purringly, hypnotically enticing. 'And I'm sure we can put ancient grudges aside to find a solution for us all.'

'You propose . . . a reconciliation? More than a truce?' Aunt Connie asks. She sounds dazzled.

'Never trust Morgans,' a low voice growls. It's Aunt Prudie.

'We are most . . . unfamiliar . . . cousins, but I believe our covens can come together. We are complimentary puzzle pieces. Our technological advancements, your . . . large vegetable. It fits.' Aunt Morgan coughs delicately when she says 'vegetable'. 'We propose installing it into our mainframe.'

'You have a frame for it?' Aunt Connie asks, and I'd be embarrassed if I wasn't so worried for my family.

Aunt Morgan's sneer returns; I can hear it in her voice. 'More than a frame,' she says. 'And we could consider a new formation, perhaps?'

But if she's asking my family to collaborate with hers, then why are her glinting eyes fixed so hungrily on my coven?

'No!' Aunt Prudie yells. 'Exploiters of magic! Breakers of rules! Crooks!' Aunt Prudie is lots of things, but she's never wrong. She furrows her brow at the Morgans.

'Ah. Of course, you still abide by the old rules,' Aunt Morgan says dismissively.

'Hidden! No harm! The only rules!' Aunt Prudie shouts.

'Archaic!' Aunt Morgan answers back. 'We may be witches but we must make progress.'

'Tradition!' Aunt Prudie shouts.

'Progress!' Aunt Morgan insists.

'TRADITION OVER ALL!' Aunt Prudie screeches.

'A typical Merlyn mistake.' Aunt Morgan continues to sneer at my family. She draws herself up, her shoulders and neck both stretching so high so that she is literally looking down on them. 'We extend a hand and all you can do is bark at it. Always the smallest dogs that bark the loudest.'

There's a menacing moment of quiet in which I realise, watching her, that Aunt Morgan seems even more dangerous when she isn't talking.

'We don't have time for this,' she announces suddenly.

Everything happens in a blink. Aunt Connie, the most won-over by Aunt Morgan, cries out first. Bright white stars pour like paint over Aunt Connie's hands, which then go stiff and motionless. The Morgans are covering my family's hands in gloves of stars, obstructing their magic.

Aunt Prudie is still fighting to free herself, getting magic ready in her mind, but the cluster of Morgan stars has already closed around her hands, sealing them so it looks like she dipped her hands in white stardust.

Mum doesn't make a sound, but she seems to be trying to tell me so much with her eyes that my own eyes water holding her stare.

I open my mouth and Mirabelle's hand clamps tight over my face, keeping the scream in.

'Clem, no!' Mirabelle hisses, but she must not be seeing what I am seeing.

'Merlyn witches have always been at risk of extinction.' Aunt Morgan's voice is bitingly cold.

'Under attack! Witches to war! Coven forward!' Aunt Prudie shrieks, hot with useless fury.

'No, there won't be a war. We can't let you go now you've created this . . . monstrous thing,' Aunt Morgan says, and I can't tell if her lips are curled in amusement or disdain.

'This is the only logical, reasonable way forward,' Aunt Morgan says. But it occurs to me that every tyrant has probably thought that their way is the only reasonable way.

'Perhaps we could discuss this—' Mum begins but Aunt Morgan is issuing further quick, chilling instructions and ignoring my family all together now.

'Morgans, to the vegetable.'

'Not my pumpkin!' Aunt Prudie shouts.

'Bring that filthy hedge witch too,' Aunt Morgan counters.

'Not my sister!' Aunt Connie shouts in turn.

'And the hearth witch,' Aunt Morgan orders. 'Take all three, they'll come in handy.'

'But, Mother . . .' someone says, very quietly. I scan the room, trying to work out which of the cloaked figures is speaking.

'Not now, Senara,' Aunt Morgan snaps.

'But there are young hags too, Mother.' It is one of the younger Morgans, speaking for the first time.

That's us. The young witch means us. Next to me, Mirabelle shivers.

'Oh, they've gone,' Mum says airily. I've never heard her lie before. 'And no one needs such weak young hags.' I've never heard her be mean before, either. She's performing for the Morgans.

'True. We need no weaklings or deadweights,' Aunt Morgan says. Even though I've got no idea how to use my magic, none of my coven have ever called me a weakling or a deadweight before.

'But, Mother—' the young hag tries again.

'Enough! We have enough with your useless sister.'

The witch called Senara wears the white cloak of the Morgans majestically, and she has the same tight lips as Aunt Morgan, the bottom one now tucked under her teeth. If we were at school and she spoke to me,

I'd be alarmed. But here, she is the least of our problems.

'Mother . . . maybe I could . . .'

Aunt Morgan's eyes sweep across the room and the rest of her coven move with mechanical efficiency, the pumpkin and my family immediately surrounded. I lose sight of Mum for a moment as the Morgan figures move into position, like lots of small moons orbiting the sun.

'I won't tell you again, Senara. Do not speak out of turn, do not step out of turn,' Aunt Morgan says, her voice icily cold, dismissing her daughter.

The star the Morgans form is large and many-pointed. It shimmers around my family, trapping them in a net of magic.

Aunt Prudie is still hissing and spitting curses at the Morgans, but Mum has pulled inwards so that her shoulders are touching her sisters'.

Aunt Morgan steps forward into her place in the new star.

I wish I could do even the smallest thing to help my mum and my aunts, but I have no idea what and I don't want to put them in more danger. My own hands are clasped so tightly together I can feel my bones under the skin and flesh and magic.

The Morgans link hands; a glow at each connection.

Aunt Morgan, commanding her troops, narrows both eyes. The room seems to darken, making the Morgans' eyes glow even brighter.

Mum's lips move in the moment of frozen silence, her eyes fixed on mine. '*The stars know.*'

Aunt Morgan holds her chin up for a brief moment, then brings it down in a deep, abrupt nod.

And just like that, they're gone. Our house stands still and empty – no Morgans, no pumpkin. Like they were never there at all. No Aunt Connie, no Aunt Prudie – no Mum.

Mirabelle releases me abruptly and I almost fall. My head is foggy and far away. It doesn't feel attached to the rest of me. My mind is reeling. I just saw Mum, my aunts and the Morgans appear to wink out of existence.

'Follow me,' Mirabelle says. '*Quietly.*'

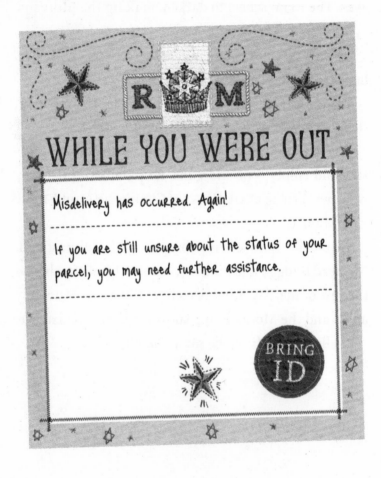

WHILE YOU WERE OUT

Misdelivery has occurred. Again!

If you are still unsure about the status of your parcel, you may need further assistance.

BRING ID

CHAPTER 14

I'm in the worst kind of shock, the state of sick disbelief kind. Mum said the truce was built on 'hidden and no harm' but these Morgans clearly don't care about keeping to that.

Mirabelle opens our front door as silently as possible. I am hopping with frustration behind her – as if seeing directly inside, instead of through the window, might make our family less 'gone' – but Mirabelle won't let me go on ahead. It's like we're on a dangerous expedition.

She inches up the corridor, silently.

'So, what are we meant to do now?' a voice says with a distinct moan from inside our living room.

'Ssh,' another voice answers.

'We're in the middle of a city. Full of humans! And I don't want to stay here, look at all this old junk.'

'Ssh,' the second voice hisses again, this time more warningly.

'Look . . . look at their tapestry. Do you think that's meant to be Merlyn?'

I frown at Mirabelle. We don't even have a tapestry.

'She looks pathetic.'

I risk a peek. There are two figures in our living room; their backs are turned towards us but I recognise them by their braids – one girl with stubby flyaway plaits, the other with a snaky elegant crown. They're even wearing the ridiculous long cloaks, but, out of formation, these two young Morgan hags are less alarming-looking than when they're with their whole pack. They're both seriously out of place here, alone, in our home. And they seem *seriously* distracted by the old throw of our ancestor that Aunt Connie put up on the wall. I try not to think about where Mum and my aunts might be right now, and focus instead on the young Morgan hags in our house.

'Mirabelle,' I hiss. 'Now would be the time for . . .' And I twirl my finger for her so she knows what I mean.

Mirabelle grits her teeth and I realise that, while I know she's been working magic upstairs, in the safety and privacy of her own ever-expanding room, I've never seen her actually doing it.

A pile of books teeters then topples, sending one of the young Morgan hags hopping sideways. Before she has a chance to find her balance, a stack of saucepans dramatically falls over and hits her, as if they're on our side – which I guess they are. Mirabelle's hand is gently swaying, tiny stars twinkling around her fingers as she brings our house to life. Like the world's best burglar-defence system.

The rug trips up the smaller of the two witches and she falls forward onto her hands. The window shutters float from their frames and clatter on either side of her head. She ends up sprawled, face-first, on the floor.

'What is this place?' she calls out in a proper stage whisper. She looks completely undignified as she staggers back upright. 'Senara! Do something! This house is after me!'

Senara is the one who called Aunt Morgan 'Mother', only to be told to not speak out of turn. I can't imagine ever calling anyone as hard as Aunt Morgan 'Mother'.

'Are you doing this?' I check with Mirabelle.

'Ward! Guard! Protect!' she answers in her Aunt Prudie voice with the slightest smile, which must be a *yes*.

'There! They're right there!' The smaller Morgan is staring right at us. 'Senara! Do! Something!' She's the one from the night in the park, the one whose eyes didn't glint. The one who didn't receive her magic.

Senara Morgan seems oblivious to her sister's nagging, and even to the enormous racket Mirabelle just caused. She's transfixed by the image of the first Merlyn, seeing something in that old throw that I most definitely do not.

'SENARA!' urges the smaller of our invaders again, 'DO!' she tugs at the bigger Morgan's cloak, 'SOMETHING!' and finally Senara's focus is broken, though she still looks slightly dazzled.

Before I can move, Mirabelle swerves in front of me, blocking me from the Morgans with both arms raised, all ten fingers stretched out completely taut. She's focused all her energy on the younger, shorter Morgan hag, who is not as intimidated as she should be, considering how Mirabelle's hands are sparking.

'Hands down, or I will be forced to use my almighty power on you! Step down, young hags!' the stubby-braided Morgan girl shouts.

I remember how, in the park, Aunt Morgan held up this girl's chin, peering deep into her eyes before turning away in disgust.

'She doesn't have her powers yet!' I call out to Mirabelle.

'They left a witch who hasn't even had her First

October yet?' says Mirabelle. 'Morgans are the worst.'

'You'd better believe that when I do get my magic,' the girl shouts back, 'I'll show you the worst!'

'Oh, yeah, it's gonna be over for us Merlyns?' Mirabelle says, baiting her. 'Yeah, no worries, we'll just wait until next year – or the year after – or the year after that.'

'It's OK,' the older girl, Senara, says from the sidelines of this confrontation. 'We surrender.'

'No, we don't!' the second witch shouts. 'Get them, Senara! Now! Just . . . blink!'

I look into Senara's eyes and immediately realise our mistake. Where the dark pupil in the centre of her eyes should be, there's a glinting gold star. Several times now, I have watched her mother use her magic. Aunt Morgan's hands never even move, and the 'wrongness' that I thought I saw in her face was *gold, flared pupils*.

Mirabelle obviously has the same dawning realisation. Senara could have used her power in a blink but she hasn't. The Morgans' power isn't in their hands, but their strange eyes.

'I'm afraid we've got off on the wrong foot,' the older of the two young hags says amiably, and holds out a hand – not as a witch, but as if to give a handshake. 'I'm Senara.' Her voice is quiet, low, very calm, in contrast to the squawking Morgan.

Neither of us take it, of course. My palms are so sensitive and full of magic, I have no idea what would happen.

Instead, I eye Senara. She's the first and only Morgan I know the first name of.

Senara is older than both Mirabelle and me and simply looks cool. It might be her eye make-up – oil-slick black – or the rueful half-smile she gives me, or that I don't really know what to say to her. Her complicated braid, ringing her head like a crown and snaking down her shoulder is as smooth as she is. Senara is also, like all the Morgans, magnificently tall.

'And who is that kid?' Mirabelle asks Senara.

Mirabelle pushed me back, she shielded me, but I step forward now.

'The youngest young hag I've ever seen,' I say. She can't be any older than twelve. She might even be eleven. Or ten.

'I'm not too young, I'm already twelve! Probably older than you,' the witch shouts. 'It should have been my year!' Her braids stick out just below her ears, making it look like her earlobes have tufts of their own hair.

'And that . . . well, that is Kerra. Mother says she's my responsibility this October.' Senara sounds tired at the very thought.

'Where are our family? What has your mother done with them?' My urge for revenge is overridden by the need to know about my family. I don't care for polite introductions right now. I saw what just happened and, even though I believe in magic, I still don't really believe my family could wink out of being, just like that. 'Where have they gone?'

Merlyns don't travel anywhere, really, but if we do, we definitely don't blink and disappear – it's too hard, too risky, as Mirabelle's accidental excursion to the Arctic proved.

Only now is my mind working through the consequences. Aunt Prudie had called the Morgans crooks but they could be even worse. Their coven is ruthless. I knew the truth of that as soon as I saw the Morgans cut off my mum's magic at the fingertips. They smashed straight through what Mum explained as the rule for all witches 'hidden and do no harm'. They turned their magic on my family.

I try to imagine my aunts and mum in the Morgans'

clutches and come up worried and blank. 'What did your coven do to our family?' I push.

What if the very worst has happened? But I would know if Mum was dead . . . surely I would know, I'd feel it. The world couldn't carry on as normal without her kindness keeping it going.

'Mirabelle, what if . . .' I try and rephrase the question to avoid saying 'dead'. 'How do we know they're still alive?'

The two Morgan witches both start speaking at the same time, the one called Kerra trying to step towards us, which makes Mirabelle's hands rise defensively again.

'Oh, the unending Merlyn stupidity,' Kerra says. 'Your family aren't dead. We're not medieval!'

'But your coven broke the truce!'

Senara is watching me carefully and she must see the horror in my eyes. 'It's not the murdering kind of bad. Mother wouldn't *waste* your coven's magic. She'll use it. And all of your Merlyn magic is still here, so we know they're . . . alive.'

'Is that how it works?' I ask.

'When the witch dies, the work dies,' Kerra says, sounding exasperated.

'Is that true?' I ask Mirabelle.

Mirabelle shrugs.

'You don't even know the basics, Merlyn! Of course the magic doesn't survive the witch!' Kerra exclaims.

I look for something that I am one hundred per cent sure Mum has made. I hear the smallest whinny.

I quickly lift Bobby out of my pocket. I'd like to give her a kiss, but not in front of Morgans.

I hold out the tiny pony, cupped in my hands. 'Mum made her. So the pony means Mum's OK?' I double check.

I catch Kerra, her hand in mid-air, reaching out to the pony without even realising she's doing it. Her eyes have gone soft. No one can resist Bobby's charms, not even a Morgan. Our eyes meet and she pulls her hand back sharply.

'It means Aunt Pattie is alive,' Mirabelle says.

'I already told you they were alive,' Kerra says with a frown.

I bend over to put Bobby the pony on the floor. I almost fell out of love with that little pony but now she's my closest link to Mum. While she whinnies and snorts and trots about, I have hope.

Suddenly, the picture of Merlyn on our wall flops forward like she is trying to tell us something.

But it's just the stars that hold her in place falling out as if they were just pins and not magic. Now, the throw has slipped, half-folded over so we can't see her handless arms or the grey tracks of her tears.

'They might not be dead, but something isn't right – what's happening?' I advance on Kerra. 'I said . . . *what is happening*?'

Kerra swallows and looks to her older sister. I recognise that look – I check on Mirabelle in exactly the same way. But I push forward.

'Hey, Morgan! What is happening to our family?'

If the magic in this house is starting to slip, then nothing good can be happening to our family, wherever they are now. If they don't have their full-throttle October magic, then they're not safe.

Mirabelle has had lots of experience at being motherless, but my mum has never been gone before. I've never really known how Mirabelle must feel until now. Without my mum, my chest is tight. My heart is heavy, and not just with magic.

My family may be alive, but they're definitely under threat – as Mum feared. And worse, they won the race to restore their magic first, yet they were still not safe from the Morgans.

Like the grains of sand in her hourglass, I feel Aunt Connie's urgency, trickling down inside me. The same anger and energy Aunt Prudie expels with every non-sentence she speaks runs through my veins. And my mum's calm is the only thing helping me keep it together.

'It'll be Mother's great plan! And Mother will definitely tell us, she will. She'll be expecting to hear from us. We will send word that we've got you and she'll be so happy she'll share everything with us, even though we're only young hags!' Kerra says in a burst.

'Well, you haven't got us,' Mirabelle points out, and Senara makes an exasperated sound.

'Mother said—' Kerra starts again.

'Kerra! Mother actually said "stop talking"! In fact, stop everything!'

They both have a little shiver on 'Mother'. I pause for a moment, interested in something other than their obvious Morgan-ness. Senara hides it better but they both flinch when they talk about Aunt Morgan.

'Thank you but no thank you, sister, you have no authority over me here.'

'See,' Mirabelle says quietly to me, 'I told you that you didn't want a sister.'

'I thought you two *were* sisters?' Senara asks.

'We're cousins,' I say and Mirabelle says, 'Oh my stars, no,' at the same time.

I sigh. She didn't have to say '*no*' quite so hard.

'Come on, Senara! Do it now!' Kerra hisses.

I look from one Morgan to the other. The younger one clearly has plans but no power and, luckily for us, the older one has power but no plans.

'Do what?' I ask.

'We're not doing anything,' Senara says, grimacing at Kerra and then turning to offer Mirabelle and me a smooth smile.

'Urgh, may the stars save you from ever having such an annoying sister,' Kerra says, throwing her hands up then insisting in an audible whisper to Senara, 'Mother would be so impressed if we brought her more Merlyns.'

'Kerra,' Senara says with a low warning in her voice.

I find myself watching Senara constantly, nervously. We have no reason to trust her, but she is at least doing a good job of not looking suspicious.

'Neither of you has any authority,' Mirabelle adds, giving me a sideways glance. 'Over us or our house or anything.'

'When we bring you in,' Kerra continues, getting more worked up, 'Mother will be so pleased with us that she'll let us be part of her big plans. Because Morgans have big plans. Important ones that I know all about and you—'

A knock at the door spreads a wide, smug smile across Kerra's face.

'There,' she says, delighted. 'I told you Mother would send for us.'

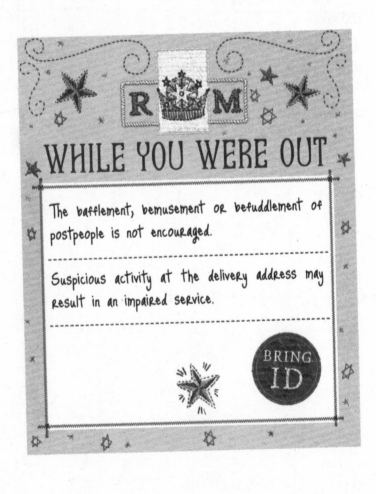

WHILE YOU WERE OUT

The bafflement, bemusement or befuddlement of postpeople is not encouraged.

Suspicious activity at the delivery address may result in an impaired service.

BRING ID

CHAPTER 15

Looks quickly dart between all of us. From Mirabelle to me: fear, from Kerra to Senara: anticipation.

'Delivery for you!'

'It's the postman.' I sigh with relief.

'The what now?' Kerra asks as I head into the corridor, where I can see the postman is hovering at our garden gate.

'Delivery for you!' the postman says again, voice bright. 'Delivery for you!' He sounds like he's stuck on repeat. And, as I peer out into the road, he looks like he's stuck just inside the gate too. Unable to move forward or back.

I hop across the path to take the parcel out of the postman's hands.

'Oh,' I say, once I see the parcel. 'I'm sorry, I don't know how . . . but you've already delivered this.' I heft the familiar parcel in my hands. It's the same long, heavy rectangle. If it were to stand on its end, it would come all the way up to my chest.

I remember Aunt Connie setting it aside, but I don't remember what happened to it then. Our house is too busy to keep track of stuff like a mystery parcel.

I slide a finger under the brown paper of the parcel then tear off a whole corner. I have to know what's inside, because I can't even have a good guess with this strange shape and weight. Underneath is another layer of brown paper.

'Yes . . . I was here . . . before?' He shakes his head in confusion for a moment, then his smile resets itself. 'Ordering a lot of stuff, are we? Online shopping – bane of my life,' he says with an odd grin.

I look at the postman, really look, for the first time. I've been so full of my own October that I've hardly noticed him.

'Hey . . .' I start.

Something about the postman gleams. I blink, looking to see what it could be, but it's probably just his gold-rimmed glasses catching the light. I try and take in details I hadn't noticed before. Dark hair greying at the temples and the sides of his neat beard; kind, though slightly dazzled eyes. He's got a crest on the left side of his shirt, a large crown above a badge which says 'ROYAL MAIL'.

The postman's mind clearly can't compute. He must be amazingly strong to even get this close to our magical barrier. He's hearing me from far away, as if I'm deep underwater.

'Have a good day!' the postman calls, readjusting the red sack over his shoulder. 'Have a good da—'

He stops dead, staring over my head into the house.

'Um,' the postman says, staring. 'You . . . um . . .'

Behind me, there's a sputtering noise.

I turn round to see where it is coming from. The cauldron is rising, thick rim and large belly glowing, floating towards us as if it is trying to make an escape. It is spurting and sending jags of tiny stars in all directions and . . . seems to be trying to leave the house.

'Um . . . ignore that, it's just . . . a cauldron,' I say quickly then immediately regret it. 'Thank you!'

I seize the cauldron, dragging it back inside with me. 'Where do you think you're going?' I hiss at it.

I kick the door shut behind me as quickly as possible, dump the awkwardly-shaped parcel on the bottom step of the stairs and pull the cauldron with me. It is bubbling and hissing sparks, and has taken on an iridescent sheen. I open my mouth to say, '*it's just soup, it's no big deal,*' when something rises from the cauldron.

As a glittering gold line begins to snake its way out of the cauldron, I don't, at first, understand what I'm seeing. It's as if an invisible hand is drawing in the air, just how Aunt Prudie did at the beginning of the month. It could be a snail trail, the way it shimmers and catches the light. But it's more fast-moving than that. And it's hovering in mid-air.

'Clem, are you doing this?' Mirabelle calls.

'No, of course not,' I say. Senara and Kerra move backwards, away from what is becoming a star. 'What are you up to, Morgans?'

Senara shakes her head, staring at the star. 'Not me.'

'And obviously me neither,' Kerra adds. 'You Merlyns are so random. Someone else is messing with that cauldron. Whose is it?'

'It's Aunt Temmie's,' Mirabelle says, keeping her eyes on the fizzing pot.

'Which one was that – the one in the overalls?'

'No, Temmie is dead.'

Senara frowns. 'But when the witch dies—'

The curious star is fully formed now and floating free of the cauldron.

We retreat from it, cautiously keeping our distance,

Mirabelle and I on one side and Senara and Kerra on the other.

'Five points – that makes it a Merlyn star,' Kerra points out.

'It can't be,' I murmur.

'But there are two others? Elders, I mean?' Kerra half-asks, half-tells.

'No, there aren't,' Mirabelle says immediately.

Watching her, I add, 'One other. Our Aunt Temmie is dead and Flissie—'

'Doesn't use her powers,' Mirabelle says.

'She never received them?'

'No, she has powers but she just doesn't use them.'

Kerra is flabbergasted. 'So your coven is split?'

'You don't know anything about our family,' I say sharply, imagining Aunt Flissie and Aunt Temmie being carried away on a tiny piece of land, split away from ours. 'That's not what happened.'

Although, like it or not, I'm now in a coven of two – just me and my 'doesn't even like me on good days' cousin.

I glower at Kerra. 'You stole my mum, you magic-crazy young hag!' I accuse her, outrage making me squeakier than usual. 'And *something* is happening to her.'

The urgency of knowing that my family is under threat bubbles and pops inside me.

'I don't know who you're calling magic-crazy,' Kerra says, 'but you had better mind your words, Merlyn, because we are two of the most fearsome—'

My hands are up, despite myself. I don't know what I'd even do with them, but Kerra has goaded me too far.

She tilts her head in bemusement. 'What are you doing?'

'I . . . I . . .'

'You Merlyns look so silly waving your hands around. You're meant to use your eyes for your magic. It's the way that mighty Morgan worked herself. We're witches of the mind, you're witches without minds.'

It's then that we notice that the outline of the star, which has been hovering and twinkling in the air, is beginning to float down towards the floor, ready for witches to occupy its points.

'Did you do that?' Mirabelle's question is directed at me.

'The answer is always going to be "no",' I tell her.

'I am not getting in *that* with Merlyns,' says Kerra firmly to the newly formed star which has settled on the floor between us. 'I don't think Mother would be best pleased, either.' She straightens her back and stalks away, her cloak flicking at her heels.

I don't much want to get in a star with Morgans, either. But I want my mum and my aunts back more than anything.

'No way am I getting in that star,' Mirabelle says. 'We don't know where it's come from. Or what it will do.'

'It came out of our cauldron. Someone sent it for us, so must be worth a go . . . come on, Mirabelle, please. For my mum?' I half-beg.

Mirabelle nods. 'For Aunt Pattie . . . yes, I'll try.'

'No,' Kerra says. 'I am not holding hands with a Merlyn.'

'Better safe than starry,' Senara says.

'Did you . . .? Was that . . .? A pun?' Mirabelle asks. She sweeps back her wild curls to actually look at Senara. She is paying Senara much closer attention than she's ever paid me. I'm suddenly jealous.

'Look, we're witches first, right?' Senara asks. 'Right? Merlyn or Morgan, magic is still magic, isn't it? Comes from the same stars and all that.'

'Yes,' Mirabelle agrees, too readily.

Kerra and I both frown, but I try and stop when we catch each other's eyes.

'We never, um, introduced ourselves,' Mirabelle says. 'I'm Mirabelle and this is Clem.'

'Clemmie,' I say, but I don't really mind having a nickname that only Mirabelle uses.

'Hi,' Senara says, her smile spreading.

'Mirabelle, can we . . .?' I say, tilting my head to one side. As Mirabelle slouches after me, I whisper intently, 'I don't trust her.'

'Just chill,' Mirabelle says. 'They're like us, two young hags who have nothing to do with their family's goings-on—'

'Actually,' Kerra interrupts, 'we young hags are vital—'

'Hagtually, we're not,' Senara sweeps in, and Mirabelle laughs as if this is the greatest joke ever.

I frown at them both. Mirabelle is starting to sound friendly to a Morgan.

'That's weird,' Kerra says.

There's so much that's weird that I'm surprised she can pick out something particular, but when I look where she is pointing, I see what she means.

It's a bird again, not even flying but casually hopping across the floor towards us. I have no idea where it came from or when it arrived.

'A type of falcon,' Senara says.

'They nest on the cliffs where we're from,' Kerra adds.

'Cliffs?' I murmur, wondering if we should be fleeing from this pumpkin-attacking bird. But there's no pumpkin here now.

'They watch us all the time.'

I look at the dark falcon who haunts the Morgans and messes with us Merlyns. 'Friend or foe, bird?'

The bird cocks its head at us.

'Shoo!' I try.

The bird does not shoo. The bird does not do anything. To be honest, it doesn't look like the kind of bird that would respond, even if it did understand me; it is too haughty.

Like Kerra and Senara, without the rest of its kind, it looks odd, and not intimidating. That beak and those yellow claws are still alarming, though.

The bird hops. Its head bobs on its neck and its dark eyes look like they see everything. Then it hops forward once again until its curled feet are on one point of the star.

R M

WHILE YOU WERE OUT

Please be aware: your item is overlarge so must be sent separately.

Your parcel cannot be returned to sender because it is extraordinarily heavy.

BRING
ID

CHAPTER 16

We all gape at the bird.

'I am most definitely not getting in a star with a bird!' Kerra looks disgusted at the thought. 'Who is leading this star? Whose formation is this?'

This is not how star formations work. This is totally what my mum told me not to do. A Morgan-Merlyn hybrid star. I doubt it's ever been done before, definitely not by my aunts.

I step forward into the star anyway, taking a point next to the one the bird is standing in. If my mum and my aunts were here, I'd be part of their star. But if there's a chance of getting them back, I'll be part of any star at all. Mirabelle steps into the point on my other side. There's a brief pause and then Senara, all icy elegance; just like her mum, swishes her immaculate white cape and finds her spot on the other side of the bird.

We stand awkwardly on the points, as if they are bases in a sport we're about to start playing, but we're a player short. The bird tilts its head up at us and chirps.

'Excuse me, I must speak with my sister,' Senara says and Kerra follows her, looking like a rebellious puppy.

They stand aside, quietly hissing at each other.

'Can you hear what they're saying?' I ask.

'I know what they're saying,' Mirabelle says. She does a low voice in imitation of Senara. *Why are you so annoying? Why do you never listen to what you're meant to do?*'

'You can hear that?' I ask.

'No, of course not. But I know that's what all older sisters think about younger ones.'

I turn and watch Senara point at the bird, point at the star, point at herself and get totally exasperated.

Kerra's hair is staticky, as if it's been thoroughly rubbed against a balloon. I wonder if her short plaits are an attempt to copy her more glamorous older sister.

When they return to the star, Senara glares at Kerra, suddenly looking a lot like her mother.

'Mother doesn't like it when we deviate from her plan. And we already have, because ... here we are,' Kerra says and shrugs at the bird, the star, us.

Slowly and deliberately, Kerra steps forward to take her place in the star and stands there formally, as if she is posing for a portrait called 'Witch on Star'.

I close my eyes for a minute and pretend to myself that my family, with the easy, experienced way they carry their power, are here, surrounding us. My mum, her warm skin and sweet lemon smell, her smile which spreads slowly and gently and always reaches her eyes with a sparkle.

Aunt Prudie's barking voice, her freshly cut grass smell, her tough, soil-covered, hands. Aunt Connie, as thick and solid as a rounded loaf. Her neat nails and neat apron. The mouth-watering smell of bread, carefully timed to be baked to perfection.

'Now what?' Mirabelle demands and I open my eyes.

Our bodies know before our brains that something strange is happening. For a moment, I think it's the magic inside me quaking before I realise that everyone is feeling it. The sensation, a soaring swoop deep in my belly, intensifies and then disappears with a pop. I reach out my hands to either side of me and realise they're glowing.

Everyone looks at everyone else, our eyes reflecting the same shock back at each other.

'What happened?'

I look around at our house. Everything looks the same. Apart from . . .

The window that Mirabelle and I were only just on the other side of has a view of nothing at all. No houses, no trees, no cars. Just sky.

I walk firmly to the front door and open it. Our street is gone; there's a flat, blurry, blue horizon far away from us and nothing else. If I was to take a single step out of the door, it would be into emptiness.

Number 15 has lost the rest of its terrace, like a small urban sheep without the rest of its flock.

I lean as far out the front door as I dare and look down. Then I wish I hadn't. Directly below me, hundreds of feet down, there is greeny-blue water. Oh. My. Stars. It's the sea.

'Clem! Get back in here!' Mirabelle calls from where she's peering out the open kitchen window.

Our house has travelled, intact apparently, to the end of the earth.

We're at the very edge of the land; on a cliff. Below us is jumble of fallen rocks and nothing else apart from the sea's white foamy border. I back away from the front door feeling sick.

'I will not die because of a falling house!' Mirabelle shouts, then, seeing my blank face, she rolls her eyes. 'We can't let it go over the cliff!'

'Where are we?' I murmur, still seeing only sea.

But Kerra's face is different. Her expression has turned wild and free. She looks like she could bite or even kiss the world she's staring out into.

'Home,' she says, rapturously.

A loud caw breaks my focus on her, and I turn round to see the bird hop straight on to Kerra's head.

'Get off me,' Kerra blurts as heavy wings flap in her face. She sputters, flailing her arms and shaking her head, infuriated by this mystery guest invading her personal space, just as it did Aunt Prudie's. It expels one final croak, tilts its head at us and pushes off Kerra's forehead, straight out the window. With a series of heaving flaps, the bird disappears among the clifftop heather.

Morgan territory. I don't know whether I should be excited or frightened at finding ourselves here. I'm even more glad now that Bobby is in my pocket. I fish her out and stroke her mane. The star on her forehead has started to fade, but otherwise Bobby still looks like Bobby. As long as she is OK, I can be too. No matter how we ended up here, we are near our family, and we have work to do.

'We have to go! Come on, Mirabelle.'

'Merlyns don't just get up and go,' Mirabelle says urgently. She's not wrong, we've never been on a family holiday, we don't own a car. We don't simply open the front door to new horizons – that's not how it works for us. Our aunts have their happy places right where they usually are – Aunt Prudie in the allotment, Aunt Connie in the kitchen, Mum at the table, yards of fabric rolling away from her.

Mirabelle has her paper map from Aunt Flissie open and is turning it around in front of her, as if to orientate herself.

'I'd really like to check my phone,' she says as she sees me watching.

With a little pang of longing, I think of how useful a phone connected to the internet would be right now. There are so, so many questions I would like to search the answers to.

Mirabelle folds up the map with a snap. 'I'm definitely not going out there,' she says, even though it is too late to stop whatever we've started.

'Why?' I ask, but I'm being thoughtless.

'I don't go out in October! I end up alone when I leave this house. Alone and cold and scared!' Mirabelle snaps at me. Admitting this in front of Senara and

Kerra must be hugely embarrassing for her. As I look at her, I finally realise how much she must be suffering.

'This is different,' I say, encouragingly. 'I won't leave your side. Which will be annoying for you – but you won't be alone.'

'Magic is wild and unpredictable, and last year when I tried to use it outside of the house, I almost died in the Arctic! The aunts make it look easy, but it isn't at all!'

Mirabelle is what happens when magic goes wrong. The trauma can live with you for a long time. All I want is to get through my First October without doing myself or anyone else huge harm. But I will also do anything to get my mum back.

'I'll show you the way,' Senara says, with a smile.

R M

WHILE YOU WERE OUT

Sorry to have missed you!
The address 15 Pendragon Road was not located.

You can apply for mail redirection in the case
of moving house.

BRING
ID

CHAPTER 17

'You're offering to help us? You know we're Merlyn witches, right?' I say.

'No! You can't!' Kerra says. 'You—'

Senara finally rounds on her younger sister, eyes flashing, cape a-quiver. 'Did Mother not say I was in charge? And did she not specifically say to follow my instructions? And did she not say to stay quiet?'

Kerra, who was staring up at her older sister, drops her eyes. 'Yes, sister,' she mutters.

'Well then,' Senara says. 'Let's take these Merlyns to their family.'

Desperation has me making strange choices, even trusting Morgans. But – I steel myself – anything for Mum and my aunts.

'We're ready,' I say. I'm already up and moving to the back door when I see that Mirabelle isn't.

'We have to go, Mirabelle, come on. We're running out of time.' We really are running out of time. The sun isn't so much setting as disappearing, the sky darkening.

Mirabelle follows me as if her feet are lead, each foot dragging. Then, at the back door which would normally open on to our tiny patio, she stops. 'I don't want to go outside,' she says as quietly as possible, just to me.

'We have to,' I tell her firmly.

I hold Bobby up to Mirabelle as proof. Her little barrel body is starting to fade. I don't know what it would mean if Bobby were to disappear completely, and I don't want to find out.

Mirabelle stands on the threshold, takes a deep breath, and steps out on to the cliff top. With the house and the cliff edge behind us, there are only hillocks of wind-blown grass and heather ahead of us.

'If we're smuggling them inside, then we should hide them – or they should at least look the part,' Kerra says.

'What?' Senara asks distractedly.

'Look like us,' Kerra says.

'Oh. Yeah, fine.' Senara blinks, and Morgan cloaks unfurl around us. 'The aunts aren't going to be around, though.' She sets off into the sky, her own cloak trailing across the grass.

It takes me a moment to realise Senara means her own Morgan aunts.

We Merlyns are jeans-and-T-shirts witches, so in the billowing Morgan cloak, I feel even more self-conscious. But, if the disguise gets us to our family, I'll wear anything.

'I can see why they like these, they're really warm,' Mirabelle says, swishing her cloak back and forth.

'I feel silly,' I say.

'You always feel silly. Come on, if I can handle the outside, you can handle the silly.'

I watch Kerra fumble with her cloak then set off with a huff after her sister and think about the risk we're taking. Even having joined these Morgan witches in a star, they could still betray us at any point.

'I have a feeling about this,' I say, staring fixedly at Senara's back.

'What kind?' Mirabelle asks.

'Huh?'

'I mean, good or bad?'

'Is it that simple?' I ask, trotting past Kerra to catch up with Senara.

'So, Kerra wants to take us back as, like, some kind of prize to make your mother happy?' I say, in a low voice. 'And that's not your plan?'

'No,' Senara says, 'that's ridiculous. There's no way Mother can be happy at all with a witch with no powers.

It's OK,' she adds and gives me a smile. 'Whatever Kerra has cooked up is not going to happen.'

Our conversation is interrupted by the wind picking up, everything except putting one foot in front of the other impossible.

I glance back at Mirabelle, whose purple curls have escaped from under her hood and are lashing around her. It's so cold it almost burns. Plaits are definitely the best hairstyle for this type of weather.

As we hike up and along the clifftop, we have to bend at the waist and lean into the wind.

Mirabelle trails behind, hunched over and looking deeply uncomfortable. The wind whips our Morgan cloaks around us ferociously. Either the Morgan witches want the wind to be ferocious, or they are so busy doing whatever it is they're doing to my family that they don't have time to use their magic to change the weather.

Kerra looks like she might be saying something to me, but the wind snatches away most of her words.

Then she points.

There, proudly atop the cliffs, is a castle; a magnificent movie-set of a castle. A whole town could fit inside it. A Morgan fortress.

I peer at the hulking castle on its craggy head of land.

I had not clocked that this was going to be an October with a castle in it.

'It's usually in ruins,' Kerra turns back to shout to us over the wind.

I can picture that. The stone walls crumbling picturesquely, rocks piled around, making it look even more desolate.

It still doesn't look very habitable.

It's the very oldest kind of castle I could imagine. I don't know a lot about history, but this looks like an ancient civilisation built and then abandoned it.

It's not just a castle, it's a statement: the Morgans are here.

As soon as we're clear of the wind, Kerra says, 'Welcome to your ancestral home! All witches originate from right here. Even you two.'

Hmm. One of the first things that Aunt Morgan said was that we should all remember 'where greater power resides'. I suppose she meant here.

I definitely don't have any homecoming feelings. I'd rather our house was back in the middle of Pendragon Road, where it's meant to be, instead of teetering on the wind-lashed cliff edge behind us.

'Morgan, our mighty ancestor, designed the castle

to repel her enemies.' Kerra's on a roll now, like an over-enthusiastic magical tour guide.

'Which enemies? You mean Merlyn?'

'No, I mean . . . um . . . all of humanity.'

Somehow, with Kerra chattering, our foursome has re-grouped. Now Mirabelle is walking ahead with Senara, matching her stride for stride, and I've been left behind.

'So, you're babysitting?' I hear Mirabelle ask.

'I think sitting on a baby would be easier,' Senara says with a grumble, and Mirabelle laughs as if this is really funny.

'This is the Iron Gate,' Kerra says as we approach a giant metal lattice which ends in menacing looking spikes that hang down over us.

'Before we go into . . . the Morgan castle . . . with Morgans – what October rules do you have?' I ask, stalling.

'Rules?'

'Yeah, you know, the ones from our ancestors that we're all supposed to follow: "hidden and no harm"?'

'I don't believe there are any rules,' Kerra says, 'though Mother doesn't like it when we run indoors. Or stand on the furniture. Or shout. But we're not hidden – all the humans round here know we're here and they know to steer clear.'

The castle is extremely castle-y. I've never been in a castle before and yet, as we walk along, I feel like I could tick off a full list of castle things that I've seen in history lessons. Massive stone archways – check. Drawbridge – check. Turrets – check, check, check.

Senara turns to give us a little nod as we cross single-file over a bridge, then over a moat, and pass between thick stone walls.

I'd probably be more interested in the imposing curtain wall that Kerra is pointing out and the gatehouse designed to prevent invasion and ransacking, if my mind wasn't constantly returning to the fact that my family is locked up somewhere inside.

Keeping any witch here against her will is brutal beyond imagining and starts my emotions wheeling between scared, angry and sad all over again.

'We can go directly down into the cells to reach your family,' Kerra says, pointing in one direction while Senara and Mirabelle sweep in another. 'The cells are all original, carved into the rock, specially designed to . . . hang on.' Kerra jogs to catch up to her sister. 'Senara, we're going the wrong way if you want to go to—'

'Kerra, please,' Senara says over one shoulder.

Kerra looks troubled.

It makes me feel shivery-strange to think that none of my family have been here for generations, technically banished, the portcullis shut against us, the drawbridge pulled up.

Our hoods up, we proceed through a courtyard, up a vast set of steps to a huge pair of wooden doors. Senara opens the doors carefully, silently.

'Keep quiet, now,' she whispers, looking back at us as she steps into the castle.

My eyes polka-dot in the gloom. There are glowing torches flickering all the way down the walls.

My mind keeps returning to our own house: its nooks and crannies, its piles of stuff. This is vast and bare, the dark brick relieved only by a sweeping, dark-red, velvet carpet down the middle of the room.

'You . . . live here?' I finally think to ask. 'This is a—'

'Our most palatial stateroom. The throne room,' Kerra says, and her voice echoes down the length of the space. If we were looking to make it through the castle in silent stealth, Kerra is not the right young hag to help us do this.

It's empty apart from us. Yet I feel eyes on me.

'And what is . . . this?' I ask, pointing at the walls.

'It's a tapestry,' Kerra says. 'Obviously.'

I get closer and the brush strokes turn into something else.

'What is this made of?' I murmur, leaning forward to touch it. It ripples under my finger. It's bumpy to the touch, every detail raised.

'Oh, the tapestry? I don't know. Thread and a spot of magic, maybe?' Senara says. She's not paying attention to me at all; her eyes are focused on the double doors at the opposite end of the throne room.

'It's wool,' Kerra says immediately. Of course she knows this. 'In non-October, it's really mangy, centuries old. Like yours. But in October we – well, not me, not really, I get to watch – but we restore it with magic.'

I glance sidelong at Kerra and her irrepressible urge to brag. She's proud. She's into her coven the way that a human might be into their football team or their hometown. The tapestry is full of beautiful images in exquisite workwitchship, with a thick border, heavy with vines, twisting around the main images. It is so elaborately woven that I don't even know where to start looking. Details glimmer all over it: a castle, a lake, a row of robot-like knights in parade, a bird like a hawk poised mid-attack above a mouse. I know I've never seen the tapestry before, but at the same time it is strangely familiar.

It features two formidable women, gilded in gold stars.

'Wool – and gold?' I ask, getting closer.

'No, that would be the magic,' Kerra corrects me.

'I'm starting to think the Morgans can't be all bad if they can make something this beautiful,' I say quietly to Mirabelle. It makes the olden days look . . . golden.

I wouldn't have thought these women made of fabric could look so lifelike. But they're better than any painting I've ever seen. The Merlyn witch looks exactly like the one on our throw at home, but with so much more colour and life; she now looks exactly like Mirabelle. She is short and sturdy and fierce-looking, with a jutting chin. She has a great billow of curls around her and two upturned hands, full of stars. The resemblance is uncanny.

'She could actually be you,' I whisper and point to Mirabelle, but anything I say at all in this room seems to carry too far.

'Huh,' Mirabelle says, as if she doesn't want to concede the truth of this but can't argue with me either.

The Morgan witch is definitely kin to Kerra and Senara. She has the same slick, tight-lipped look, with those glinting eyes.

The tapestry runs chronologically down the room, starting with two small witch sisters and then showing some of the stories I've heard about as they grow – Morgan bearing down on Merlyn, who is now a spider almost underfoot. A bee buzzing around Morgan's head. Seeing them elaborately sewn into the tapestry gives them a mythic quality.

There are other legends too, ones we Merlyns didn't grow up being told about. Morgan is wrapped in the giant coils of a dragon, its sharp teeth right at her neck.

And then things get worse. I can only glimpse the rest of the panels down the length of the room, but I know that Merlyn and Morgan's sisterhood blew up. The tapestry is everything we witches would become, if it all went badly. All-out, spectacular war, with massed humans huddling and running away.

'See there – that's our blessed ancestor, the first witch, Morgan, who was born with all the world's magic. Right, Senara?' Senara doesn't answer but Kerra ploughs on. She seems like she could happily boast all day about her coven-family. 'But then her trickster sister, Merlyn, attempted to steal it from her and cursed them both. Your family are descended from the great betrayer and it's your fault that we're stuck with this October problem.'

I squint down at the end of the Morgans' great tapestry but it's too far away. The first panel, closest to the castle's entrance, shows two sisters holding hands while stars play around them. They have identical looks of wonderment on their faces. This was how it all started – the first witches receiving their power. They look young and beautiful, glowing with stardust.

That is not what stops me in my tracks, though.

Just behind the two original witches, Merlyn and Morgan, there's a familiar face staring out at me. It's a serious, bespectacled face, somehow kind and trustworthy.

'I've seen this person before,' I mutter. There's something jarringly recognisable, something I need to examine more closely. I want to say there's something on the tip of my tongue but there isn't, it's more like an itch at the front of my brain. *Why do I know that face?*

'Hey, Merlyn, you're not here to admire our art, OK?'

'My name is *Clemmie*,' I tell Kerra, and hear the tiniest neigh, almost a squeak I might have imagined. I reach into my pocket and stroke the soft downy star on Bobby's fading muzzle.

And then I'm trotting from image to image, moving faster as the story unfolds, trying to track that face and find it again. From panel to panel of the tapestry, I follow the witch sisters.

There are so many scenes of the two witches at war. A flock of dark birds whip around Merlyn as she flies at her sister. They must have really hated each other. I can feel the animosity in their facial expressions. Morgan is taller, more regal looking. She'd be better at sneering.

And then, abruptly, the story ends. There's Morgan, hands wrapped around a sword which is pointing straight up to the sky, looking down at nothing at all. That's it.

The tapestry seems to be unfinished, but before I can ask why, Senara and Mirabelle are gone.

'This way,' Senara calls from the darkness, the double doors opening into what looks like a black pit.

WHILE YOU WERE OUT

Please note that there are prohibited and restricted items that should not be sent by mail such as batteries, liquids and matches.

Also perishables, such as live animals or oversized vegetables.

And weapons of any kind are banned.

We recommend extreme care if opening a parcel that may contain any such prohibited items. If you receive any such prohibited items, good luck to you.

CHAPTER 18

If that's where Mirabelle is going, I'm going too, I tell myself firmly, and follow them into darkness, immediately tripping down the first step. It's a staircase, barely lit and twisty enough to put even the one Mirabelle installed at home to shame.

We wind down and down and when I think *surely the stairs will end*, we keep going down.

Then we emerge into an impossible space. It takes me a moment to work out where we are.

Even after all those steps, we haven't hit the bottom. We're on a platform, like a balcony, that runs around a cathedral-like cavern.

I'm light-dazzled for a moment, and reach forward to hold on to the railings because this new place is gleamingly white and bright. It's the complete opposite to the dark, ancient castle.

I immediately feel the space: the floor far below us and the ceiling yawning above us. It's bigger than a department store, though just as glossy. Bigger than a theatre, though the balcony we're on reminds me of one.

I immediately feel exposed and step backwards into Kerra, who is bringing up the rear with a frown.

'Wait here,' Senara says with a smile. 'I'll check – and come back.'

I step forward again quickly. 'Where are they?' I whisper to Mirabelle.

She lifts up a shaky finger and points below us.

I almost don't see them at first. The pumpkin – our pumpkin – sits beneath something that looks like a large helmet with wires entering it. It is dwarfed by the massive room, but still enormous compared to the figures around it. There's a flock of Morgans, caped and busily moving, and three static figures, their curly heads in a row; Aunt Connie's white and Aunt Prudie's grey sandwiching Mum's dark head. Though we're far away, Mum's hair still looks immaculate and, somehow, that simple fact makes me breathe more easily.

There's a buzzing noise, echoey against the cavern's curved walls and I peer down to see. It's coming from machinery which looks particularly unwitchy.

Two large robotic arms are suspended from the vast arced ceiling. They are orbiting the pumpkin like a sun, occasionally pausing to rest against its orange surface, as if they're measuring its heartbeat or listening to its lungs. It reminds me of the *beep beep beep* of a patient's heart hooked up to a hospital machine.

The air around us crackles. The coils of wires spark, as if with electricity but it must be magic. Every surface is covered in screens and interfaces and buttons. Rubber suckers are attached around the pumpkin, connecting it with loops of wire in every shape, colour and size to devices that look like they are monitoring it. Our school has a big new IT suite the headteacher won't stop going on about but I've still never seen this much technology in one place.

But what really matters is the trio of witches, looking so small at this distance and in this unhomely space.

'Mum!' I whisper and my nose immediately goes tingly with the feeling of tears coming.

'Is this human-made?' I hear Mirabelle ask. She'd better not be asking me because I don't have any answers. I had no idea that the ancient castle was squatting on top of somewhere like this. It looks a bit like one of those gleaming white shops that sells the latest digital equipment; it has the same air of efficiency and wonder – and money.

"Cos we fry all our human-made stuff in October,' she adds. I think about our phones, our clocks, our lightbulbs— all exploded.

'No,' Kerra says immediately. 'Witch-made.'

'A factory,' Mirabelle murmurs.

I'd been embarrassed when Aunt Connie hadn't understood what a mainframe is but looking at this thing now, I realise I didn't understand either.

'No. An actual evil-villain lair,' Mirabelle corrects herself in a whisper.

Aunt Prudie must have been more than horrified when she first saw this. This breaks every rule I've ever known about being a witch. My family believe that our starry power comes directly from the night sky, not a laboratory.

'Mirabelle,' I say quietly. 'I'm not sure about this – or anything.'

The scale of the Morgans' work makes my eyes so wide they start to smart a little bit. But I'm here for our family and our family alone.

My mum and my aunts are standing, braced, with hands above their heads against the pumpkin.

They each have a guard of two Morgan witches on either side of them and as I watch, another three Morgans peel away from the pumpkin. There are too many Morgans to keep track of.

Even from up here, I can see the gold vein of magic flow from Mum and my aunts, from their chests and through their hands into the pumpkin. But . . . that's not how it worked at home. The sparks seem to pulse steadily, the magic moving with a rhythm. Merlyns alone never did anything like that. There's a buzz like a current moving and the pumpkin is glowing from the inside as the robotic arms circle above.

The thin metal floor of the balcony starts vibrating with a quiet thrum. It's the sound that makes me realise – my coven doesn't need to form a chain to pass through their magic because it's being pulled out of them individually. This whole place is a machine and my family are a part of it.

'What are they doing?' Kerra asks.

'Your coven is using our coven as their source,' Mirabelle says sharply.

For the first time, I realise how difficult this is going to be. We can't just walk down there.

'Why aren't the Morgans using their own powers?'

I ask despairingly. What was a race between our two families to each reclaim their full year of power has turned into a war.

'They're charging the pumpkin like a battery full of magic,' Mirabelle says, shaking her head in horrified admiration.

I scan my family from our bird's-eye viewpoint. Aunt Connie is still wearing her apron but her head is bowed low. Mum is in her yellow dress and Aunt Prudie is, of course, in her green gardening overalls – but as we watch, Aunt Prudie turns and tries to wrestle free.

'That screaming hedge witch is making a fuss again,' Senara says and she sounds far too casual about it. She turns away easily, clearly not compelled to stare like I am.

'That's Aunt Prudie you're talking about,' I say defensively, craning forward to see.

'The angry wrinkly one in green overalls?' Kerra checks.

Aunt Prudie is furious, but that is her natural state. She howls something that we can't catch the exact words of but can hear the raw sound – and then she tries to pull away from the pumpkin.

'Yeah. And then Aunt Connie is that one. The one

in the apron. The one who welcomed you all at first.'
My heart aches for Aunt Connie.

'The hearth witch.'

'Yeah. That's her. And then my mum.' But I can't
say any more because my sadness dries into a splinter
of fury.

Aunt Prudie seems to be leaning back, as far away
from the pumpkin as she can get. But she still hangs
there, hands glued to its surface. Then she does what
looks like a little stomping dance on the spot, a toddler
having a tantrum, and finally boots the pumpkin.

Aunt Prudie, who tenderly nursed that pumpkin for
thirteen years . . . just gave it a walloping big kick.

The Morgans are younger, quicker and much more
numerous than our coven and they cluster round.
Without even touching her, Aunt Prudie is stilled.

'They're going to hurt her!' I cry, much too loud.

'Mother hates mess,' Kerra says, unhelpfully.
'She won't want to waste a single star.'

Above Kerra's eyes with their non-magical black
pupils, her eyebrows are drawn tight together in worry.
Both hands hover at her mouth.

That makes Aunt Prudie sound like a cup full
of some precious liquid – the cup might be useless but

they wouldn't want to break it until they can decant the liquid into something better.

But Kerra's eyes are trained on Aunt Prudie. 'But that doesn't look . . . it doesn't look right,' she says, tearing her eyes away from Aunt Prudie to check where Senara is and then immediately turning back.

She's not wrong: the way that Aunt Connie's head is bowed, the way Aunt Prudie is fighting back.

An even taller Morgan witch appears: Aunt Morgan. I suck in a hiss of cold air through my teeth.

Whatever she says ends the kerfuffle as quickly as it began.

'They should be putting their own magic into their own stupid pumpkin!' I protest. I remember saying to Mirabelle at the beginning of the month – a lifetime ago – that magical shortcuts were like cheating. This is definitely cheating.

'What is Mother planning?' Kerra wonders out loud.

'I thought you were a vital part of her plans?' I say, snarky with pain. I heard the way her family dismissed her, calling her a 'weakling' and 'deadweight'. My family would never speak to me like that.

'I'm trying to be,' Kerra says, and she seems to try and steady herself with a breath. 'An all-natural magical vessel. So it slowly diffuses the magic throughout the year . . . experimental. Smart. But, Mother . . .'

It isn't a real compliment.

'The young hag didn't disappoint, would you look at this?' Behind us, a voice I've never heard before purrs, and my heart sinks.

Kerra whirls round first and I hesitate, wondering if I should keep my face turned away. Our 'disguise' of Morgan capes won't withstand close inspection from actual Morgans.

'Aunts!' Kerra says, probably aiming for happy but coming out squeaky. 'We are—'

'Hold your tongue!' one Morgan snaps at Kerra.

I glance backwards. Three white-caped Morgan witches have appeared behind us.

'Powerless young hag!' the second says.

'That's enough from you, deadweight,' the third and final one adds. All three of them speak in the same sharp tone. They could be mirror images of each other, tight-lipped witches with matching smirks.

Just when I think Kerra's own lips couldn't tighten any more, they go even thinner.

'Oh no,' Mirabelle breathes.

I didn't see where the Morgans came from but

as they advance on us, I see another figure behind them.

'Sister?' Kerra asks.

Senara keeps herself half-hidden behind the newly arrived Morgans. She looks away for a moment and doesn't answer Kerra.

'Where's Mother? I thought she'd like to see what I've brought her,' Senara asks the trio of her coven elders. Like a cat who thinks it's done a good thing by dragging in a bird, Senara seems to be waiting for praise.

She hasn't taken us to our family, she's taken us straight to her own.

CHAPTER 19

I feel so frustrated with myself I could scream. *Of course* Senara has betrayed us. I don't know why I thought any Morgan could do anything other than turn on Merlyns.

But the older Morgan witches smile coolly. 'If your mother is distracted from her work, then there will be very, very big problems, young hag. Now – scram.'

If Senara is bitterly disappointed that she can't show off her capture, she doesn't show it. She looks slightly scared about the idea of distracting her mother and turns away quickly.

'You devious, double crossing...' I shout, taking a big, angry step towards to the Morgans. Mirabelle's hand on my arm tingles with warmth and holds me back.

'Stay where you are, Merlyns!' one of the Morgans commands, her gold eyes flashing.

I hold my breath, making my heart hammer without oxygen. A coven is just another word for a gang and the Morgans are not just bullies, they're bullies with celestial power in their very eyes.

One of them looks like she winks for the briefest moment, but other than that, the three Morgan witches are motionless. I feel the cold catch of fear, because even though they're not moving at all, their magic is.

It's our hands. The Morgan witches' icy magic is slipping over our hands. Mirabelle is so close behind me that I feel her breath on the side of my neck when she gasps.

So hot and heavy this month, my hands are now cooling fast. A cold, brushing sensation moves up each joint of my fingers and I look down to see white gloves, just like my mum and my aunts had, growing up my arms.

Mirabelle and I look as if we are wearing flawlessly white gloves – like we work in a museum and are about to touch something really old and important.

As the light shifts, I can better see that what looks like gloves are actually a network of hundreds and thousands of tiny pinprick stars. Like lace or chainmail, our fingers, our palms, right to our wrists — all covered with cold nets of the Morgans' making.

I've had a bad case of October incompetence since

the beginning of the month but now – now it feels like we've all fallen off a cliff into a horrible new world. I try and lift my hands, but they won't move.

'Release them!' Kerra says grandly. 'I demand it!'

It doesn't work. Nothing Kerra says ever works.

'Aunts, please, these are my Merlyns,' Kerra tries again, as if the Morgans are cats who might break out in a hissing fight over who gets to claim us.

The Morgans remain motionless, as if Kerra never spoke.

'The littlest one doesn't even have any powers!' Kerra shouts abruptly. 'She hasn't had her First October yet.'

Kerra is pointing at me. I know this is a lie but it's also quite close to the truth. She is standing with legs apart, her chin tilted up at her aunts.

Mirabelle moves in front of me, protecting me, our bodies still touching. I can feel she is shivering. 'So scared of the hands of young hags? What are you going to do? Drown us? Or burn us? Like the bad old days?'

Senara is still there, lurking behind her coven elders. Now her star-pupilled eyes are focused on Mirabelle but I can't immediately read her expression; she looks like she might be about to cry.

And then she's gone. Kerra's face screws up at the sound of her sister retreating.

'We wouldn't threaten young hags. In fact, we wouldn't bother threatening any Merlyn,' one of the Morgan elders says.

'Weak witchery,' another of them says. They must see us as small, insignificant, out of place. I realise now how ridiculous we were, thinking we could walk in and reclaim our family.

Mirabelle takes a breath. 'What are you saying about our family?'

'I said,' one of the tall Morgan witches begins to repeat, 'that your mother is—'

'My mum is an angel,' I interrupt fiercely from behind Mirabelle, 'and anyone who says differently can take this up with me in November.'

The threat is pathetic but all I'm trying to say is that I'm willing to use more than magic.

'There isn't going to be another of *your* Novembers,' one of the Morgans says with a sneer. She turns to Mirabelle. 'Your mother is also an angel?'

And now I wish that whatever they were going to say, they'd said it about my mum because I would have known it was untrue and I'd be able to take it.

Mirabelle looks frozen, unable to jump to her mum's defence. Aunt Flissie never wants to spend any time at home in October – and home is where Mirabelle is.

'Not angels,' the second Morgan witch says, 'and not witches. Your family are *mice*.'

'Darn clothes, make soup, tend the garden!' another says in a sing-songy voice.

The Morgan witches say all these things as if they're completely absurd. I glance at Mirabelle to see how she's reacting, because, painfully, there is truth in it.

But just because these are small things doesn't make them bad things. I remember what Mum said: over the years, Merlyns have become peaceful witches leading quiet lives, that we might look unambitious but we're careful. In my mind, I'm rehearsing all the things I should say. I want to perfect my comebacks, script the digs I should make.

'Your family is pathetic, that's what they are. Little domestic witches, trotting about with their *vegetables*,' the third Morgan says with a predatory smile.

'And you're – you're *crooks*!' I exclaim. It's not what I wanted to throw back at them but it is, at least, what Aunt Prudie would have said.

'You claim these useless young hags as "your" Merlyns, powerless one?' All three of the older witches turn their heads to Kerra like they are one being. 'You'll never be welcome in the Morgan star at this rate.'

Kerra's jaw hardens. 'I have been the best and most loyal young hag,' she says. 'For twelve years, I've done everything the Morgan way. And now, you're going to exclude me because I haven't come into my power yet? Because when I do, you're going to regret that and—'

All three of the Morgan witches laugh. They're just as cruel to Kerra as they are to us.

And that is when Mirabelle lashes out.

She swipes with a leg, hooking one of the Morgan's ankles with her own and taking both herself and an enemy witch down. It must be costing her extraordinary effort to move at all with her hands under the Morgan's icy-cold magic.

She's a thrashing human whirlwind but it can't last. Not against three pairs of starred eyes.

There's a tug at my cloak, dragging me backwards. 'Come on,' a voice close to my ear urges. 'Now!'

As the felled Morgan witch rights herself, Mirabelle goes still, pressed against the railings, her back to the vast expanse of the cavern below. All three Morgan witches are staring down at her.

'Quick!' The voice hisses again. It's Kerra, wrestling me away from Mirabelle, trying to drag me backwards. She's pretty strong for a powerless witch.

I stumble along behind her, my forearm squeezed in her grip. 'What are you doing?' I cry. 'That's my cousin! They're taking my cousin!'

'Shush!' Kerra hisses as she pulls me back into the darkness of the staircase. 'The thing about magic eyes is you can only look at one thing at a time – now, come on!'

I came here to get my mum and now I'm losing my cousin too. I feel so close to giving up. Temmie went first, then Aunt Flissie, then my mum and Aunt Prudie and Aunt Connie. And now Mirabelle. At this rate, I could be the only Merlyn left.

'No!' I snarl. 'We have to go back! I can't lose any more family!'

'Come on!' Kerra urges. 'I don't have magic, but I do have you. I couldn't let Senara hand in both of you – then she'd definitely win.'

'Win!' I exclaim, shrill with derision.

'Mother can only have one favourite,' Kerra replies, looking back the way we've just come where the white gleaming cavern holds everyone who matters to me captive.

'You're using me to try to score points against your sister?' I ask, already knowing the answer is *yes*.

Kerra stops mid-step. 'Look,' she hisses, pulling the back of her hand across her face which is damp with sweat, 'I'm helping you – actually helping you, OK? Grateful, much? It'll all be OK as long as Mother doesn't come for us. She'll be busy *obsessing* over that pumpkin. And she never has time for young hags anyway.'

Abruptly, a tall and imposing cloaked figure appears several steps ahead of us. I have a wild moment when I consider charging at her; she is only one witch.

But then I see she is *the* witch. Kerra shrinks back against the curved wall of the staircase.

'Young hags,' Aunt Morgan says.

CHAPTER 20

My heart sinks.

Aunt Morgan's hands are neatly folded in front of her, but this time I know better – it's not her hands I need to watch. In the darkness of the stairwell, the gold stars in her eyes glint at me.

'I was perfectly clear with you and your sister. Monitor, don't acquire,' Aunt Morgan says crisply. 'We'll be overrun with spare witches. I expected better from Senara.'

As if on cue, Senara appears in the doorway, slowing from a run into a stiff walk, looking from her mum to her sister and back again.

'But you, a deadweight in this coven . . .' Aunt Morgan says to Kerra with quiet viciousness. She is speaking low and calm but that only makes her anger more ominous. '. . . you force me to intervene, interrupting my important work, chasing around like *children*.' She hisses the word 'children'.

Kerra is quaking slightly but still insists on talking. 'But Mother, you sent the star for us and we—'

'Star? What are you talking about?'

Kerra doesn't quail and keeps going, her stubby braids quivering above each ear. 'It came out of the Merlyns' old cauldron – a five-pointed star – but it brought us here so I thought you wanted us involved in your plans and —'

'You had one job: to keep the young Merlyn hags from interfering. That was all.' Aunt Morgan's voice is buttery for a brief moment. 'All young hags were meant to stay out of our way. Bringing them here was a bad enough decision, but helping one . . .'

'But—'

'Silence!' Aunt Morgan says. She sounds perfectly calm but she gives Kerra a sharp blink.

Kerra's mouth is still open; she is in the middle of protesting. I can even hear the 'But Mother' she would have said. But she's been silenced. She opens and closes her mouth a few times, but nothing comes out.

Her hands go to her throat, then her lips, as if feeling for her voice. Her shocked eyes are watery and huge, then her forehead crinkles and her shoulders move as if she is sobbing but I can't hear any sound.

Aunt Morgan is now completely ignoring the daughter

she's zipped into silence. Senara hovers, starry eyes darting from her mother to her sister and back again, her bottom lip trapped awkwardly between her teeth.

I knew Kerra was foolhardy but, as I watch her take a deep breath and then approach the dragon that is her mother, one hand outstretched, I realise that she is next-level stubborn.

Aunt Morgan side-eyes her youngest daughter and before Kerra can even touch her cape, Kerra disappears with a faint pop.

'Now I have three spare witches,' Aunt Morgan says. 'I hope not all of them are deadweights.'

Senara releases the lip she was biting and steps forward. She doesn't want to be one of the 'spares', I can tell.

'Mother – the two young Merlyn hags . . . they do have magic. Even . . . that one. I heard them talk about it,' Senara, the betrayer, stutters out and I half-growl at her.

Aunt Morgan suddenly swoops towards me and seizes my hands, the freezing, white-starred gloves peeling back so she can see my skin, and evidence of the magic beneath it. I want to pull away but her hands are like icy claws. She turns my hands this way and that, gold-pupiled eyes narrowed.

'Untested young hag,' Aunt Morgan says disgustedly. 'You may join the rest of your sad little coven.' And she closes one gold-starred eye at me.

I, too, magically swoop out of her sight. I have that disorientating sensation I did when our house popped out of the city and to the coast; while my body knows that I've moved, my brain has to scramble to catch up.

This time, I don't go far. I reappear with that faint pop, right in front of the pumpkin.

'Oh no,' Mum says weakly as I'm added to their row. Mirabelle's head is down, her hair hanging forward. Aunt Connie's eyes are shut. All of them have starry nets around their hands, peeled back just enough to press palm to pumpkin.

'Young hag!' Aunt Prudie leans around Mum to shout.

'Not happy to see me, Aunt Prudie?' I ask, thinking I'm funny but she looks horrified.

I can feel the Morgans' eyes on me, but more than that, I can feel their eyes steering me to the pumpkin. I'm a limp little puppet as the Morgans manoeuvre me with the same amount of care that a human would take sticking a battery in a television remote control.

The bare palms of my hands meet the pumpkin and

a rush of warmth returns, along with pins and needles. I'd forgotten how hot and heavy my October hands are without the Morgans' nets of ice over them.

'Ouch,' I mutter, and the Morgan nearest to me snorts.

I focus on all ten of my fingers, pressed so hard that the orange of the pumpkin almost seems to come through them.

Each of my family have their hands pressed directly against the pumpkin, too, a Morgan witch standing close to them: monitoring, threatening. I will myself to pay attention, to observe the Morgans and learn how to escape them.

'Now, Merlyns! Send through those stars!' one of the Morgans demands, her voice loud and clear and even a little amused.

Above us, the robotic arms start moving, spinning, and a humming noise fills the entire cavern. I feel like a lab rat. Of course, Aunt Morgan wouldn't want to risk her own witches on an experiment this wild.

And then, instead of me leaning into the pumpkin, it feels like it is pulling me in. I can feel the suction on my very soul; the machine reaching into me, trying to get a hook into something.

I can feel the stars deep inside me starting to rise.

We are only here because of the magic inside us, not because we are people as well as witches.

It shouldn't matter – to give up the stars inside me. I don't want them anyway, and so far they haven't done me any good. But what will the Morgans do with my magic?

I know what my coven wanted to do with a full pumpkin: guarantee their safety from the very witches now ready to experiment on us. Sending magic into the pumpkin for my family was one thing, doing so on command of the Morgans is another.

I will not give them my stars.

I can't believe my first time using magic properly is going to be to not use it at all. But then, of course, I can believe it. Everything is upside down and back to front this October.

Go numb, go limp, I will the stars. Stay there. If I can't pin my own magic down, then this machine definitely won't. For the Morgans, I will be more than just blocked, I will be full-on magically constipated.

My hands are heavy, I feel exhausted, but nothing inside me is moving. My magic is dormant and not even the Morgans can force it awake. When I feel sure that nothing is happening, no gold sparks are making it to my hands, I look up.

Stars are seeping from Mirabelle's hands into the pumpkin. Her face is furious but closed and I know she is not willing the magic inside her to do anything; the stars are being slowly sucked out of her. The sparks pulse from her slowly but steadily, with a heartbeat rhythm.

The magic seems to be pouring out of Aunt Connie, a flood of sparks filling the pumpkin so that the entire orange wall of the vegetable in front of her turns gold. Aunt Connie's face is mask-like, her usually apple-round cheeks loose and exhausted looking.

I don't know when they think it will be full, but the pumpkin looks it from here, crowded with hopping sparks of magical light. This is meant to be magic that will see the Morgans through for a whole year. How much will be enough for their greed?

'Stop!' the Morgan witch closest to me says testily. 'Something is lopsided, not all witches are working properly.'

The Morgan witch takes something that looks like a thermometer, but with stars instead of numbers, and proceeds to shake it.

It occurs to me that if they'd been even a little bit nicer, they could have had so many more answers out of Aunt Connie. But they weren't patient.

'A Merlyn deadweight over here,' one Morgan calls to another. Me and my magicless hands have been spotted. None of the rest of my coven can hold their stars down but my hands have been blocking me all month.

'How can you tell? They all look like deadweights to me.' Another Morgan laughs as she approaches me and frowns for a moment into my brown, ordinary eyes.

'Defective young hag!' she reports back.

Another Morgan turns my hands this way and that, squints her uncanny gold eyes at my fingers then gives the skin of my hand a pinch.

'Ouch,' I say, louder this time.

'Send her back to join the other deadweight, there's no magic in this one either.'

The nameless, interchangeable Morgan witch leans down to stare at me and her wink could almost be friendly before I remember – oh no – and I'm gone again.

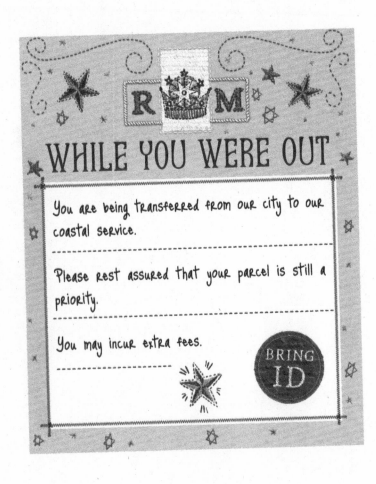

R✦M

WHILE YOU WERE OUT

You are being transferred from our city to our coastal service.

Please rest assured that your parcel is still a priority.

You may incur extra fees.

BRING ID

CHAPTER 21

One of the Morgans blinked – and I've moved. The white laboratory is gone. I hate how they do that.

I am facing the sea and the first thing I notice is that I am even colder than I was before. The chill is general though, not specific to my hands, and I look down to see that the spangled, white, glove-like things have gone.

I'm in a bare and empty cave, the complete opposite of the bright, white space I've just come from.

The cave looks like it is hewn from the cliff itself with cold, black rock on either side of me. In front of me, the third side is wide open to the ocean, like a huge window someone forgot to put glass in.

All the Morgan magic, channelled into a cavern. How hard would a window have been? I get as close to the open edge as I dare. Which, to be honest, is not that close.

My cave – my prison, I suppose, as I glance back to where the fourth side of the space is sealed by bars

– has an endless view out to the sea and down to the jagged rocks below.

Something hunched by the bars moves and I jump away, from both it, and the sheer drop out onto the rocks and waves.

Aunt Morgan didn't send me here alone. Kerra is straightening up, touching a hand to her throat sadly.

'They said I was a deadweight,' I tell her coldly.

Kerra grabs both of my hands and holds them up for me. Her mouth is moving but I struggle to understand what she wants to tell me.

That sparks a huge series of gestures, back and forth between us, up and down. Kerra points at my chest, my head, opens and closes her fists fast as if to make them flash. She wants me to know something, but she doesn't have the words and I don't have a way to let my power out, only to hold it in.

I have a flash-of-guilt headache that I'm here, undrained, while the rest of my family is plugged in as if they serve the pumpkin instead of the pumpkin serving them.

The cave is dank and chilly. It's a witch's cave, there's magic all around us, so there's no reason for it to be this uncomfortable. The Morgans could have made it nice and cosy, but they left it cold and bare for a reason. It's a deliberate choice.

A stalactite drips. I'm sure I'd think this cave was impressive if I could just peek inside instead of being stuck here. With just a few flicks of their fingers, my coven would make this place so homely.

My coven. My double failure: to make my magic work and to bring my family home safely stings my eyes like a spray of sea water.

Suddenly, the tight silence between Kerra and I is broken by familiar voices.

'Con!'

'Aunt Connie!'

'Accursed—'

A tangle of witches arrives in the middle of the cave with that faint Morgan pop.

It's Mum, Aunt Prudie and Mirabelle, all in motion, all shouting. They've been instantly transported by the callous Morgans but Aunt Connie is silent – and wobbly.

She begins to topple, tree-like.

They all dash to her and, everyone fumbling, hands thick and useless as they are wearing mittens, they manage to lower her to the floor. I catch Aunt Connie's shoulders to support her down.

Aunt Connie looks so small, her energy all drained, her hair floppy. Her eyes are shut, her limbs all loose. My aunts are old, of course, but I never thought of them as fragile.

'Mum! Is she . . .? Is she . . .?' I try to get out.

Mum sits down and lays Aunt Connie's head in her lap as best she can with her hands; hands with Morgan magic spun around their fingers, caging her power.

Come on, Aunt Connie, don't stop bossing us around now, I pray.

Mum listens carefully, her dark head bent over Aunt Connie's white one. 'Her pulse is steady – let her rest,' Mum says quietly, and I feel jelly-like relief in my knees and in the bottom of my stomach.

Next to me, Mirabelle's head dips and a big, ragged sigh escapes her. She falls backwards out of a squat and wraps her arms awkwardly around her legs.

'Mum!' I want to throw myself into her arms. We manage a semi-hug, and, even here, Mum smells like sweet lemon and home.

I want to hug Mirabelle too but I don't even know where to start.

'What do we do now?' I ask.

I feel . . . leaderless. I never thought I'd miss Aunt

Connie's nagging. And I have so many questions to put to her – the cauldron, the floating star, how we got here – but she will say even less than Aunt Prudie now.

Aunt Connie is always warm, busy, bustling, but now her skin is cool, her eyelids bruised-looking and thin and her eyes underneath darting about in anxious sleep.

I thought I was angry before. Now, I'm alight. I didn't get the opportunity to lash out at the Morgans like Mirabelle did.

'It's OK, Clemmie, it's OK,' Mum says as I reach out one of my bare hands to touch one of her covered ones. I can't leave my hand there though, the lattice of stars sealing in her magic is too painfully cold.

It is spectacularly *not* OK. Mum's diplomacy and kindness won't help us now. We need an angry witch. We can't all be resigned to this.

'They broke all the rules, Mum! They're hardly hidden in this *castle*! And they're doing great harm.'

Mum nods. 'We were afraid of this . . . we were trying so hard to prevent . . . *this*,' she says helplessly.

All my anger is pulled out of me, as if by a machine as strong as the Morgans'. The pumpkin is what brought the full force of the Morgans down on us, but that's not my mum or my aunts' fault. They were trying to protect us Merlyns, wrap us up in even more magic. But more magic just means more danger.

'This is all because of that pumpkin,' I say. 'I wish we'd never managed to put any magic in it at all.'

'Magnificent pumpkin! Masterpiece pumpkin!' Aunt Prudie shouts. Her magic might be fading but her voice isn't. And everything is shoutable if you're Aunt Prudie.

This isn't an 'I told you so' situation because I could never have known this would happen. But right now, I hate that pumpkin; the thing that my coven made is now being used to punish us, and is incredibly dangerous. Who knows what will happen when it is full of power – and that's why Aunt Morgan's using Merlyn witches instead of risking her own.

'My brave young hag,' Mum says. Then she pulls back to look at me properly and, even in this bleak cave, I can see her face drop a little further in dismay at my hair.

I laugh with a snivel as Mum attempts to sort out my topknots, but it can't be done with magically gloved hands. The knots have sagged beyond recognition. Any magic holding them in place is fading too and so my natural, wilder hair is pinging loose.

'*Accursed* Morgans,' Aunt Prudie says, because . . . of course she does. I glance up to see that she has cornered Kerra near the bars of our cave and is scowling very directly and deeply into her face. Kerra is doing her level best not to flinch from the close scrutiny.

'Oh,' I say. With Kerra silent, it's up to me to explain her presence. 'That's Kerra – she's a Morgan, but she tried to help me. I think. Really help, not trick me like the other one.'

At the mention of Senara, even without naming her, Mirabelle hunches deeper, her pointy chin between her knees.

'When they caught us, I think Aunt Morgan took her voice, Mum,' I say and glance back at Kerra.

Kerra reaches one hand towards her throat but gives up halfway. She nods.

'She did what?' Mum exclaims and reaches out to embrace Kerra – another clumsy half-hug, but Kerra squeezes her eyes shut and stays there for longer than you'd normally hug someone you barely know.

'To their own,' Aunt Prudie says, sounding disgusted.

Aunt Connie usually takes her self-appointed role as Aunt Prudie's translator very seriously. But now she is silent and her silence makes me feel sick. She has always said we are "running out of time". It's even truer now. She may not be able to count down and tell me how much time is ticking away but I can see that for myself.

'This world is never quite big enough for our two families. This October, the Morgans triumph,' Mum says and her lips manage to make the smallest of smiles for me. I know underneath her smile, she must be holding down her fear, hard.

Mum gazes around the cell. 'And maybe we were always destined to return here, to where our ancestor was penned. The legend says that this was once the cell where Morgan kept our mighty Merlyn.'

Kerra looks like she is absolutely bursting with things to say in reply to this. I'm sure she wants to declare that legend says no such thing.

Mugs of soup arrive in the middle of the cave with a faint pop. An afterthought.

Mum shoves one in Mirabelle's direction. 'Here!' she urges her. 'Drink! It is just about possible with the . . . gloves on.'

'They're not gloves, Mum,' I say.

Mum gently supports Aunt Connie's head and I help her drip a little water against Aunt Connie's lips.

'Gave most! Suffers most!' Aunt Prudie mutters, watching us.

I glance down at Aunt Connie where she is still curled up asleep.

Mum nods. 'Constance has always given the most to this plan,' she whispers.

'Inferior soup!' Aunt Prudie mutters, sampling the mug then kicking it away from herself. She gazes at me fixedly.

'Ha! Hands!' she exclaims, bending to crouch close to me and my free hands.

'Yes,' I admit. Now that my hands are unaffected by Morgan magic, I need to learn how to use my magic more urgently than ever before. I wish I could craft something out of stars. Even just a mattress would help Aunt Connie, but, of course, freedom is what we all need.

'Flummoxed?' Aunt Prudie asks as I stare at my hands. When I don't immediately reply, she pokes me as best she can with her own captive ones. 'Magic bewilder! Magic perplex!'

I look at Aunt Prudie. 'Yeah, I am, I guess. Flummoxed.'

'Magic true and easy! Magic deeply felt!' says Aunt Prudie. 'Stars know!'

'I don't know anything,' I say. 'The stars know it all.'

'Must know!' Aunt Prudie says.

'Must know what, Aunt Prudie?'

'Must know *self*!'

I guess that's the main problem. Even though most of the month is gone, I still don't know what kind of witch I'm going to be.

'Aunt Prudie . . . you did say hands don't matter,' I say.

'Piffle paffle!' Aunt Prudie exclaims.

Mirabelle unfolds herself a little, raising her head from her knees. 'Mind matters!' she adds quietly in Aunt Prudie's voice.

'Pfft!' Aunt Prudie condemns us both.

'Can the stars come out of somewhere else? Like, the Morgans use their eyes?'

'Accursed Mor—' Aunt Prudie starts.

'OK,' I admit quickly, 'bad example. But like, what's to stop you having a magical elbow?'

Kerra has her head in her hands, probably in despair.

'Or maybe you could just . . . bypass your hands?' I suggest, even though Aunt Prudie is almost vibrating with fury.

There's a snorting noise. It's Mirabelle and she's trying not to laugh. 'The magicless teaching the magicless,' she says.

'We are going to get you out of those *things*,' I tell my family firmly, glaring at the icy gloves. I nudge Kerra because I said 'we' and I meant it.

She raises her head, gives furious Aunt Prudie a tiny glance, and nods.

'Come,' Mum says, squatting down and giving us all the best attempt at a smile, 'eat, and let's be grateful we're together. It's not as bad as it looks. The pumpkin is in the wrong hands but it is still safe. And the stars will provide their light.'

I look at Aunt Connie's small, curled form. She is the one who would push me and my hands, if she was awake. But it's as if, without her power, Aunt Connie would rather just not be at all.

'Witches welcome wilderness!' Aunt Prudie shouts and a particularly loud wave crashes against the rocks below us, punctuating her words.

'Yeah, yeah, Aunt Prudie, you're very tough, I know. But . . .' I stop. I don't need to tell her that I'm missing Aunt Connie's cosy kitchen, the fire making the soup bubble, the bread baking. I'm sure she is too.

I lift up a mug and drink the inferior soup and, while Aunt Prudie might not like it, it is warming.

The sky here is different from the sky at home.

There are so many stars and I don't think they're there because any witch willed them to be. They wink and glow and glitter and I can see why they are our emblem, the origin of our power.

Stars are bright little spots in the sky. Or they're giant hot balls of light-emitting gas. Or they're where ancient magic comes from. Or all three of those things at once.

Far, far above me, each of those tiny specks is a nuclear reaction, happening all the time. Stars are full of pressure, one gas turning into another.

I'm full of pressure too, the magic inside me turning into something else as I focus my mind.

I look up at the night sky and consider shaking my fist at those tricksy little lights. Instead, I send up some questions. My family have been saying 'the stars know' ever since I was born. But now more than ever, I am at a loss to know what that means.

'I hope you know what you're doing,' I whisper up at the stars, then add, 'no disrespect or anything.'

And I think the magic hidden inside me chimes in response – or it could just be the wet echoes of the cave.

I rest my forehead against the rock, which is so cold that, for a moment, a chill rushes down my whole body.

I had wanted time to look at the sea. Now that's

all I have. Our already-narrow world just shrank even further. I gaze out at the frothing turquoise water as Mirabelle turns on to her side, facing the cave wall, and Kerra flumps down, also staring bleakly out to sea.

A single bird wheels past. There's been a lot of birds around, lately. I watch it suspiciously as it loops back around the cliffs, its wings flashing in the sun. It's no pigeon, and there must be so many birds in the sky, but . . . what if it's the one that divebombed our pumpkin? Or hopped into our star?

I shake my head. It can't be. Surely not. But then the bird's high-pitched squawk rises in tone, as if it's trying to warn us of something.

The single bird is slowly joined by a whole flock. From far away they are silent, but as they flap closer and closer, they're noisier. They chatter with a *kack-kack-kack-kack* sound. Aunt Prudie squawks back at them.

The birds circle, hover, chatter. One seems to sing.

I gaze out at the sea for long enough that my eyelids begin to droop, my family's quiet voices murmuring in the background.

'Should have known!' Aunt Prudie mutters. 'Should have seen!'

'We couldn't have seen it,' Mum whispers back.

'We don't have any ability to see further than the October we're in. We could never have known.'

'Greatest triumph! Greatest downfall,' Aunt Prudie sighs, settling next to her sleeping sister.

'Rest, dear sister, rest,' Mum is saying, soothingly. Even though it's not directed at me, I lie down too.

Just as my eyes are closing, I see a flash – not of gold starry magic – but of a tail: square-cut, cream and brown. Almost asleep, I blink myself awake and see a bird tilting its head horizontally to look me full in the face.

The bird is perched right at the edge of the cave mouth, unafraid of the drop behind it. I guess I wouldn't be afraid either if I had wings.

The bird cocks its head like it has asked a question and is waiting for my answer.

CHAPTER 22

It must take about a week for our lives in the cave to become routine but I lose track of the days quickly. Sleeping on the hard floor is a challenge, but that's not the worst bit.

'You're so squirmy. Can you just chill, please?' Mirabelle complains, but it's on me to make my family comfortable and I wish I could do more. A stove for Aunt Connie might help.

Even without magic, we've made the best of it. I've lumped the sand on the floor into pillows and have made a small toilet in one corner, closest to the open sea air. Feathers from the birds on the cliffs, patterned in gold-brown and white, float in on the breeze and we pile those up too, to lay on. They're surprisingly warm and comfortable.

Kerra and I are as busy as two useless witches can be. We try to sharpen rocks against the solid floor then use them against the bars of our cell. It makes a painful screeching noise, but luckily doesn't bring the Morgans down to find out what we're doing. After hours and hours, we've made a small groove in one of the bars – we might be able to cut through it completely in a hundred or so years. I keep myself busy to avoid having to work on the disappointment that is my 'magical' hands.

Every time the Morgans take my family away to be part of their monstrous experiment, all I can do is watch as a bright star appears from nowhere and swiftly closes around them with a pop, magically transporting them back to the pumpkin against their will.

I pace, terrified for them and the state they will come back in; I'm scared that without their magic, my family might not survive. Aunt Connie is now so weak, it's as if her very essence is being drained away too.

And, even worse, part of me – a part I am not proud of – is relieved to be so useless to the Morgans.

Mum beams as she is taken away and I stay safely in the cell, but it always feels like forever until she and the rest of my family reappear. And when they materialise out of thin air again, clutching their magically encased hands and wincing, they all collapse to the floor in exhaustion.

Kerra is as miserable as me, if not more so,

but just having someone there – even if they are a Morgan– helps when my family are gone.

And, voiceless, Kerra can't endlessly complain.

'So you thought that star – the one that appeared out of nowhere, you thought your mum made that? To bring you home?' I ask her one evening, backtracking through all the things I did wrong to end up in the cave.

Kerra nods sadly.

'Oh, great,' Mirabelle says bitterly. 'More witches with mummy problems.'

Kerra looks like she could almost spit with fury, but she doesn't have the words.

'You're lucky, Morgan,' Mirabelle says. 'You're lucky not to be forced into witchhood yet.' Her shoulders are tight with anger.

Kerra opens her mouth and tries to talk over her but Mirabelle ignores even that and turns away to face the cave mouth.

Mirabelle points. 'Look there – from a distance, stars are just tiny dots. But up close, they're huge and hot and heavy and that's what's in us. And now, we might have to deal with it all the time. When your body fills up with power from the night sky and you have to deal with the consequences – that's just not fair.'

Kerra's lips are still working in silence.

'I don't even want to be a witch.' The confession tips straight out of Mirabelle.

'You don't want magic? At all? Like, not even in October?' I ask.

'We were never asked if we wanted it. The power just descends on us. You can't . . . opt out. Being a witch doesn't come naturally to me.'

Mirabelle's confession almost makes me blurt out something similar. I didn't know that any other witches felt like this.

'I'm scared of my own magic, my own fingers. My hands don't feel like my own, they've been . . . weaponised. And what I think about it doesn't matter. Magic is so selfish,' Mirabelle says.

It's true. Our family of witches aren't big do-ers. We stay tucked away in our own little house, ignoring the rest of the world and its problems. There's silence while we all watch the stars out of the huge open window over the cliffs.

I jump up. I've been focusing my energy on the bars of the cell but perhaps I should be spending more time considering the opposite side – the one that is already open.

'Come on,' I say, 'help me out. We can't go down, but maybe we could climb up!'

Kerra jumps up too, nodding frantically and pointing at me, the cliff, herself.

I stand at the very edge of the cave, facing inwards, one arm in Kerra's grip and the other reaching along, out of the cave, patting down the cliff-face, searching for a handhold.

'You're not serious,' Mirabelle says and it's not a question. 'Two young hags, one with no magic, one with dodgy magic and you want to – what?'

I don't answer as Kerra grasps hold of my forearm even tighter and I put one foot out of the cave so that half of me is still inside, half of me out, the sharp corner edge of the rock right in front of my nose. Blood, or stars, fills my head with dizziness and I stretch further across with one arm and one foot, feeling across the cliff face for anywhere to grab on.

'I'm going to wake up your mum,' Mirabelle threatens but she is immediately drowned out by the screech of birds.

I am facing inwards, trying to think and move like a rock climber when I feel a soft but insistent pressure close around my back.

Feathers, not loose but attached to thick, muscular

wings, are surrounding me. It's a wriggly, writhing, slightly poky sensation but I'm being held in a hammock of wings.

The birds aren't attacking but they aren't letting me leave the cave, either. They've formed a huddle at my back and are pushing me, with caws and scratches and the occasional sharp nip from a beak, back up and in.

I fall forward, back into the cave and onto Kerra, whose eyes are ginormous in shock.

One bird lands at the corner I was hugging as I tried to climb free and chatters angrily.

I put up both hands in surrender and back down into a squat.

'Of all the foolishness,' Mirabelle says then sees me shiver. 'You cold?'

'Nah,' I say. The wind is still there but it's brisk and salty and, with the risk of the cliff edge, makes me feel awake.

I glance back at Mirabelle and realise I need to return the question. 'You?'

'Yeah. Always.'

I shuffle closer so that we can huddle together, like penguins for warmth. Kerra waits a moment then shuffles in too.

'It's really, really cold in the Arctic,' Mirabelle says, her voice serious and low again. 'I know that sounds obvious. But it's colder than I could ever have imagined. I tried to make myself things but all I could think about was the cold. That's why they used to use fire on witches I think, because if you're on fire, I bet you can't think about anything else. That's how I felt in the Arctic; my mind went completely blank, I couldn't create anything at all. At first, I couldn't even make myself a coat because I couldn't imagine a coat. The cold took over everything.'

I keep my eyes on the stars and let her talk.

'And sometimes I think that cold sunk into me, that it's still inside me. I'll just be living my life, doing my thing, and the cold will roll straight over me. And I've been really cold since we arrived here.'

I hunch even closer to Mirabelle to try and help. Kerra looks like she might roll her eyes but she penguins up again too.

'Hey Morgan, I get you and your sister were trying to impress your mother. But if your mother doesn't care for young hags, especially the powerless kind, then she just doesn't. If she's not there, then she doesn't care,' Mirabelle tells Kerra. The last line sounds rehearsed, like something Mirabelle has repeated to herself a lot.

I know that Mirabelle, like everyone who can be startlingly mean, is talking more about herself and her own situation. It occurs to me that maybe she doesn't even need magic when she's got words that blunt. Kerra looks wobbly.

'I was wrong about your sister. Another mistake,' Mirabelle tells her. 'I liked her vibe. I thought she was all right.'

That is as much of a compliment as Mirabelle ever gives and, for a moment, I'm jealous of Senara again.

'Hey,' Mirabelle says, watching me closely. 'You're *actually* all right. Ordinary, but all right.'

I glow with my own "all rightness". I didn't know I was all right in her eyes, so it feels like an unexpected gift.

Sometimes, someone says something and the words are so warming that you take them and hold them close. My mum is like that all the time, everything she says glows with kindness but Mirabelle . . . isn't.

So when she says I'm all right, I really must be. And when things aren't all right, I'll probably remember that Mirabelle thinks that I am.

I feel a tiny thump inside my jacket pocket. Miniature hoofbeats. Bobby shimmers slightly in my palm, and stamps as I take her out.

'Would you . . . like my pony?' I ask Mirabelle. I feel very silly offering up Bobby like she's a teddy bear we could share. But I want to offer something – something to show her that yes, I am all right. And she is too.

We watch Bobby parade up and down and it makes me smile, even though she is now fuzzier around the edges than she should be. Her soft, snack-seeking lips and her warm hay breath are almost gone, but she's still full of pony-spirit and tosses her head this way and that.

'At least we're together,' I say, and regret it as soon as I see Kerra wince. I might as well have said, 'At least we're not Kerra Morgan'.

'First Octobers are the worst,' Mirabelle says into her hands. 'And this one is pretty bad. Almost as bad as mine. But not as bad as my mum's.'

'Your mum's First October . . .?' I ask, finally. 'What happened in Aunt Flissie's First October?'

Mirabelle doesn't answer. I never set out to pester my cousin but somehow I always end up bothering her. This is big information to withhold. If I was ever going to hear it, now, at rock bottom, would be the right time.

'What do you know?' I insist. 'Why do they always say, "The stars know" but I can never know?' There's a small sting in the fact that she knows something about our family that I don't.

'Cough up all the secrets,' I say immediately. 'You can't hold out on me when we're . . . here.'

My family have never answered any of my questions. As soon as I could talk, I asked a lot, but Mum would distract me with tiny treasures or treats, Aunt Connie would tell me the answers would come when I wasn't a young hag and Aunt Prudie would shout 'No'. Mum says that secrecy comes with the craft and the coven. That only the stars know.

'Aunt Connie calls it . . . a great mistake and a great tragedy. And Aunt Prudie doesn't talk about it at all – she hasn't spoken, y'know, properly since,' Mirabelle says in a low voice.

I give a little shiver and lean in. Mirabelle seems to catch it, and shivers too.

'My mum, your Aunt Flissie . . . she was the youngest. So they were all waiting on her coming of age. And they were impatient, I guess.'

I know that feeling. Aunt Connie has been waiting for me to become the fifth point of the star for years. The pressure on her sister must have been even worse.

'Poor Aunt Flissie,' I say.

'And they . . . had a plan. Something to do with that cauldron. Their first time of putting magic into a thingy. But . . . my mum didn't have control of her magic and Aunt Temmie was in the wrong place at the wrong time.'

'And?'

'Temmie died. And her body disappeared among the stars. The aunts say that when witches die, our bodies return to the stars. We're made of stardust.'

I know this, Mum has said it before: *Like magic, nothing is forever*. We give everything back to the universe eventually, even our bodies.

'But how did she . . .?' I try to think of a time that I've even seen Aunt Flissie using her magic.

'She didn't have control of her hands, or something. She still wears gloves all October now,' Mirabelle says, looking down at her own hands.

I feel so tight and tense, holding my own hands desperately hard, that I might shatter at even a prod. I wonder if all families have these secrets and problems, or whether this is particularly a witch thing.

And that is the end of Aunt Flissie's story, I realise. There might be more to say but either Mirabelle can't say it or she doesn't know it.

'That's why my mum . . . goes away. Aunt Connie

said it's her terrible guilt. Because Mum believes she's the reason Temmie died.'

My brain is rickety with magic but I try and make sense of this. I imagine Aunt Flissie, the youngest of five sisters, with grand plans. She probably couldn't wait to join in. She would have excitedly taken her place in the five-pointed star – and then one of her sisters died that very First October. Because of her enthusiasm.

If anything happened to Mirabelle or my mum or any of my aunts because of me this autumn, my life would stop. I would freeze, I would never be able to look at my family ever again, knowing what we lost.

'And that's why you hate her?'

'I don't hate my mum!' Mirabelle protests. 'And I don't think she's a murderer! Well, maybe she was, I don't know. But she didn't mean to be.' Then she goes quiet. 'Or . . . I don't hate her because of the accident, but because she's still running away from it now. And that means running away from me. Obviously, no one was going to actually banish my mum – but she does it to herself. You and I weren't even born and yet, we're still the ones who catch this family foolishness.'

I've never cried for Temmie's death, any more than I would cry for the very first Merlyn, because she's been gone my entire life and I never knew her. We've never talked about the how or the why before, because it's just been a fact.

But now my nostrils are stinging for Aunt Flissie, whose life stopped when she lost her sister. There used to be five sisters but then there were four, and that really turned into three and a half.

I hope I don't look as sad for Mirabelle as I feel. In among the hubbub of our household, Mum and I have something private that is just ours. And I never meant to leave Mirabelle out, but I did. Aunt Prudie and Aunt Connie aren't exactly cuddly and so, of the five of us who stay every October, Mirabelle must be the most alone. I feel that, more than ever, as we huddle on the floor of the cave.

'Where does Aunt Flissie actually go in October?' I ask.

'I don't know,' Mirabelle says with borderline despair. 'Wherever I'm not – as far away as she can get. Mum doesn't use her magic anymore. So I can't track her. Aunt Pattie once told me she thought my mum spent a lot of time in Scotland. That's where I was aiming for . . . when I ended up in the Arctic.' Mirabelle shivers again. 'I reckoned you and me . . . we couldn't hang out because of . . . the Arctic and stuff. I didn't want to do that to you, too.'

I blink. I had never thought Mirabelle might be ignoring me to protect me.

'We'll stick together now,' I say lamely.

'Our family has never stuck together,' Mirabelle says, then pauses thoughtfully. 'Why do you think the Halloween party matters to me so much?'

'Because parties are . . . cool?' I try, and it's the wrong thing, obviously, because she shuts down.

'Well, this has been a delightful treat,' Mirabelle says, sounding snuffly. I glance up to see if she means it – she doesn't. 'But you can take your Morgan paws off me now, thank you.'

Kerra has one hand resting on Mirabelle's shoulder, staring at her intently. She doesn't back off in the face of Mirabelle's sarcasm and lays her head on Mirabelle's shoulder instead.

If Kerra didn't already feel sorry for us, she definitely does now.

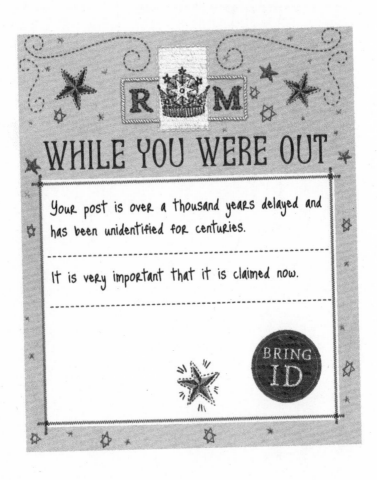

WHILE YOU WERE OUT

Your post is over a thousand years delayed and has been unidentified for centuries.

It is very important that it is claimed now.

BRING ID

CHAPTER 23

Everyone has gone to be plugged into the pumpkin again. Kerra is slumped on one side of the cave and I'm on the other, just waiting, when a head appears between the bars of our cell.

I wasn't expecting to see anyone, but this head definitely doesn't belong to anyone I want to see.

'Senara?' I exclaim.

Kerra leaps up, a variety of expressions passing across her face before it settles on excitement.

'Shh!' Senara hisses, unnecessarily in the case of her sister.

I can't go anywhere but I can turn my back on her.

'Hey, Merlyn! I'm not asking for your forgiveness, OK? I just need you to see this.' Senara half-clears a throat that doesn't need clearing, and I peer over my shoulder at her.

Senara looks down at the heavy locks on the bars and her eyes narrow then gleam. The locks neatly slide away.

'Come on,' she says, beckoning me. Kerra has instantly gone to her sister's side and is nodding and tapping her throat at the same time, like a dog sitting and wagging its tail, waiting for a treat.

'Yes,' Senara says to her little sister. 'I know. Just a minute.' Her voice is kind – but she betrayed us.

'No way am I going anywhere with you,' I say. Any tenuous trust between our two covens has already dissolved.

'It doesn't matter what happened before,' Senara says.

I toss my hair over my shoulder to better show her my 'You've got to be kidding' look.

'Um. Maybe it does in some ways and then, it might be important that someone says sorry. But I mean, what matters is what happens next. And I need your help with a thing. A Merlyn thing.'

Neither her glowing, gold-pupiled eyes nor her track record make me want to trust Senara.

'You're a . . . a crook!' I say, echoing Aunt Prudie uselessly. 'What Merlyn thing?'

'I think I've found a way to get you out of here,' Senara insists.

I don't want to encounter Aunt Morgan again. I don't want to have my hands plugged into her machine again either.

'Come on, Mother won't even notice, she hasn't really acknowledged me since you arrived. She's got four fully fledged witches to experiment on. And you're like Kerra to her: low priority.'

Kerra's eagerness dies away completely and she looks a bit wobbly.

'I mean – that's not what I meant . . . no . . . it's just . . . Mother underestimates us. You know that Mother thinks that young hags are worthless. I'm . . . sorry, Kerra. And I'm sorry about you, too, Merlyn.'

I glance back at Senara, the betrayer. She is flushed with embarrassment. But she apologised.

Senara's eyes close, her brow all crinkled. 'I just wanted Mother to . . . that doesn't matter. She'll never . . .'

I realise, with surprise and a touch of panic, that Senara might be about to cry.

'It was when your cousin . . . it was when Mirabelle stepped in front of you. To protect you. Twice. I've never done that for you, Kerra. But I should. Young hags should . . . stick together.'

And I realise there's nothing for Senara to gain from betraying me again, nor anything more for me to lose.

I turn round further and hesitate at the edge of the

freedom she is promising. 'I need to wait for my family,' I say.

'No,' Senara says immediately. 'This is already a risk, I can't take a whole coven.'

'I can't trust you,' I insist. 'I have to at least check with Mirabelle.'

Conspiring with Morgans. Aunt Connie would have something to say about this.

But then, with a catch, I remember Aunt Connie, looking ashy with exhaustion, her health draining away along with her magic.

'OK, forget it,' Senara says and turns to go but Kerra is blocking the way.

Senara sighs. 'Yeah, I know, I haven't forgotten about you, sister. But – and I say this because I care, OK? – I don't trust you enough to give you your voice back here. When we get outside.'

Kerra rolls her eyes at her sister, then pantomimes something, spreading her hands wide in appeal. Then, she draws herself up as tall as possible, taps both eyes, and makes a furiously angry face. I'm not completely sure, but I think she's trying to do an impression of her own mother.

'Yeah, I know. But Mother is always angry. And I'm

officially giving up on trying to please her. You should too, Kerra, she'll never listen. I'll always just be a young hag to her, no matter what I do. If we're going – it's got to be now, come on. The elders of both covens are down with the pumpkin.'

'What do you mean "outside"?' I say. 'I thought you said you were going to help us?'

Senara crouches down to look me levelly in both eyes. 'I saw a witch. Out on the clifftops. She wasn't a Morgan. She went into your little house. And,' Senara's voice dips into secret significance 'I could have told Mother but I'm telling you instead.'

'Are you sure?' my heart double-beats for Mirabelle. Could Aunt Flissie have come for us?

'I can't guarantee she was a Merlyn, but she had "The Hair".'

'What do you mean "The Hair"?' I ask, reaching up to touch my own pinging curls.

Senara gestures a hand around my tangled head.

Everything about Senara is smooth: her sleek braid, the way she moves, her quiet, polite voice. I don't know if I can believe her. But I know Mirabelle would have believed her, before, especially if there's any chance Aunt Flissie might be involved.

I think of our little house teetering on the cliff-edge and of all the small things my family do inside it to make it more beautiful and fun in October: the kitchen full of Aunt Prudie's greenery, Aunt Connie's cosy fire, the windy stairs, Mirabelle's purple den. I want to go home.

'If you're coming, we need to go now,' Senara steps back out of the cell. 'That witch isn't going to be there forever. And . . . I am, you know, sorry. I didn't even see you to start with. I just saw Merlyns. We've inherited Merlyn-hate as standard.'

I look at Senara's eyes. I shouldn't trust anyone with eyes like that. But Kerra and I, the deadweights, have got nowhere by ourselves. Even if Senara does betray me again, at least I'd be on the other side of these bars.

'Prove it,' I say. 'Do something for my coven. They're stuck here and they can't even use their hands.'

Senara sighs, shrugs, winks one eye and her offering is so small, I don't notice it at first. A stack of pillows, small but fluffy looking.

Small, but enough. I stand, brush my sandy pyjamas down and follow.

Senara pauses her smooth glide to eye my pyjamas. She gives me one quick wink and I'm wearing a white

Morgan cloak again. The heavy warmth of it and the way it swishes at my ankles is more comforting and less strange this time around.

We race across the courtyard, over the bridge and back out on to the clifftop's scrubby grass. Our house looks so dinky against the vast seascape.

We slow down as we approach the house. I realise we don't know who we're going to find inside. I blink back at the castle looming behind us and I just want to be out of its sight.

We sneak inside through the back door.

We're trying to be quiet, but as we let in the fierce wind from outside, the copper pots and pans hanging from a rack from the ceiling jostle each other. This poor house is always being invaded. We pull the door shut behind us and crouch down in silence, straining to listen for any proof of life in the house.

It is so strange to be at home without Mum, Aunt Connie or Aunt Prudie making a noise somewhere. I keep expecting one or all of them to walk in any minute. I wish Aunt Prudie was here bringing in vegetables for the soup. I wish Aunt Connie was here bossing us around, waving her wooden spoon, demanding we chop the vegetables. I wish Mum was here, laying the table in pretty gold colours and handing out bowls with a smile. I'd like a bowl of soup.

Hedge or hearth, they're all home witches and they should be here, in their favourite place.

But all we can hear is the house creaking in the wind; the only Merlyn witch here is me.

Senara drops a tiny wink to Kerra, who immediately bursts out, 'There is so much I need to say! Urgh! I have so much I need to tell you! The things you Merlyns believe in, my stars . . .'

Kerra carries on lecturing us but I carry on past her into the living room. It's empty too, apart from a cream and brown feather floating down to the ground.

'There's no one here,' Kerra says, stating the obvious. 'Your imaginary witch is gone.'

'I did see someone,' Senara bites back at Kerra. Then, 'I swear!' she says, more sincerely, to me.

'What now?' I say. 'Lock us back up?'

There's more than enough going on already – but looking at our house now, I still feel a tiny touch of embarrassment at how shabby it is when almost stripped of magic. Everything that is tatty and grimy the rest of the year becomes shiny in October, but it isn't shiny anymore.

'Your house is cosy,' Kerra says and I turn to her

with an immediate glare – but she's not sneering.

It is, even though every October thing my mum and aunts so joyfully made has receded. So much has changed that it takes me a moment to see one thing that hasn't: the throw has been pinned back fully against the wall. Someone has been here.

The three of us stand in the middle of the room, staring at the throw. Well, two of us are. Kerra is looking around wildly.

'Look, Kerra, do you remember?' Senara says and points at the throw. 'When we were here before, we saw it. It's a piece of our tapestry.'

'I never noticed . . .' I say, my breath catching a bit. The dirty old throw that usually hangs over the back of our sofa pales in comparison to the majestic tapestry in the Morgans' throne room. 'Though, does hanging a blanket on the wall make it a tapestry?'

'How very Merlyn of you,' Kerra says.

'Don't make me regret giving you that voice back, sister,' Senara says and, surprisingly, Kerra doesn't reply.

'It just used to be on the back of the sofa.' I point at the squishy sofa for emphasis, where several other blankets are piled up. 'I mean . . . Mum said she was Merlyn – maybe – but I never really . . . looked.'

Because now, looking is all I can do. Merlyn's face is a grimy grey and hard to see. There's not a lot there: a woman in side-profile looking up, arms outstretched, the picture cut off at her wrists.

And the background, which I'd never noticed at all, the shimmer of rows and rows of approaching figures on horseback.

Horses.

I pat my pocket gently, then more frantically.

'She's gone! Bobby's gone!'

But then my fingers make contact with a soft bristle. I gently pull Bobby out.

I stroke the last remains of her forehead star with the tip of my finger. She looks even more fuzzy round the edges, and she's losing her colour.

She has almost completely faded away. She was magic-made, so, looking at her, I know my mum has very little magic left. The idea of Mum, weak and magicless, is a gut-punch of pain and worry.

Senara takes Bobby's four faintly shimmering hooves on to her own palm, holds her up close and blinks. Bobby is suddenly a full, solid pony again.

'I never had anything like that,' Kerra says wistfully, reaching out to run a finger down Bobby's velvety nose.

It's too hard to explain how Bobby came to be, out of Mum's kindness alone. Senara sets Bobby down and the pony shakes herself.

'Stay here,' I tell Bobby. 'Protect the house – or something.'

'We need to take the tapestry to the throne room. Come on,' Senara says. Her eyes are wide, the stars in them bright.

***

Back in the gloom of the throne room, Senara uses her magic to effortlessly float our Merlyn throw towards the abrupt end of the Morgan tapestry. The entire tapestry shimmers as our portrait of Merlyn finds its place on the wall in front of us. Our small, shabby piece of the tapestry is a dirty scrap compared to what the Morgans have kept. And they've made their history central to their castle, while we flung ours over the back of the sofa.

My breath catches in an almost-hiccup of excitement.

The threads of their tapestry and our throw weave together. It's the most magical jigsaw ever, but with only two pieces: one huge, one small. The embroidery reforms and my eyes dart between the two ancient ancestors as they are drawn back together, one stitch at a time.

Mum would love this so much. As the two pieces entwine, the end of their story is unravelling for us.

There, still roiling through the earlier panels of the tapestry are the battles that we all know about already. Witch sisters using their magic on each other through dozens of magical transformations, stars flying.

Crowds are swarming towards them from every side of the tapestry. The humans on horses look small and insignificant compared to the central figures of Merlyn and Morgan but there are hordes of them, shiny with armour and weapons.

Their story is building to a crescendo, racing to the disaster that we all know about. Because while we don't agree on who started it, all Merlyns and Morgans know: the sisters each tried to strip the other of their powers and created our one-month-only problem.

Something other than magic clenches painfully inside me for a moment.

The two halves of the final panel: Morgan, standing, large and dominant, looking down in judgement at her sister, sword ready to swing. She looks like the victor. Merlyn, gazing up so helplessly, looks like she is crying, begging for mercy.

But as the two halves meet, I hope the others are

seeing what I'm seeing. I'm breathing too quickly to put it into words.

Because, as colour floods back to our tapestry, the centuries-old bobbly fabric tightening and glowing as it is magically restored, I see that the grey splodges on Merlyn's face aren't tears. They're stars.

And I feel like we've discovered the most important secret of our witches' world. But . . . it was never a secret. It was right here in front of us, hiding in plain sight.

'The things that Mother has told us about your family . . .' Senara shakes her head.

'We thought Merlyn and Morgan messed this whole thing up for us all, and we're here dealing with the consequences,' I say.

My eyes rove all over the tapestry, taking in every detail, seeing how the two pieces come together and confound what we all thought.

The past has been murky, dark stories handed down. But this couldn't be clearer.

'We have it so, so wrong,' I say.

The stars might know but our families definitely don't.

R★M

WHILE YOU WERE OUT

Please, please, PLEASE accept delivery of this parcel.

This will be the final attempt!

BRING ID

CHAPTER 24

We're still all standing in front of the tapestry when we hear the heavy doors at the end of the hall creak open. My heart drops as the outline of a figure appears, but then we hear the call.

'Delivery for you!' a faraway voice calls. 'Delivery? For . . . you?'

Kerra is wide-eyed with horror but it's not her coven coming for us.

'I think . . . I think it's the postman,' I say.

He has a blank face and yet, he's moving, as if he's being steered or has been put on autopilot to complete tasks.

'Careful,' Senara whispers to Kerra, stepping in front of her.

Our magic bars all humans from entering our orbit in October, and yet here he is again, breaking another of the rules. Again.

I can see he's wearing his familiar uniform – a red plastic jacket emblazoned with the Royal Mail logo.

He's carrying a large red post sack on his hip.

Somehow, our postman has travelled all the way here and crossed the threshold into Morgan territory, into their stronghold of a castle. There's something superhuman about him, I think, even as he peers around looking dazed.

'What are you doing here?' I ask.

'I . . . have a delivery!' he calls.

He rubs at both eyes with his fists and takes another step forward, like he's in trance.

I move back – and he moves forward, like we're on a strange magical see-saw. He takes a deep breath and another step and then plants his feet firmly.

We stand facing each other and, as I take in his serious bespectacled face, somehow both kind and trustworthy, my jaw truly drops.

I turn back to the tapestry, scanning until I find it. The postman's face! It is right there on the wall, just behind the central figures of Morgan and Merlyn. He must appear a dozen times, in the background. And in a panel near the end, he is reaching towards them both in exactly the same way that he is reaching towards us now, only today, he's offering a long thin parcel I've already taken delivery of three times.

'Who are you?' I ask. My eyes dart back and forth between the tapestry and this figure. He looks so out of place, but he clearly belongs here.

'I'm your postie, Arthur. Nice to meet you – again.' The postman holds the parcel out for one of us to take. None of us do. Even witches should be careful about gifts from strangers. 'I just deliver what comes into the depot.'

It's the same parcel I propped up in the hallway, the same parcel he put over the garden gate. The same one I put on the bottom step of our stairs and never even thought about again.

The postman turns the parcel round, lowers a small pair of reading glasses to the end of his nose. 'Morgan Merlyn,' he says. 'I don't know – that one of you?'

The hush that descends on us is solid.

Eventually Senara steps forward.

'Will you sign for it?' Arthur the postman asks valiantly, as he passes it to her.

Before I can warn her, Senara takes her sharp nail to the strip of Sellotape that runs down the middle of the box, sealing the two sides of the cardboard.

It doesn't give. I thought it was just me, having a case of October incompetence, but there must be something more than that.

She grunts in annoyance, then hisses and withdraws her hand quickly. Her nail has broken.

She blinks to conjure a knife then tries again. The knife bends immediately, as if meeting a stronger metal.

Senara passes the undeliverable box to Kerra who tries to find the end of the Sellotape, but just as quickly she passes it back again, as if it's a party game and whoever opens it wins what's inside. Sparks gather around Senara's eyes, but though the parcel seems to be made only of cardboard, no matter how much she widens her golden eyes, it doesn't open.

I slide the box from Senara's arms and return it to the postman who doesn't look pleased about it being returned to him.

'You open it,' I suggest.

'I can't!' Arthur the postman protests. 'It's not addressed to me.'

'Can you open it for us?' I say. 'Please?'

He shrugs, then with a quick, practised gesture he rips the Sellotape off, all the way down the box.

Part of me is smug that I've figured out there's something special about the postman, but I still gasp as he knocks the packing stuffing out of the way and carefully lifts something long and bright from the box.

'What did you do?' Senara asks.

'I just . . . gave it a little tug. It's only Sellotape,' the postman says with another shrug.

We're all dazzled.

Held aloft in the postman's hand is a huge sword.

I look from the postman to the tapestry and back again. There he is. Holding the same exact sword, handing it to the ancestral sisters.

Kerra follows my eyes and does a very dramatic double-take, as if she's forgotten she has her voice back and is still pantomiming for us. 'Wow,' she says simply, looking from the woven picture of the sword on the wall to the real sword in front of us.

'There you go,' Arthur the postman says.

'I don't think that is meant for us,' I say, shrinking backwards from the sword.

'It was addressed to us. All of us. Any one of us could take it,' Senara says.

'I'll take it,' Kerra says immediately.

'Not every one of us *should* take it though,' Senara says, but Kerra has already stepped forward.

'Yeah, yeah, my power hasn't come in, I'm just a deadweight. But if you're just going to stand there, I might as well try.' She brandishes the sword aloft.

It's the most majestic thing I've ever seen. Almost as long as she is tall.

'What do you feel?' Senara sounds apologetic for even having to ask.

'I can't feel anything,' Kerra announces. She shifts her grip on the sword, gazing down its length and at its spectacular handle, ornately carved and embedded with all kinds of stones. I catch a glimpse of a different Kerra as she stands there, plaits poking out behind her, sword aloft.

'It's very shiny,' I say as Kerra frowns at it and makes a stab at the air, as if she could summon something with it. I turn to Senara. 'You have to take it. You're the only one in control of your power. Even though you're a Morgan.'

Senara glances up and down the throne room nervously. 'I can't . . . I can't take this,' she says. 'Mother might sense it.'

'Then I think this is yours to return to sender,' I say, gesturing as if we're going to return the giant sword to Arthur the postman.

He jumps back immediately. 'Oh no, I just deliver things, I don't think I can return this. It wouldn't be safe!'

Kerra twists the sword around and presents the pommel to my hand. In that moment, I know we can trust each other. I give my hands a little warm-up shake and then hold my breath as I take the sword. I lift it out of Kerra's hands with only one of my own. I immediately realise my mistake as the weight of the sword takes me by surprise. By the time I've brought my other hand up and round to hold it, the point has already doinked the floor.

Arthur the postman and the two Morgans all stare at the new dent I've just made in the stone floor. I feel a bubble of hysterical laughter and try to pop it.

I don't know if the delivery is actually for me or not. But I've finally taken it – his job is done. The giant undeliverable sword is in my hands, kind of. Arthur the postman breathes a sigh, maybe of relief.

'Um. Thank you for delivering this,' I say, grimacing at the hulking great sword by my side. 'You don't know who the sender is?'

'No, but I'd like to have a word with them, to be honest. Makes me wonder how much other funny stuff comes through my depot.'

'In October, there's a lot of funny stuff,' I say with a small smile.

Arthur nods, his suspicions confirmed – we are the funny stuff.

'Ta ra then,' Arthur says and he ambles away.

I've never even seen a real sword in real life, let alone held one. It's just a giant pencil, I think. An extension of my arm.

'It must mean something,' Kerra says. 'If it's in the tapestry, then it's a sacred piece of witch history.'

'Yeah, so if it's historic, then it's just ornamental?' I say with distaste. 'It's just so . . .' I give it a wobble, both hands on the hilt now. 'It's not actually for . . . using, right?'

'You can't wobble a sacred vessel!' Kerra exclaims. 'The stars only know why you got your powers this October and I didn't.'

'Does it come with a shield?' I ask, scanning the tapestry. The hordes of knights have shields.

My hands feel warm around the sword's handle and I suddenly whip one hand back, causing the tip to clank noisily to the floor again.

'Can we stop with the incredibly loud noises, please?' Senara says, taking another nervous look over her shoulder.

'There's something inside it,' I say. I can feel a humming; this sword is filled with a staticky buzz of power.

'Of course. It must be loaded with magic,' Kerra says, sounding like Aunt Connie when she's talking about soup: hungry.

I feel a sudden urge to show the sword to my family. I can imagine what they would say as clearly as if they were here with me.

Mum would admire its beauty, if not its purpose.

'Overgrown needle!' Aunt Prudie would shout.

'No piece of metal, no matter how magical, will decide the fate of this family,' Aunt Connie would say, resolutely. 'We need no such destiny-shaper.' She would be all prim about it, too.

And Mirabelle – she would make some joke about the great inconvenience that comes with great power. But for the first time, I *do* feel the very, very great power here. And I feel the very, very great responsibility that comes with it.

'We need to get out of here,' Kerra says and starts towards the doors. 'We can hide back at your house and come up with a plan.'

'Wait,' Senara says and her eyes guide the Merlyn side of the tapestry back down. Kerra wraps the sword quickly and neatly in the throw and then hands it back to me.

'Keep it safe,' Senara says. 'Mother will be able to sense any disruption to magic.'

'I hate saying this, but you have to take us back to the cave,' I say catching Senara's eye. 'My family will be sent back soon and we can't risk being found out now. Plus, Aunt Morgan will definitely find out if we're not back where we're meant to be.'

Senara nods in agreement. 'I think you're right, Clemmie, but we're going to need a plan. And, sister, you're going to have to be *quiet*.'

Kerra looks like she might actually grind her teeth, and a tiny glimpse of a smile appears on Senara's face.

'You're both going back to that cell,' Senara adds. 'So no talking, remember? Now, come on, quickly.'

CHAPTER 25

I follow Senara's lead, out of the throne room. My mind is spinning and the sword is weighing heavy in my hands.

'What would your mum – Mother – do with all that power? The stuff in the pumpkin, the stuff in *here*?' I ask, hefting the sword up.

'Exceed even our ancestor,' Senara says with finality. 'Mother wants to restore the old way of life for witches. Shape-shifting and seismic wars and not having to hide at all. She doesn't want to be stuck in a ruined castle eleven months of the year. She wants to rule the world. Subjugate humans to witches.'

'It's not evil to be ambitious,' Kerra adds hurriedly.

'But it is maybe . . . tricky . . . to want to overthrow every human government, for example,' I reply.

'Witches were made to be different. You must know that,' Kerra says, but with less certainty.

It was rude, the way Aunt Morgan just rocked up at

our house. And then it was sneaky and devious how she made off with my family and their hard work. And then draining their power, putting them in danger – that's really bad news. But, threatening world peace and having global domination? That's definitely a super-villain vibe.

Back at home, my aunts might have used this pumpkin for eleven months of growing plants and new dresses and soup over a cosy fire, but here, in the Morgan's clutches, it's too much for all of us. Magic is too big. It's already too big for us for one month; it would be far too big for the world if we had it all the time.

'Eternal power is our family's mission, our mantra, our everything. To have an always-October. We work towards it from when we're babies. It's all Mother cares about,' Senara shrugs, and I feel a flash of tight anger at her for saying it so casually. But it's so easy to still be angry with people who haven't made the problems but have inherited them.

'But she has gone too far. We have to stop her,' Senara says and, though she normally looks so grown up and effortlessly cool and magical, now, as she puts one hand in her mouth, worrying at her broken nail, she looks like Kerra – guilty. Her family have a lot to answer for.

'We just have to explain. Carefully and clearly. We can show Mother the full story, tell her about the ancestors and how we were wrong,' Kerra insists.

'I'm afraid it's too late for that. The more full of magic that pumpkin gets, the more I can see it in Mother's eyes,' Senara says.

'See what?' Kerra asks impatiently.

'I . . . I think it's greed.'

'Nothing wrong with wanting magic,' Kerra says. 'I do too.'

'Why would you want something that hurts so much?' I ask.

'It hurts?' Kerra exclaims.

'Yeah, of course.'

'How? How does it hurt?'

'Um. So, I get cramps. They come in spasms, they make my hands seize up. It's heavy, the magic. It's uncomfortable all the time. But, I've inherited it from my mum and she got it from her mum and it goes back generations of women having cramps and heaviness and pain and stuff. I think all witches get it.'

'Witches are where biology meets astrology,' Senara says. 'All bodies are made of stardust, big bang and all that, the stars simply have a more direct line down to us.'

And stars are hot. The pain is like the steady heat of a sunburn.

Kerra turns to her older sister to ask, 'Why doesn't Mother tell us about magic hurting?' She suddenly looks a lot younger than her twelve years.

'She's . . . ambitious,' Senara says. 'And the pain isn't the worst bit, it's the loneliness.'

'Really?' Kerra says, crinkling her nose. 'You feel lonely? There are so many of us. Mother and all her sisters.'

Kerra and Senara have even more aunts than we do. An excess of aunts is not what any of us need.

'A witch can be lonely even in the biggest coven,' Senara says. 'Now – Kerra, I'll come back for you. But stay here for now – and *please* stay quiet. Or try, at least.'

'Urgh,' Kerra says, and her older sister's expression is right on the line between infuriated and entertained.

I look as deeply as I can into Senara's gold pupils (which still unnerve me). But I'm the one holding our ancestors' sword, which is throbbing with magic. If she can trust me with that, I should trust her with this.

I faff with the sword and the tapestry around it. I should have asked the postman if I could keep the big cardboard box. The sword looks sparkly, but it doesn't feel sparkly – it feels heavy. Everything is more of an effort now that I'm carrying it. It's like I've had extra weights strapped on to me, or like I'm moving underwater.

'Remember – Mother can't get her hands on the sword,' Senara says, then turns to Kerra with a serious expression.

Kerra steps backwards, hands to her throat.

'I'm not going take your voice, sister,' Senara says quietly. Kerra gives her sister a huge hug, their braids tangling. Senara regains her low, serious tone with a struggle.

'I wouldn't use my magic against you. Or you,' she adds to me, 'but you must, must be silent. They can't know I was here.'

Senara has barely gone before Kerra turns to me and starts talking.

'Now. I can see that this is all going to be up to me – so listen.'

CHAPTER 26

'So,' Kerra says, 'let's get into it. What's wrong with your magic?'

I try to splutter out my indignation but instead I sputter into silence. I don't have a comeback. My magic is like a car starting; I can't get it in gear. Stars might be inside me but I can't channel them into actually making anything.

If anyone had asked me before October, I would have said I don't give up easily. I've spent a whole year trying to make Mirabelle my best friend again. But, this month, I gave up on my magic quickly, too nervous about what it might do. Now it sits inside me, heavy and useless.

'I mean, there's a lot wrong with all the Merlyns, but you – you don't work at all.' Kerra reaches out and pokes one of my hands then cranes her neck so she can peer up into my downturned eyes. I keep staring at the rock so I don't have to look at her.

'There's stars in there, but you can't get them out. Not with your hands, not with your eyes. Like someone screwed the lid down too tight,' she muses. 'Hmm. So, we start with the basics.'

And then she makes me do something that, in all their demonstrating and hollering, my family never did – she makes me breathe.

Kerra offers a hand to pull me up off the floor and we stand. She gestures and I copy, putting one hand on my upper chest and one just below my rib cage. She closes her eyes and breathes in a deep inhale.

Then she exhales even more slowly, even more deliberately. Kerra breathes with me and I match her rhythm and because she's busy breathing, she doesn't talk at all.

My mum is patience itself. I am not. I screw up my eyes – as if that will help.

I breath in – and out – and in – and just as I'm about to open my own eyes and tell Kerra that this is ridiculous, I feel something inside me. There's the steady pulse of my heart, regular and reassuring, and under and over it, and maybe even dancing through it, there's a fluttering.

I press the hand on my sternum harder down,

feeling the solid bone and underneath it – yes, there! – the dancing. I am full of stars.

They're sparking and bouncing around inside me the way that that one tiny light was inside the pumpkin. If this is 'the Morgan way', then it's working.

I press my hand down harder still, feeling the pressure of it glow in my palm.

For just one month, I am home to all these busy sparks and I've never felt them inside me before with such clarity. My breath, strong and steady and filling my whole body, catches the stars and carries them up and down inside me like a tide.

Hello, I want to tell the sparking stars, *I'm your host. I'm Clemmie and I don't know how to use you all properly. But I'm learning.*

I open my eyes, dazzled by what's happening inside me.

Your mind's eye, Mum had said. *See it exactly how you wish it to be.* Maybe she would have been a great October teacher if only I had given her the chance.

I stare at Kerra, still feeling the dancing inside me. Her wide brown eyes make sense to me. *Can you feel it?* her eyes are asking.

'Oh my stars,' I breathe.

'You can hear them,' Kerra says with a smile which then turns thoughtful. 'So the problem isn't the stars. It's how to get them out.'

'Thank you,' I say, and we share the smallest of smiles.

'My problem isn't talking, it's getting people to listen,' Kerra says, smile widening. 'So, what are you going to *do* with the stars? What do you want?'

I feel like I've been doing nothing but talking about what I want, all October long.

'A happy, ordinary life!' I exclaim. 'Just my cousin saying, "Hey, let's watch a movie or go to the park – *not* to collect magical powers from celestial beings – just to hang out".'

Kerra raises her eyebrows and I feel hot with embarrassment.

'Fine, what do *you* want?' I ask her.

'For Senara and Mother to say, "Wow, Kerra, thank you, we can't do anything without you".' Kerra holds my eye and, for a moment, I think she might cry but then she bursts out laughing. 'But we now know that is never going to happen in a star's lifetime,' she says, and she makes a zipping motion across her mouth which makes her laugh more.

'So,' she continues, 'not the Morgan way, through

the eyes. And apparently not the Merlyn way either. Some other way to channel your power.'

'I asked Aunt Prudie if I could have a magical elbow,' I say.

'Why not?' Kerra smiles. 'While we're breaking rules. Let's start with the elbow.'

I put out my elbow dubiously.

'Anyway,' Kerra says, frowning at my elbow, 'they're lucky to have us. Older siblings like ours *need* younger ones. Who else would they ignore, otherwise?'

Mirabelle isn't my sister but I don't correct Kerra.

There's a pop – not my elbow – and Kerra and I have been here for long enough to know exactly what that means.

I shove the sword in the tapestry and push it flat against the wall like an uncomfortable pillow.

'Quick!' I say, and Kerra and I sit down, squeezed tight next to each other, the sword along both of our backs. Concealing it like this won't hold up to a close look and we're only just in time.

As my family appears out of nowhere, this time a guard of Morgans accompanies them, *carrying* Aunt Connie.

She lays on a net of starry magic strung between

the Morgans. I knew Aunt Connie was old the way I knew our house is made of bricks – it was part of life. But now she looks so ancient that I don't know how the Morgans can keep using her. It makes me wince to see her like this.

'Aunt Connie!' I call out as my aunt shifts uncomfortably.

The Morgans, nameless and shapeless under their cloaks, each bend over my family's hands to secure them. The gloves wrap back around Aunt Connie's hands easily.

Kerra's mouth is open again, and I can tell she wants to say something, but I elbow her into silence.

This time I can see how depleted my family are. Mirabelle's look of exhaustion is beginning to match my mum's.

Mirabelle is the furthest away. I want to tell her what I know the most but she's keeping her distance from the Morgans, from us all. She'd probably like to shut her bedroom door on all of this, if only she could.

She gives the cave a baleful look. If only she knew what we learned today. If only she knew what we're sitting on.

One of the Morgans suddenly straightens and the stars in her eyes narrow almost completely away.

I don't know if there was a sound of metal on rock or if she could just sense it but she asks immediately, 'What are you hiding, young hags?'

Kerra stands first – I don't know how we ever thought that we could cover this sword – her hands out, not in attack but appeal.

'What have you done, young hag?' one of the Morgans asks in a hiss.

'What have you done, deadweight?' another chimes in, closing in on Kerra who, any minute now, is going to reveal her voice. I can't risk that.

'Hey!' I call. 'Stop!'

The final Morgan begins to approach me. I grab the sword, the tapestry shaking loose, and stagger up.

The Morgans pause, all of their eyes on the sword as I try to bring it upright, attempting to look like I know what I'm doing.

'Where did you acquire that?' one of the Morgans hisses. They're spreading back out again, moving to mark my mum and my aunts. 'You thought you could hide things from us?'

When I see the white-caped Morgans clustered around my family, the thought of Senara having betrayed us again crosses my mind.

I don't answer, Kerra doesn't either. Her shoulders are still but her chest is rising and falling.

I breathe. In, and out. I can feel the magic in the sword, dancing the same way it is in me, and I will it to respond.

I listen and I can hear the stars chime inside me.

My hands and my heart are so full. Magic ready to beam out of me. I think huge. I am full of awe. I breathe, just as Kerra showed me, feeling the stars inside me jump with every breath.

'Clem!' Mirabelle calls, but I block her out.

I can feel the Morgans' eyes on me and the sword, but their jabbing eyes, their magic, is no more than a nudge.

I shift my feet, spreading them wider, trying to hold the sword so that it doesn't topple me. And then, I lift it. I don't really know what to do with the sword but I want to look like I do. My arms quivering, I bring it up, up, to shoulder height, then further so that the handle is at the level of my eyes, the sword pointing straight up to the cave's rocky ceiling.

At first, it feels like a little bump of power, a nudge. Like how Mum passed her magic on through me. But it's quickly more than a bump; it's a shove and there's nowhere for the power to go.

It's not me and a surge of bravery, it's the sword, full of ancient energy.

So I bring it swishing down on nothing at all and it cuts through the air like lightning.

The flash is blinding – like an atomic blast. Everyone and everything is knocked backwards. Mum and my aunts are pushed back against the walls of the cell. The Morgans are knocked off their feet, capes flying, slamming to the floor.

But Mirabelle had her back to the ocean.

Mirabelle's arms don't flail, she doesn't try to reach out and grab on. She doesn't have time, it all happens so fast.

Mirabelle didn't even startle. She was just there – and then she wasn't.

She fell silently. She didn't even scream.

For a moment, I'm the only one standing at all. Even though I'm not sure what my legs are doing because surely they can't still be holding me upright.

Then, behind me, Kerra heaves herself to her feet. She is staring at me, her dark eyes as wide as eyes can go.

It feels like my ears should be ringing but they're not. I can hear Kerra's silence perfectly.

The sword drops from my hand with a huge reverberating clang.

'No, no, no!'

The only answer is my own voice reverberating in a rolling echo from the cave around me.

I feel sick and empty and the wrench is so physically real that I feel as if I've fallen off the cliff myself.

'No! Mirabelle!'

But Mirabelle is gone.

CHAPTER 27

As soon as Mirabelle is gone, the sky cracks and it begins to pour with rain.

I run to the opening where our cell becomes cliff and, dropping to my knees, grab the edge.

No matter how far I crane outwards, I can't see anything.

There's the crash of the waves, the whip of the rain and the wind is so loud that for a moment I don't hear anything at all and it's just me, on the edge, in a moment of extreme clarity. The enormity of what has happened rings clear: I had the sword, I tried to use it, I pushed everyone back, Merlyn and Morgan alike – and Mirabelle is gone.

Mirabelle's own words come back to me: '*I don't think she's a murderer! Well, maybe she was, I don't know.*'

For a chest-tightening, breath-speeding moment, I think about jumping after her. I don't, but I still feel like I'm drowning.

There's a popping sound behind me but I ignore it. I'm hollow, all empty. By my side is a big hole where Mirabelle should be.

'Where is she?' a voice behind me demands.

I turn round and there is a new figure, wild-haired and wet, right there. She's so Mirabelle-shaped that I almost lurch straight into her in relief.

But it isn't Mirabelle and for a moment the crush of that is overwhelming. I can't be cousin-less.

Then my stricken brain makes the connection. I haven't seen her all October. I've never even seen her use magic.

My eyes widen as I stare at Aunt Flissie.

It's uncanny how much Aunt Flissie looks like her daughter in the dim light of the cave. Same posture – confident and casual at the same time. Chin up, shoulders back, feet firmly planted on the ground. They have the same big hair, same sharp chin and identical dark eyes.

Aunt Flissie is soaking, one hand streaming stars, the other clutching a wet glove.

'Where's Mirabelle?' Aunt Flissie is furious, waving around a huge dripping concertina of a map. She's almost completely winded; wherever she came from and however she got here, she lost her breath on the way.

'Where is she? I can't see her anymore. She's vanished off her map.'

Aunt Flissie doesn't wait for a reply, she glares about the cave and then at the map again. Her chin jutting just like Mirabelle's, she rips her other glove off, exposing long, powerfully magical fingers. She waves a single hand above her and disappears with a pop.

Almost immediately, she reappears, wetter than before. Her hands steam. 'She's not out there. In the water, on the rocks. And she's not there. She's not . . .' my aunt waves her map furiously, 'she's not anywhere!'

If Mirabelle was still here, I'd ask so many questions. I'd want to know how Aunt Flissie got here, how long she'd been watching Mirabelle on her map, where she's been.

Aunt Flissie isn't looking at me, she's looking at her sisters. 'I – had to keep tabs on her after last year,' she says, frantic, still waving her map. 'Where *is* she? Where has she gone now?'

Aunt Connie would be so much better at this than the rest of us. I glance at where she is lying but she can't help us; she can't even help herself.

'*Where* is my daughter?' Aunt Flissie demands, sounding like she is trying to master her panic.

Mum, who is always smiling, now isn't smiling at all. Her face is set, all the muscles that would normally be moving in and out of a hundred different smiles are frozen. I watch Mum's eyes for any judgement but she only looks sad.

'Felicity,' Mum starts, rubbing her head and struggling upwards. 'Sister, the Morgans—'

But I can't let Mum explain my actions. 'Aunt Flissie, it was me, it was my fault that Mirabelle—'

'What happened to Mirabelle?'

'She's gone,' I say. *She's dead*, I don't say. 'It's my fault, I'm responsible,' I say to the floor, my shoulders tight, with a big heave of a sob which, when it comes, takes all my breath.

I wish I had fallen, I wish it was me bursting into stardust against the rocks or in the waves. I don't feel the cold like Mirabelle does.

Of all the people in all the world, I would want to hurt Mirabelle the least. She was my blueprint. I was watching her to learn how to be not just a witch, but a person.

There's a long silence while I look at the floor, which has turned blurry. I wonder what Aunt Flissie thinks of what she sees: the glittering white gloves that are keeping her weakened sisters captive, the Morgans unconscious on the floor of the cave.

'I . . . I've been away too long. I thought I was the biggest threat to my daughter.' Aunt Flissie is breathing fast. She looks exactly like Mirabelle did on the threshold of Number 15: big hair, big nerves. 'But Morgans? Keeping her here? Keeping you all here?' Aunt Flissie looks around the cave in disgust.

Then, turning business-like, she asks, 'Did you see her turn to stardust? Mirabelle?'

'We didn't see anything, love,' Mum says.

'We failed,' Aunt Prudie says, voice low but still echoey in the cave. 'History repeated. We failed.'

'It's not your fault, Aunt Prudie, it's mine. It's . . . that sword.' The sword is still there, gleaming against the dark rock floor.

Firm arms loop around me and hold me close, so that when the big cry starts, I have someone to quake against. It's not Mum, it's Aunt Flissie.

Aunt Flissie and I have never hugged before, but her hands are as warm and kind as my mum's.

I cry, noisily, but it feels like that belongs to Aunt Flissie. If anyone is going to make a noise, it should be her. Daughters mean more than cousins.

'Whatever happened, it wasn't you,' Aunt Flissie says, her magical hand on my shoulder getting more vice-like. 'You need to know it wasn't you, do you understand? I leave every October to keep her safe from me – but we Merlyns aren't good at carrying our power. Or balancing it. Something always goes wrong. Our First Octobers have been cursed for a long time now.'

I would love for it to not be my fault. It would take one of the bubbling emotions out of the mix at least.

'But—' I say.

'No,' Aunt Flissie says firmly. 'I don't believe it and I don't accept it.'

Aunt Flissie pulls back from me to look deeply into my eyes. I call her 'Aunt' but she's never really been much of an aunt to me. I didn't sit on her lap when I was little, she never played any games, she kept her distance. But she's here now.

'I gave up on my sister. I will not give up on my daughter. We will get out of here and we will find her,' she says. 'Last time I gave up all hope. I refuse to do that now.'

Mum stumbles upright but she doesn't touch Aunt Flissie with her own gloved hands. 'Keep your hope,' she says. 'But sister, you're not safe here – you should leave.'

'We all need to get out of here,' Aunt Flissie says, and I feel a momentary relief in being able to follow the instructions of a grown witch with her powers. It's exhausting to be in charge.

Then another thought occurs to me: I should be banished. I have to leave the coven. I can no longer be here with my mum and my aunts. I look at my mum and now I could cry for myself. An honourable witch would banish herself, but I don't know if I can. The loneliness is already bitingly sharp. My hand goes to my pocket but then I remember that Bobby is in our little house, alone on the cliff.

When Mirabelle was gone last October and I didn't have my magic yet, life was normal but miserable. Now I'm to blame for our misery.

I think I'm suffocating with the shock of it.

'Being afraid of yourself is the very worst thing,' Aunt Flissie says to me and looks down at her hands. 'Mirabelle wouldn't want that. For either of us.'

'Clemmie?' a small voice asks. It's Kerra. She has the sword and she has turned the pommel towards my hand.

'No,' I say, backing away. 'No.'

'May I?' Aunt Flissie asks.

Kerra looks from me to Aunt Flissie and back again. She doesn't know this witch – but then, neither do I.

One of the white cloaked Morgans is stirring, groaning, but as she looks up and sees Aunt Flissie, she gapes then blinks once and she and the others disappear in a pop.

Mum's forehead crinkles. 'That's it,' she says. 'The Morgans will be down on us soon.'

'Not if we get to them first,' Aunt Flissie says. 'This was the . . . thing – the weapon?' she asks Kerra, still inspecting the sword.

Mirabelle wasn't safe in my hands. Nothing is safe in my hands. I am helpless. I don't want to touch that sword again.

Aunt Flissie takes a deep breath then takes the sword from Kerra. 'The worst has already happened. Sisters, you need your powers back. And the Morgans have royally broken our truce.' She lifts the sword and draws the tip down sharply, just in front of Mum's gloved hand.

Mum whips her hand back and I almost expect to see blood but instead, two fingers, freed of the white gloves, are glowing. Mum rips the glove from her other hand. Then she reaches for my hand and gives it a squeeze and I instantly feel warm with a gathering of magic.

'Freedom! Retribution!' Aunt Prudie shouts and flexes her long thin fingers, raising them high in the air and cascading sparks everywhere. 'And now! Revenge!' Aunt Prudie looks grimly pleased.

My family are no longer restrained. But Aunt Connie hasn't moved. Maybe she can't.

I desperately want her to get up, dust herself down and pull her rolling pin out of her pocket and smack it in the palm of her hand.

'Can you get us back to where the pumpkin was?' I ask Kerra.

'Yes,' Kerra says immediately.

'Young Morgan hag ally?' Aunt Prudie asks suspiciously.

Kerra nods, and Aunt Prudie nods brusquely back then turns straight to Aunt Connie, who she gently lifts upright with her magic. Mum steps forward so that Aunt Connie can lean against her.

Kerra watches for a moment then leans forward too. Aunt Prudie grunts, which is as close as she might ever get to thanking a Morgan, and Kerra slips a shoulder under Aunt Connie's arm to steady her.

'We're going to need you, Con,' Mum whispers to Aunt Connie, my aunt's wilted cauliflower head still sagging between Kerra and Mum. Aunt Prudie stands by herself, looking particularly fierce but particularly tiny.

'Come on then, Morgan,' Aunt Flissie instructs Kerra. Aunt Flissie slices the blade through the cell bars as if they are butter and charges ahead. After everything that's happened, the coven can't split now. I chase after Aunt Flissie because she still has hope.

It takes a moment for my eyes to adjust to the gloom. There's a light somewhere, guiding us. It takes me a moment to realise it's coming from the sword, aloft in Aunt Flissie's hand.

The Mirabelle in my mind is more real in the dark. I can picture her heavy dark eyebrows. The way they rise in surprise when she smiles.

Her huge purple hair, the way she throws it forward to cover up her eyes.

Her sharp chin.

Her knees pulled up tight under her purple blanket.

The way that she, and only she, calls me 'Clem'. *Called* me 'Clem' . . .

Mirabelle, for whom even leaving her bedroom

was a big deal. Mirabelle, who never wanted to go beyond the threshold of our house. Mirabelle, who had stepped so cautiously since she got lost in the Arctic. Now we might as well all be there too, because we are so lost.

And I realise, too late, that I'd never complimented her. On her magic and how she used it. Everything she made was perfectly and thoroughly detailed. And her room, annoyingly split from my room, is the best one in the house.

They are a whole coven of crafters: Mum's clothes, Aunt Connie's soup, Aunt Prudie's garden, Mirabelle's furniture. Clever, delicate magic-makers. So far I've only destroyed things.

The corridor winds downwards; I can feel the slope in my feet where my toes meet the tips of my trainers. It feels like we're burrowing down, down to be entombed with the Morgans.

Because Aunt Morgan simply transports our coven with a nod and a blink, none of us have seen these winding passageways before. I try to keep Aunt Flissie in sight ahead of me, but go slow enough for the rest to still follow. I feel so very, very responsible for them.

We pass under an iron arch at the exit of the tunnel.

'Towards an always-October' it says in curly writing over the top of the gate. The Morgans didn't just write their mantra, they carved it deep into metal.

The tunnel starts to widen out, filling with more light, and suddenly there are the Morgans, so desperate for it to always be October.

CHAPTER 28

'Merlyns!' Aunt Morgan shouts. 'Stay where you are, Merlyns!' A white wall of Morgans is breaking apart, turning towards us.

The Morgans knew we were coming, of course they did. Those witches I knocked aside must be back, lurking in their coven's formation. And they could probably sense the disturbance we made when we – when I – did the thing with the sword.

They're protecting the pumpkin, I realise. Against us.

We are a rabble, they are an army. None of them are drained, none of them has lost anyone. Our two covens face each other in a tense stand-off.

Then Kerra surges forward, waving her arms. Senara breaks rank and advances to meet her. One of the Morgans sucks in air in a hiss.

Kerra is, I can see now, filthy. Her white cloak is dirty after a week in the sandy cell, her hair loose and tangled.

'Mother, she has to speak, I—' Senara says.

But Kerra has already begun. 'Mother – no one respects the Morgan way more than me, but we were wrong! About Merlyn and Morgan and everything that happened between them. Our powers were restricted and hidden for a good reason. Mother – I think we've been too wrapped up in our ancestors and their old war and we haven't ever really connected with this generation of Merlyns . . . and we should!

'Please, Mother!' Kerra pleads. But her mother has silenced her before and might do again.

Senara takes over. 'Mother – we have to stop thinking of this as a pumpkin. It's an extremely dangerous magical device that could put everyone at risk. In the wrong hands, it could be weaponised. Even in the right hands . . . infinite amounts of magic cannot do a body good,' she finishes lamely.

Aunt Morgan greets the speeches of her daughters in absolute silence. Her eyes are narrowed and she hasn't looked anywhere else but at the sword in Aunt Flissie's hand since we arrived.

Aunt Flissie is the one who breaks the silence first. Her earlier composure is gone. We are all angry witches, in our own way, but she is furious, her brown eyes burning.

'Where is my daughter?' Aunt Flissie demands.

'You lost another Merlyn? I can't pretend to be surprised,' Aunt Morgan replies coolly.

'She is missing from your castle, Morgan, and so—'

'You Merlyns are so careless, aren't you? You killed your own sister, did you not?'

Behind me, Mum gasps.

Aunt Morgan arches a cruel eyebrow. Her eyes are full of meanness. 'You have no *temperance*,' Aunt Morgan says.

The cave is darkening.

Aunt Flissie sets aside the sword and brings her hands together, as if she was going to wind a skein of wool, even though, in our family, if anyone was going to be winding wool, it would be my mum.

As Aunt Flissie's eyebrows come down, so do clouds. The entire cavern is filling with them.

She's building a tempest, her gestures getting bigger and bigger with each spin.

The Morgans remain completely still. Immobile in the face of all of Aunt Flissie's work, even when lightning crackles above us.

Aunt Flissie's storm is epic and, for a moment, I believe in it.

Then Aunt Morgan simply purses her lips and blows,

with less force than you'd even use on a birthday candle. A tiny puff.

It's worse than if she'd used all her force, somehow.

The wind blows Aunt Flissie backwards and, like a pinned butterfly, she is held in place against the vast cavern's wall.

I glance at my coven. Aunt Connie's white hair – usually so stiff and halo-like – is limp and bedraggled on her face, as she almost hangs between my mum and Aunt Prudie. Mum's dry-cleaner's uniform is filthy, her face deeply lined with exhaustion, her natural smile completely sunk. Aunt Prudie is, well, exactly the same level of dirty she always is, but the crisp snap has gone out of her too. They're witches in mourning, not witches ready for war.

Then I think about Mirabelle and ask myself what she would do here. She wouldn't cry, that's for sure. She'd be fuming with everyone. Mirabelle would be angry, so angry she'd be ready to . . . tear it all down. To confront that brooding, pinch-faced Morgan who calls herself 'Aunt'.

And before I even know what I'm doing, I rush forward and grab the sword.

CHAPTER 29

Aunt Flissie's storm may be fading, but now the cavern floor is beginning to vibrate. The vibrations get bigger, turning into regular juddering jumps that I can feel through the base of both feet.

I turn round to see the floor-shaker charge in. It's silver and it's moving fast. It's a horse, supersized, glinting all over with plates of armour. A golden star on its forehead.

It's Bobby, erupting into the cavern. I can tell it's her by the fluffy feet, the sturdy legs, the way she tosses her head. I almost drop the sword.

Bobby charges straight through the Morgan witches, who scatter in all directions.

As Bobby's gallop slows, I see the figure on her back.

Fierce and beautiful, screaming at the top of her lungs, is Mirabelle.

'Clem!' Mirabelle hollers, as Bobby's now huge hairy hooves wheel towards me. 'Whoa, Bobby!'

Bobby slows but doesn't stop and Mirabelle leans all the way down to throw an arm out to me.

I almost pull back away from her but, at the last moment, I manage to shift the sword to one hand and reach up with my other. She grabs all the way up to my wrist, until our hands are tightly interlocked. Mirabelle's hand in mine is strong and warm and real. She pulls me upwards with a force that can only be magical and makes my hands tingle.

Mirabelle swings me behind her effortlessly and I grab her around the waist, her hair a big purple-streaked pouf in my face.

As for Bobby . . . I haven't ridden Bobby since I was very little and she was part of my magical childhood. To swing up behind Mirabelle now feels strange, not just because we're riding a pony the size of a car and I'm trying to keep the sword's sharp pointed tilted away from us, but because Mirabelle is here. She's back and I cling to her.

Bobby is large and unstoppable. Even though I know she's on my side, I'm still scared. Scaled up as a giant pony, she has lost the playfulness of when she was petite. Just as she didn't know she was tiny, she clearly has no idea how massive she is now.

Her little legs don't usually do anything you could call "galloping" but she builds up speed, and the rhythm of her hooves alone begins the destruction. The entire room is vibrating, some of the wires and cables of the Morgan mechanics swinging loose from their sockets and twanging under the pressure.

'Come on, girl!' Mirabelle shouts, and Bobby brays squeakily then kicks her rear legs up, jolting us on her broad back.

She tosses her head and charges back again through the regrouping Morgans, some of whom throw themselves backwards to get out of the way of the rampage.

'Is it really you?' I ask Mirabelle.

Mirabelle blows her hair out of her eyes in exasperation, which should be proof enough.

'I came back as soon as I could,' Mirabelle shouts back over her shoulder, almost apologetically.

'You don't have the manners to be even a little bit deceased?' I lean forward to shout back, and Mirabelle laughs. I haven't seen her laugh for . . . a whole year.

I'm so angry there are no words. Everything I just went through. Finding Mirabelle not dead is almost enough to make me want to kill her.

'I was mourning you,' I hiss furiously into her hair.

Mirabelle pulls backwards to try and look at me. 'Not for very long,' she says. 'And your eyes aren't even red and puffy, so not well enough.' Then she turns back round, lowering her head to Bobby's mane.

'We would have been here sooner but she had a lot of explaining to do,' Mirabelle shouts.

'*We*?' I shout back. 'Who's we? What happened?'

'Look!' Mirabelle says, dragging on Bobby's mane to turn the now-huge pony about. Bobby squeals and wheels round. I almost lose my seat, tilting desperately to stay behind Mirabelle, who leans right forward.

Behind us, the cavern has erupted in black wings. Except, I know now, they're not completely black, they're flecked with cream and brown too. The largest falcon at the front of the flock swoops low to the floor. I watch carefully and the very shape of the bird twists.

Then the bird slips elegantly into the form of a witch.

She looks like storybook witches are meant to look: bedraggled hair, dirty, torn clothes, alarming eyes. I've never seen her before, I know that. Apart from . . . I have seen her before. I've caught a hundred tiny glimpses of her, throughout my life.

I think about how the dark birds have been haunting us. How they tried to attack the pumpkin, how they burst through the windows, how they were circling the cliffs waiting for us . . .

Not haunting. *Helping*.

It was her all along. One of us. If I wasn't still out of breath, *this* would have taken it away all over again.

'Temmie!' Aunt Flissie says and her voice sounds like I've never heard it before. It sounds sore, like she's been singing or shouting at the top of her lungs. It's thick with a deep, deep happy-sadness.

I stare at my almost-namesake.

'Sisters,' Temmie says, low and serious as the birds swish and flap among the Morgans. Her voice is gravellier than anyone else in my family. 'May I join you?'

No one says anything for a painful thump of a heartbeat, then almost all my aunts start speaking at once.

Mum: 'It's not possible – not possible!'

Aunt Flissie: 'Temmie . . . Temmie?'

Aunt Prudie: 'Missing sister! Returned!'

Mirabelle is beaming. Just beaming. I've never seen her smile this widely. She looks smug as anything.

'You knew?' I ask, outraged.

'She saved me,' Mirabelle says. 'When I fell. Straight into a pillow of birds. Caught me and landed me safely.'

I have enough time for one heart-pounding moment

of gratitude that they're both safe. We've got a pile up of witches, all missing Merlyns returned.

'I would have died,' Mirabelle says, her voice suddenly as shivery as when she speaks about the Arctic. 'But Temmie saved me. I think – maybe – she's been saving us all for a long time.' Mirabelle points up at where the birds are swooping and diving, targeting the Morgans with their sharp beaks and claws.

October is always rammed full of strange things, the birds just one of them. I thought I had to roll with it all. I should definitely have been questioning the strangeness.

I squeeze Mirabelle now, not sure how to even begin to apologise.

'Oh, but hey – the way you swung that sword!' Mirabelle cries. She shakes her head. 'That was the most un-ordinary thing I've ever seen.'

'Says you, second member of The Death-faker Club.'

Mirabelle laughs delightedly. 'Clem,' she says, 'I was so wrong about the ordinary thing.'

'Nothing wrong with ordinary,' I say.

'Sisters!' Temmie calls, and exactly as it started in our home, a shimmering line is forming in the air, as if a huge, invisible hand is holding a glitter pen. At the corner that will make up the first point of the star, the line takes a sharp angle and continues.

Temmie is sheltering her sisters, especially my still-weak Aunt Connie, in the protection of her star.

I'm hypnotised by the sight – my mum, interlinked with all her sisters, with no more gaps. Our star was never truly broken.

Mirabelle whistles to Bobby, long and loud, startling me away from Temmie.

'Mirabelle!' I shout one last time. 'The pumpkin!'

I realise I have one job. To maintain the balance of this world, that pumpkin and the plans for eternal power have to be destroyed.

I feel silly as I try to adjust my hold on the sword. I can feel the tug of its weight in my elbow and my shoulder, but if I can hold the stars inside me, I can hold this. I'm sure it would be better suited to a tall and elegant Morgan like Senara but, for now, it's mine and I have to use it as best I can. One more time.

There's no stopping Bobby now that she's at full pelt. She's a sturdy, thick-bodied pony, not an elegant horse, but now that she is supersized, there is a huge amount of power in those legs.

Mirabelle urges Bobby forward.

I don't really know what's in my mind but I cling on to Mirabelle with one hand and heft the sword up in the other, and hold it as high and focused as I can. I don't have time to feel silly.

The Morgans are too slow to realise what we're doing, still under attack from Temmie's enormous flock.

Mirabelle charges straight at the giant orange target. At the last moment, Bobby veers round the pumpkin and I lunge forward.

The sword hits the hard skin of the pumpkin and, in a panic, I think it's not going to break the surface, but then, with a great slicing sound, it slides through the buttery insides of the pumpkin, all the way up to the hilt.

But Mirabelle can't stop Bobby, who rears up and carries on. I can feel them both slipping away from me and before Mirabelle's waist can be wrenched out of my grasp, I throw myself towards the sword, swinging like I'm a kid on a climbing frame, and cling on to the sword with both hands.

The sword is stuck about three quarters of the way up the pumpkin, and I'm left dangling from it.

'Clem!' Mirabelle shouts, but Bobby is galloping away. Like a bumblebee, I've stung the pumpkin and now I'm stuck myself.

I heave on the sword to bring my knees up and scrabble to find purchase on the pumpkin's surface. I slip and slip again until I manage to brace myself so that, with both hands on the pommel of the sword and both feet flat against the pumpkin, I'm crouched on its side – a giant spider on an even more giant vegetable.

I can see my hands glittering around the pommel while glowing stars gather, as if queuing up to be let loose. I don't know what is going to happen when I finish cutting this pumpkin. I only hope it won't detonate.

I don't know if this will end October or not.

I hunch my shoulders, pulling myself inwards to the sword, then push as hard as I can with both feet, straightening my legs. The sword is long but I lean back, pulling it away from the pumpkin, and with a huge, squelchy rasp, the sword pulls loose.

Then, of course, I'm falling. I topple and roll backwards and try to keep the sword with me but not on me.

I'm winded from the fall but neither I nor the sword are hurt.

And then, there is chaos everywhere. For one blinding moment, there is only a bright white light and through the light, everyone's voices – Morgans and Merlyns all shouting.

As the light begins to focus, the air is full of stars. For another infinite moment I can't see anything. The blaze of light is too strong, and I have to blink and blink again to clear my eyes of glitter.

The magic in the pumpkin is escaping, streaming out.

CHAPTER 30

For a moment, the stars hang in the air. The witches in the room seem to go silent – or maybe it's only me, because everything seems to hang, suspended, as the tiny sparkles of magic float as if undecided.

Stars prickle in the air and in my eyes, and I can barely see, but I squint though the brightness. The stars are whisking back to their rightful owners. My mum, aunts and Mirabelle are all glowing with star clusters, which dance all over them and then sink into their skin.

And the Morgans aren't attacking. Some are making frustrated or furious movements, trying to lash out, but most have their hands at their eyes. They can't see.

For a triumphant moment, I think the stars really do know where they belong.

Aunt Connie positively flips into life as the stars reinvigorate her. Her white hair pings back into its cauliflower shape and her apron straightens itself. 'We don't have time!' she shouts immediately, and quickly throws out her hands on either side of her. Her cheeks are dark-berry-coloured with excitement.

It is only for an instant, but with the light of the pumpkin making the entire cavern glow orange, I can see my family, magic restored, and they look spectacular.

Right at the beginning of the month, Aunt Connie had talked about how the first Merlyn and the first Morgan had been magnificent. Then I saw it for myself in the tapestry. Now, for the first time ever, I can see it in real life.

I realise, in this moment, that I've never seen the full scale of my coven's magic. While I was busy taking down the pumpkin, my family were getting ready and now, they are . . . enjoying themselves. I can hear Aunt Prudie's conspiratorial cackle. Her fingers seem to have got longer, more twisted, mossier.

'Grow!' Aunt Prudie shouts as greenery sprouts. 'Grow and grow and grow!' She is having the most delightfully messy time of her life. She has erupted into foliage. Her hair has turned leafy, and green vines are racing from her in all directions, worming into the walls, up and down all the Morgan machinery.

Aunt Prudie's plant-work is intricate and beautiful. Even though the cavern was full before, now it is filled with a lattice of greenery and feels more alive than ever.

'Earth! Soil! Friend!' Aunt Prudie shouts, digging her hands into the grass and mud. The very ground is quaking beneath me, mud erupting through the tiled flooring. My aunts have been patient for a long time but now, in their revenge, they are joyfully destructive.

The Morgan's cavern is becoming a forest of spiny leaves and, even numb from my fall, I can feel them poking me in the back as they spread. Above us, I hear a thunderous rumble and I feel almost certain that the castle is collapsing around us. Aunt Prudie has always said that "nature provides".

'Tender root!' she hollers, gesturing plants up and along with her fingers. Ivy sprouts and lurches, golem-like, tearing down wires, crashing against keyboards.

And if I wasn't seeing it, I wouldn't have believed that Aunt Connie, so frail and crinkled, could now be flaming red. Aunt Connie is positively crackling with magic. Her hair looks electrified at the ends. She looks healthy and whole, and I am so happy to see her alight.

She is melting the Morgan's precious October work with relish, flaming in the same way Aunt Prudie is drawing forth green stems and sending steaming runnels of hot liquid throughout the cave. It could be lava but, on closer inspection, it looks a lot like steaming soup.

Aunt Flissie is . . . trying hard. 'I'm out of practice!' she shouts to my mum. She sounds flustered. Storm clouds gather in fits and spurts, occasionally raining.

Puddles are forming on the floor. They don't look impressive, to be honest, but if a Morgan witch was running and wasn't looking where she was going, she could definitely slip over. Though, for a witch who left us all to avoid being a witch, Aunt Flissie still looks incredibly witchy right now, miniature lightning bolts in her hair.

Aunt Flissie's thundercloud cracks above Aunt Connie's fire. 'Sorry!' she squeals across the cave, and hail begins to fall in fits and spurts.

It would be funny if it weren't so immense.

Their magic is like my family itself – shambolic and wild and absolutely the work of five individuals instead of an organised coven. And none of the Morgans, squinting, rubbing their magic eyes back into sight, seem to know what to do with these wild Merlyns, free and making magic right here in the middle of their space. The Morgans might do cool, invisible things in a wink or a blink but they could never manage this kind of creative frenzy.

Not to be outdone, my mum is stitching gold thread through the air. Mum is the most sensible Merlyn, which I'm realising doesn't mean much because she is currently closing the exits with giant gold zippers.

But by far the most powerful force filling the cavern is Temmie – I can't quite make myself call this stranger 'Aunt' – who also has her hands aloft, encouraging her birds to cause chaos.

I watch, mesmerised, as they beat their wings rapidly, hovering in place, before tucking in their wings and dive-bombing downwards.

I wouldn't want to be raked by those claws, magical or not. On the attack, they look more like gargoyles than birds, forcing the Morgans to stumble, duck and run for cover.

The birds twirl and whirl, forming a tower in the air, calling their *'screeah'* song all the time.

Some of the Morgan witches are trying to defend themselves, but the blinding stars have cut through their organised ranks and they're still recovering their magical vision.

Then I hear Mirabelle loud and clear. 'Charge!'

she cries, and, with one big roaring neigh, Bobby does exactly that.

I blink starry spots from my eyes and stagger onto one knee. Mirabelle has one arm raised in a fist, defiant joy on her face.

This time, Bobby goes directly for the pumpkin. Armoured-head down, the giant pony rams it. Then she prances backwards and rears up.

'Mirabelle!' I shout, but I don't need to because Mirabelle keeps her seat as Bobby strikes forward with two huge hooves.

I don't think it'll give, until she rears again, bringing both hooves back down heavily on the pumpkin, and cracks begin to appear down the its sides.

Aunt Morgan makes an unearthly kind of howling noise which becomes words as I get to my feet and heave the sword up with me.

'Protect the pumpkin!' Aunt Morgan is shouting at her disorientated coven. 'Protect that pumpkin now, witches, or I will drain your power to fill it!'

Up until this point, the Morgan coven has been a creepy, white, swishing mass of witches who move as one.

But now, as Aunt Morgan threatens her own witches,

I realise there are lots of different personalities among their coven. A few witches actually pull away with revolted expressions, a few look meekly terrified.

Aunt Morgan is ruthlessly determined, but it's too late for her plans for the pumpkin.

The third time Bobby rams the pumpkin, it bursts spectacularly, splitting in at least five different places at once. I don't realise what has hit me until I lift my hand to my cheek and scrape away a handful of thick, stringy pumpkin flesh and seeds.

There is pumpkin everywhere. Every single Morgan witch is covered, head to toe, in thick orange gloop. There was enough pumpkin flesh in the middle of Aunt Prudie's masterpiece to keep all the nation's witches fed with soup and pies for years. Instead, we all look like we showered in it.

Bobby is frolicking through the smashed pumpkin. She trots back and forth through the squashed remains, her rider still clinging on around her neck, whinnying and lifting her hooves high.

Aunt Morgan has abandoned her coven and is stalking through the devastated pumpkin, her eyes glowing with fury and focused on Mirabelle.

Mirabelle is patting the giant pony. She has already

dismounted and has her head low against Bobby's neck, her back to Aunt Morgan.

I look from Aunt Morgan to the remains of the pumpkin and back again. I can't and I won't turn the sword on her. No witch has died yet and no witch will die now. Not Temmie, not my cousin.

'Mirabelle!' I call.

I start running, but I'll never be fast enough, so I lower my arm and skid the sword across the floor. I have a moment of feeling ridiculous for throwing the sword as if I'm bowling and could ever hit my mark, but Mirabelle turns away from Bobby, squats and is ready . . .

The sword, which didn't kill Mirabelle before and might save her now, whizzes across the room and Mirabelle is lunging forward—

And Aunt Morgan stomps straight down on to the pommel of the sword, which screeches to a halt under her foot. She bends, seizes it with an elegant sweep and stares deep into its mirror-like surface.

I was running and now I'm skidding too, trying desperately not to slide right into Aunt Morgan who is raising the sword with a confidence none of us young hags had.

I try to flail backwards from Aunt Morgan who is raising the sword high above her head and almost slip in the pumpkin mush on the floor.

'Mother, no!' Kerra shouts desperately, and I look up to see both the young Morgan hags, also skidding their way to their mother, their hands tightly together.

Senara is staring at her mother with outright revulsion. 'She's a young hag, Mother. It's only her First October,' she calls.

But the sword has pushed Aunt Morgan over the edge.

'A Merlyn,' Aunt Morgan hisses. 'That's all that matters.'

I hunch, expecting to feel a lightning strike of magic or metal, or both, any moment. The sword's tip is so very sharp, its blade so very long. I reach out reflectively, as if my hand alone could possibly block the sword's fall.

'Clemmie!' I hear my mum call, but it feels as if only Aunt Morgan and I are in the cavern, she so tall and so much like her ancestor, me reaching helplessly up.

And it's like we're replaying the wrong history, because in the tapestry of Morgan and Merlyn, we had thought the final scene went something like this.

The panel where the Morgan and Merlyn parts weaved together after so long apart lives in my mind.

I think it always will. Our two families have been working so hard to restore what was lost. But nothing was lost. It was given away.

Because when we put the two pieces of the tapestry together, we could see the picture's true meaning.

In the tapestry in the castle, there was Morgan, standing stiff and magnificently tall, covered in stars. Both of her hands were wrapped around the blazingly bright handle of a sword, pointing straight upwards as she was about to swing it down in judgement. And in our half, there was Merlyn, crying, arms outstretched, begging, the frayed edges cutting off her hands at the wrist.

It was only when the two pieces came together that it truly made sense: it wasn't a final battle. It was a truce. Standing so much taller than her sister, Morgan looked like an aggressive executioner but she wasn't, and she wasn't banishing her sister, either.

Morgan was not holding the sword on her own.

Merlyn's hands couldn't be seen in my coven's part of the tapestry, but I had expected they would be turned up, begging for mercy. But now we could see there were four hands, entwined in a burst of light, around the pommel of the sword. And both sisters had *stars* streaming from their eyes, not tears. The sword wasn't a weapon to turn on each other, it was a tool to redirect their magic back up to the stars.

We've always assumed that what we live with now are things Morgan and Merlyn did to each other in hate and fear. But, when we young hags saw the complete tapestry, it was clear that the sisters chose to return their magic to the stars. They sacrificed their power together.

However, Aunt Morgan doesn't know that, she hasn't seen what I've seen. She is not going to turn the sword handle to me now and offer to wrap our hands together. She sees us as being impossibly different; the branches of our family tree have grown so, so far apart that she's forgotten we have the same roots.

***

Everything goes calm and still, both inside me and the cavern. I don't know where everyone is looking because my eyes are shut.

I think of Kerra and aim to be centred and full of oxygen and focus. I breathe with Kerra's solid rhythm and my chest releases with a tiny bit of relief. I can feel the fizz of the magic inside me.

I am not scared, not at all. I'm so full of stars, there's no room to be scared.

I look at Aunt Morgan and see that she is just a witch, and a snooty one. She's greedy and mean but she isn't the worst thing that could happen – yet. With unlimited power, *then* she'd be something to really be scared of.

I focus on the sword, not the witch. I was meant to be called Clemency and that means *mercy*. I don't have to forgive Aunt Morgan for being a greedy witch but I don't have to punish her, either.

The sword is the thing. It has served its purpose and now we don't need it anymore. That deeply magical ancient artefact is too much for us. Year-round power is too much for us.

Any magic I am channelling won't come through my hands, I know that now. I've never successfully used my magic the way the rest of my coven do. My heavy hands drop and, instead, I try and pull all my power in. Stars stand out like sweat all over my skin; I can feel them prickling all over my body.

'*Must know self*', Aunt Prudie had said.

I still don't know what kind of witch I am. I'm impatient like Aunt Connie, while trying to be as kind as Mum. I ignore my Merlyn hands and forget about Morgan eyes. Those ways are not the only ways. A witch can be both – or something entirely new.

The stars do know everything and that's how they can be anything. They know what I know, they know what I want. The stars are humming and I'm in tune with them now.

This is what I want: to protect my family.

I call up every single flicker of magic and mould it in the middle of me. I can feel the magic as well as if I was actually holding it in my hands.

I focus my eyes and stare at the sword, staring so hard that I can only see the sword and the rest of the world turns blurry. It is beautiful as it catches the shifting light of the cave. I stare, and I breathe . . .

The magic beams out – not from my hands, or my eyes, or even my elbow, but straight from my heart, out of my chest.

Then, with one more breath, the sword explodes.

CHAPTER 31

The tiny fragments look like stars in the air. Shards graze past me but they feel soft and warm.

Every witch, whether Morgan or Merlyn, has a shimmering gold outline around them.

I can see specks of light coming up through my sleeves. The magic is leaving me. The magic is leaving all the witches.

One of the Morgans even reaches up above her to try and make a grab for her magic. But there's no pulling it back into ourselves.

I feel instantly lighter, like I could bounce – whereas before, I could only trudge. It's as if I've taken off a really heavy coat that I'm happy to discard, because underneath, I see me.

But maybe I'm too light . . . there's also an ache where the heaviness used to be, like the magic is a vital organ that has been removed, leaving a hollow.

I don't even know it's if the end of October yet, and,

as I've never experienced the magic leaving, whether this emptiness and silence in its wake is something I just need to get used to. My nose tingles – not with magic, but with tears I'm squashing down. The sadness I'm feeling is strange.

Some of the Morgans are covering their eyes or clutching at their chests. I wonder if they feel the same pang of emptiness that I feel. I made room for the magic inside of me and hadn't even started to use it properly.

Then the magical light comes together over our heads, forming a streaming column, exactly as it did on that first day of October. The beads of light are gathering and they are . . . leaving. The light forms one solid ray and ascends, straight through the ceiling.

As the light fades away and the cavern turns dim, Kerra is, of course, the first to speak.

'Join me, sister?' she shouts. She has shed her white Morgan cloak and now begins to move in front of her mother, who has been left holding just the pommel of the shattered sword.

The Morgans are scattered and don't seem to know what to do. No one is marshalling them. Most of them are turning hesitantly to their head witch, and I realise that greater numbers don't actual mean greater power –

there might be eleven of them, but Aunt Morgan's voice is the only one that matters, and Kerra is now talking over her mother.

'Stop, young hags!' Aunt Morgan is screaming at her daughters, who are darting about in front of her, not letting her get a clear line of vision.

'Mother! No!' Senara shouts. Aunt Morgan has stepped forward, pushed through her daughters and her eyes are wide open. She looks like she's about to direct a killing blow at my aunts.

But there can't be an epic showdown because the magic has left. Her eyes produce tiny sparks but they fizzle away to nothing, revealing the woman under the witch.

Still gasping, I turn round to see where my family are. In the middle of it all is what is left of the pumpkin that caused all this chaos. Mirabelle, her hair blown back from her face so that I can see, is smiling the widest smile I've ever seen. Beyond her, I can see my mum and her four sisters and I don't know who to run to first.

Bobby is smaller than when she charged in. Mirabelle slaps Bobby's shrinking, fading flank and the pony prances into the pumpkin. Then she gives me another full-beam grin and heads towards her mum who pulls her so tight their foreheads touch.

'Hags!' Aunt Morgan roars. She is covered in stringy pumpkin goop.

There's a collective gasp at this name-calling. 'Young hags' is one thing, but coven elders don't disrespect each other like that. Temmie and Aunt Flissie, heads close together, turn in shock.

Aunt Prudie sweeps in. 'Words!' she shouts, even louder than usual. 'Pah! Hags! Witches! Angels! The same!' Aunt Prudie shakes a finger at Aunt Morgan. It doesn't matter that it doesn't have magic in it; she gets very close. Aunt Prudie's hair is especially wild, her face craggy, the wrinkles all pointed angrily downwards.

'Witch! Hag! Demon! Sorceress! Cat! Dragon!' Aunt Prudie hollers then turns round, fast, to face Mirabelle and I. 'Labels! Same thing!'

Then, she goes quiet. 'Words for women of power,' she says and gently touches her long, lined fingers to Aunt Morgan's face.

'Women don't fight women! Witches don't hurt witches!'

It's the best way I've ever seen anyone end a fight.

Aunt Connie claps her hands to take control. 'We're leaving now. And we expect not to see you darken or destroy any doorway of ours again,' she says, directly to Aunt Morgan.

It makes me want to whoop and cheer.

'No! *We* banish *you*!' Aunt Morgan says, her accusing finger shaky. 'You and your preposterous vegetable!'

Senara clears her throat. 'Mother . . . I—' she says.

'Traitor!' Aunt Morgan howls. 'You are no witch daughter of mine!'

Senara is still for a moment and I wonder if she might cry. Instead, she turns away from her mum with a shrug.

'In that case, I'm coming with you,' she says, and Mirabelle holds out an arm for Senara to dip under.

'You lot are mad. We'd better not see you in our neighbourhood again,' Mirabelle shouts at the Morgans, who are raggedly pulling themselves into formation – but without their cloaks, they are half the witches they were before.

'Your family gave up eternal power for you,' Kerra says quietly. 'My family would never do that. Not for me, the deadweight.'

'Sis – it's OK,' Senara says. 'Or, I mean, it's not OK – but October is ending.'

'Yeah,' I say, 'and you can come with us too.'

'All this *pumpkin*,' Kerra says, surveying the orange wreckage.

'Could have been a wonderful soup, right, Aunt Connie?' Mirabelle says, eyes sparkling as if full of stars.

CHAPTER 32

Aunt Connie turns away from Aunt Morgan as if she simply doesn't exist, to focus on the witch who appears to be my no longer long-dead Aunt Temmie.

Temmie is definitely part of the same set as her sisters, though with her sharp nose and pointy chin, she is most like Aunt Flissie and Mirabelle. Her eyes are the darkest of dark browns, so dark they're almost black and mirror-like. They're Mum's eyes.

The rest of her is tough and lean and really dirty. And I realise for the first time that I don't know how old any of my family actually are. Aunt Prudie is old enough to be very crinkly. My mum is just 'mum' age. And Temmie – it's hard to tell under all that dirt, but she's old enough to have lived a whole life outside of our coven with a whole history I don't know.

'Are you hurt?' Mum asks, eyes roving all over her sister. 'I can't tell under all . . . this!'

Temmie bursts out laughing. 'Not clean enough for you, Pattie?'

'Of course not love. You're filthy and I can't wait to dunk you in a bathtub.'

Aunt Flissie leaps forward, embracing Temmie.

'You really are her? You really are Temperance?' Aunt Flissie asks, tilting her head this way and that to take in her sister. 'Because I thought . . . my First October – the accident . . .'

Temmie returns Aunt Flissie's embrace, but awkwardly, pulling back to say, 'I never died. And I never really left. It was a trick, Flissie. As soon as our coven might have the power of the full five-pointed star, I had to leave. I lied to you – to you all.'

There is a horrible gut-wrenching moment while we all watch Aunt Flissie thinking about what Aunt Temmie has just said. She's already shaking her head, back and forth.

'It doesn't matter how you're here, only that you are here. That's all I need.'

'I'm sorry,' Temmie says, still quiet, still tender, speaking to the child that Aunt Flissie must have been when she thought she had killed her sister.

'So am I,' Aunt Flissie says and turns, her eyes

finding me and Mirabelle. 'I've spent all this time trying to undo what I did in my First October, and really I should have been thinking about our young hags and their Octobers instead.'

Mirabelle wades through a particularly large patch of stringy pumpkin goo to wrap an arm round me as we watch our mums and their sisters rediscover each other. Constance, Prudence, Patience with Temperance and Felicity now returned to them.

'Sisters reunited!' Aunt Prudie shouts and then, unexpectedly, she bursts into tears. The other four cluster around Prudie, putting hands on her. Something fizzes between them.

'What Prudie means is—' Aunt Connie starts but Aunt Prudie puts out a gnarled hand. Not to use for magic, but to halt her sister.

Aunt Connie falls silent and we all watch Aunt Prudie.

'Speak for myself!' Aunt Prudie says. 'I am ... I am ... I am happy you are back.' The end of the sentence comes out in a big rush but it's a whole sentence. I have never heard Aunt Prudie say a whole sentence.

Temmie throws her arms around Prudie. My mum hugs them both. Flissie tucks herself into Prudie's side and Connie wraps her arms around them all.

That's a star, I think. It doesn't matter how many points it may have, it's what's in the burning hot centre that makes it glow.

I interrupt it anyway. 'Mum, I have to show you something.'

The castle is shrinking and fading around us. The tapestry is still there but it is now tatty and torn, dirty. It looks even more familiar now, like the ragged scrap that we've always had in our house. The figures of Merlyn and Morgan are flat again, no longer popping with colour and magic.

'Glorious,' Mum says. 'Just glorious. The needlework!' Her eyes are roving across the Merlyn and Morgan story. 'So this is where it all came from.'

'This is their story,' I say, pointing to the final panels. 'I was thinking maybe we could fix it, together.'

'I think this might be stealing,' Mum says as I pull tapestry panels down from the walls.

'Mum, they stole you from me,' I say, bundling a panel of tapestry into her arms. 'I'm just taking something back.'

Mum looks dubious but as I rip down panels, she rolls them up. 'The dry cleaners,' she says with a huge smile. 'I'll get it sorted out.' I give her back the biggest grin I can.

'Magic departing! Make haste! The house!' Aunt Prudie says with a shriek then corrects herself. 'The magic is departing! We must hasten back home! The house can't leave without us!'

'Quick! Run!'

All our October improvements will be disappearing. Our house will soon fade back into its place on Pendragon Road.

With rolls and rolls of tapestry under every witch's arms, we race out into the air, which is fresh and cold.

As we run back through the ruins of the Morgans' ancestral home and the ruins of their October plans, I think, *November must be almost here.*

R★M

WHILE YOU WERE OUT

Your parcel has, finally, been successfully delivered. When giving feedback on the service you have received, please consider a five-star review for your postperson, who made delivery in exceptional circumstances.

BRING ID

CHAPTER 33

It is ending. With every minute, the magic is fading from the world and we make it through the back door just in time.

The magic isn't quite gone, it's just not ours anymore. The mass of stars has left but I can still see the odd tiny glimmering spark, hovering around.

The last thing I see through the kitchen window is the Morgan castle returning to its natural state. The stone walls are crumbling back to picturesque ruins. I can see why this castle might be on hundreds and thousands of postcards, but I don't think the Morgans are going to be very comfortable for the next eleven months.

Aunt Connie, walking into the back-to-normal kitchen, looks more upset than when she was aunt-napped by the Morgans. When the sparks of magic dissolve away, my aunts usually enter a deep winter gloom. Now, in the middle of the room, she picks up what remains.

It's a battered tin pot, no longer shimmering or spitting stars.

'You kept my cauldron!' Temmie says and dings it fondly, just like my mum did.

'Of course,' Aunt Connie replies.

I look from her to Temmie and back again as something deep and serious passes between them. I realise that there are probably many more secrets that our house and family haven't given up yet. For the first time, I feel there's so much more to learn from their five-pointed star.

Aunt Connie hands the cauldron to her rogue sister and picks up the once-magnificent hourglass that counted down our thirty-one days of magic, now back to being a small egg-timer. She brushes a few grains of sand from it.

I can see now why she uses the hourglass. Even in an egg-timer, those tiny grains of pale sand look like sparks of magic as they fall and filter away. Aunt Connie must feel like they are racing through her fingers, no matter how much she tries to hold on to them. Magic and time are both uncontrollable.

'Everything takes longer without magic,' sighs Aunt Connie.

'You should try growing a pumpkin from seed for thirteen years,' Aunt Prudie says. 'Tricky.'

'So, sister, every time our magic went wrong, it was you?' Mum asks Temmie. Her smile is as eternally welcoming as ever. And maybe just a little teasing.

'Every single time,' Temmie agrees and bows her head so that her long straggly hair shakes forward. 'We witches were never meant to have eternal power. It is too much.'

When she looks back up at us, I can see she is still glowing with purpose. 'I decided that I couldn't stop the Morgans. But I could stop you.'

'Those birds!' Aunt Connie and Aunt Prudie screech together. Neither tries to translate for the other.

'Yes,' Temmie admits. 'I've hindered you – and sometimes tried to help. The shape of the bird that I took on – I thought it was dashing. A Merlin falcon.'

When she smiles, Temmie has an impish grin.

Aunt Prudie chuckles. 'A Merlin bird! Merlin, the bird. Ha! Yes, very good.'

'You did help us,' I say. 'You made the star that brought us to the castle. And you put the tapestry up on the wall for us so we wouldn't miss it.'

Temmie raps a knuckle against her cauldron, making a deep, sonorous vibration and nods.

'Ask your young hags, they know that eternal power would corrupt. Because in the end, I didn't achieve anything. It was them.'

'I don't think they're young hags anymore,' Aunt Connie admits.

'Yeah,' I say. 'We're not young hags, we're our own hags.'

Temmie looks warningly at us. 'And it's never finished between our two families. The Morgans may well return for us. Or for you two. But October is over for now.' She shrugs. 'I believe what covens say – if I'm allowed – is ... "the stars know".'

Around the circle, my coven family echo this back to Temmie and I watch them all.

The stars know. The stars know.

WHILE YOU WERE OUT

In an attempt to remove errors, duplicates and gaps in the customer address information, we confirm the below are now resident at your address:

- ☑ Temperance Merlyn
- ☑ Felicity Merlyn
- ☑ Prudence Merlyn
- ☑ Constance Merlyn
- ☑ Patience Merlyn
- ☑ Mirabelle Merlyn
- ☑ Clementine Merlyn

CHAPTER 34

'Halloween,' Mirabelle says, and her grin lights us both up.

'What's "Halloween"?' Kerra asks.

'The best night of the year. You must know! All Hallows' Eve? The night the magic leaves us. And before it fully returns to the stars, it's spread thinly across everyone and everything. Humans can feel it and they celebrate by pretending to be witches. We usually have a party. An epic one,' I say, feeling pleased to be able to teach Kerra something for a change.

'I've never been to a party,' Kerra says, her face brightening. 'It's not really the Morgan way.'

'No,' Mum agrees. 'But maybe witches have got too stuck in one way of doing things – I think you young hags can change that.' She gives me a thoughtful look. 'There are, maybe, as many different ways to use your power as there are witches. Or stars, even.'

'Yeah, because Clem didn't use her hands to let her magic out,' Mirabelle says.

'Or her eyes,' Kerra adds.

'I'm fuzzy on some of the details,' I say, remembering that feeling of a burning channel inside me.

'You were only just getting started, love,' Mum says, almost sounding sad for a moment but then her brightness bursts back through. 'Ah, but we will try the generosity of the stars next year. I don't know if our powers will ever return. Only the stars—'

'*Yes*, Mum. They're up there right now, being all twinkly and knowing,' I say, and Mum laughs a sweet up-and-down kind of laugh like a song.

'About the magic, Mum . . .' I say, sidling closer to her. 'This isn't how we usually say goodbye to it . . . are you sad?'

'Oh no, love. And your aunts aren't really, either. Magic is wonderful, of course. But we were more successful than we thought possible this month. We brought our family back together. Even the ones we thought long gone.' Mum says this in the same kind of voice you might use if you were pointing out a rainbow in the sky – all happiness and wonderment.

I don't know who I admire more. Mirabelle and Temmie for resurrecting themselves, Senara and Kerra for standing up to their mother, or my aunts and my mum for going full-scale fantastic.

'Halloween!' Aunt Flissie exclaims, swinging into the living room and grinning at Mirabelle. 'This year, I can help with the party instead of just showing up in the middle of it.'

'Oh,' I say, as I finally understand why Mirabelle has always been so keen to organise the Halloween party every year: Halloween marks the end of October when Aunt Flissie returns home! No wonder Mirabelle is so particular about her party – she's not throwing it for herself or her friends, it's how she welcomes her mum home.

'And, hey, Mirabelle, I was thinking maybe we could go away *together*,' Aunt Flissie adds. 'Not in October. And on the same map.'

'Yeah,' Mirabelle says shyly.

My heart does a little hop for them.

'Oh, but it's too late for costumes!' Mum exclaims.

'Costumes?' Kerra echoes, sounding like an alien adjusting to Earth.

'Come on,' Mirabelle says, 'let's see what we can conjure without any magic.'

Mirabelle usually cares so much about the details. But this year, she doesn't care about perfection at all. She's happy to just dig around among my aunts' clutter. Not as happy as Kerra, though, who pulls out each bit of junk as if it's a marvel to show to her sister. We leave them to it.

'I bet you can't wait for ordinary life again,' Mirabelle says. She's teasing me but it's not mean.

'Yeah,' I admit, 'I want to be able to leave the house, walk around like normal and not leave a trail of destruction behind me.' I glance at Mirabelle, who, when it mattered, did finally leave the house.

Our house. In the fading away of magic, Number 15 was restored to its normal spot on Pendragon Road. When I look out the window now, I see streetlights and cars instead of endless ocean.

'You, um, you're a really good witch, you know,' I say. 'You make cool stuff. You rock it.'

'I know.' She inspects her nails. They are long and sharp and black, and I think that might be Senara's doing. There's not a single chip in the polish.

'I don't rock it,' I add.

'Not yet, little cuz. But you will. You've got to find the thing that will help you get through the Octobers to remind you who you are when the power hits. And you've got to find something to get you through the rest of the year, too.'

I realise now that planning her epic Halloween party

for when her mum came back home helped Mirabelle get through October.

'Mirabelle?'

'Yeah, Clem?'

'Did I . . . actually do anything? With the whole sword thing?'

Mirabelle rolls her eyes but smiles at the same time. 'I know you can feel self-conscious, Clem, but just . . . don't.'

'But did I end October?'

'October always has to end,' Mirabelle says. 'Aunt Connie's hourglass shows us that.' She offers me a hand. 'So, are we going to do this? Show these Morgans the Merlyn way? Throw a party they'll never forget?' The way she says 'we' makes me glow inside, like a pumpkin stuffed with magic.

'Yes,' I say.

'We have to go big or . . . gourd home,' Mirabelle says.

I stare at her and another realisation about my cousin clicks into place. 'Is a gourd . . . a pumpkin?' I check. 'Are you . . . punning?'

'I am the Hallo-*queen*,' she replies, straight faced. 'I know, my jokes are seedy.'

'You didn't.'

'I've got lots more *pun*-kins where that came from.'

'No, Mirabelle.'

'Don't *squash* the fun,' she says.

'I thought you were the only one who wasn't embarrassing,' I say, tugging my hand free and moving further away from her.

'Aw, getting all *mushy*, are you?'

'You are the worst.'

'We can *pumpkin-patch* it up . . .' she says, reaching across the corridor to grab me.

'No!' I shriek, protesting the puns but not the cuddle.

'Hosting a Halloween party is the best bit of my whole entire life,' Mirabelle says. 'Of course I know all the Halloween puns!'

***

Compared to previous Halloween parties, the decorations aren't very good. The aunts dig around and bring up some non-magical junk. Aunt Flissie shows Aunt Connie how to blow up a balloon. Aunt Connie can't get the hang of 'these humanmade nonsenses' so they keep popping, but every time a balloon does pop, they both laugh, which is worth hearing.

The food isn't October-great either. But Aunt Connie gathers up all the old, gnarly vegetables that she can find and brews up a soup using a familiar, battered, old tin pot, which might have once had its glory days as cauldron.

And of course, our costumes aren't the best. Mum finds me an old orange sheet and together, we 'style' it into a pumpkin. Mirabelle says that she's obviously "too old and too cool" for an actual costume, but Senara gives her a slick flick of black eye-makeup which transforms her. Kerra doesn't seem to understand the point of fancy dress but enjoys her tinfoil-shiny cardboard sword.

'I think they're your best Halloween costumes ever,' Mum says as we gather in the living room and drink some apple juice from Temmie's now shrunken cauldron.

'Mum . . .'

'I mean it,' she insists. 'You made these costumes with love and care. And magic is the same. However it comes out, it comes from your heart.'

Mum is back in her beige dry-cleaning uniform, but she doesn't seem bothered. Her magical yellow dresses are gone for at least the next eleven months.

'But it's easier with magic, isn't it?' I ask.

'Yes, magic makes it easier. But witches treasure the making, all of it.'

Aunt Prudie talks non-stop, starting with Kerra. 'Welcome to the Merlyn household, young Morgan hag ally! Happy Halloween! We're celebrating the departure of our magic and hope for its return next year! The stars know!' And no one needs to translate for her at all.

Even Aunt Connie perks up when she does a headcount. 'Nine!' she crows. 'A coven of nine! Never have there been so many Merlyns.'

'Connie,' Mum says with gentle reproof.

'Yes, well . . . yes. Not all Merlyns by birth.'

'But you are both welcome here for as long as you care to stay,' Mum adds.

And so I let Kerra tell us about the things she's going to do now that she doesn't have to follow the Morgan way. Mirabelle leaves and I worry for a brief moment until I realise she's showing Senara our street from our freshly restored front garden.

'I don't know if I'll ever live this one down,' Mirabelle says, returning to stare at the floppy balloons and tin pot of soup, but she lets her mum pull her into the middle of the room to dance anyway.

There's no live band of goblins this year, just Mirabelle's phone, which she's finally dug up from the neighbours' garden and plugged into a single speaker, but it's enough.

By midnight, my Aunt Connie is dancing so wildly, I wonder if I can see sparks of magic flying from her heels. Aunt Flissie, Temmie and Mum join arms and dance in a circle, beaming at each other. Kerra and Senara have never really danced before, or at least, not like this, so Mirabelle and I show them some moves and, of course, Kerra has to learn a full routine and be the best at it.

I watch my coven dance – and these witches can really shake it – thinking that now is not the time to tell them, but I've got big non-magical plans for this family. We might not have magic for the rest of the year, or maybe ever again, but tomorrow is November and that means we get to start again.

There's a shiver of cold in the air. But that means Christmas is just around the corner, with the festive kind of magic.

'Hey,' Mirabelle says, flopping down next to me, so close that her shoulder smacks mine. 'You know it's ordinary all the way out from here, right?'

'Yeah.'

Mirabelle grins but then turns serious. 'But that . . .

could actually be a different kind of difficult. Because we are witches all the time, even without our power. And we are extraordinary. Even you. You get that too, right?'

I guess young hags can't know absolutely everything – but I know more than I started the month with.

'The stars know,' I say with a smile. 'And I know, too.'

ACKNOWLEDGEMENTS

There are almost too many thanks to be thanked. This book being made real is dream-come-true stuff and really, everyone I've ever met and everything I've ever read has been part of it.

Thank you to the brilliant Hazel Holmes for giving these witches a home. To Emma Roberts for helping me get what I could see in my mind's eye straight on the page (especially that wonky sword) and fixing all my terrible grammar. And thank you to everyone at UCLan Publishing, including illustrator Heidi Cannon and designer Amy Cooper.

To my incredible agent Jenny Savill (AKA the first and greatest of Jennys), thank you so much for guiding me from October to October, it truly is the best month and I was so lucky to meet you in one! The Merlyns would be lost without you.

Thanks to all my wonderful friends, especially: The Crowther Club: Alan Ward, Isley Lynn & Stevie Hopwood for all the tea, biscuits, retreats. You are the kindest and best folk. The Illustrious Eleven: Dyna, Kris and Mylo Barnes, Katie, Kevin, Evie & Mira Webber-Tsang for all of our amazing adventures from Hong Kong 'til forever. You are all blazing purple comets in my sky (I mean . . . you're wonderful). The WIE Collective: Becky Johnson, Frances Lane-Ho, Kate Gilbert and Holly Piper. Strongest and most brilliant of women. Special mention to Florence, Henry and Ottilie Piper and Rosa and Sid Lane-Ho for being the most fun, especially on the dancefloor. The Little Bears: Charlotte, Hazel, Sam and Russell Bailey, Emma Dennis-Edwards, Louie Keen & Jordana for your inspiring creativity. Sarah 'Little Teapot' Dacombe, Hannah 'My life would suck without you' Gumbrill-Ward, 'Knockout' Nina Pottell and Keara 'are you kidding me, five stars?' Fulton – thank you, I love you, let's get lunch.

To all of the amazing teachers and schools, theatre folk, all the lovely people in E17 and everyone at Abney Park that I've had the privilege of working with, thank you for your time, energy and support (especially talented young Mousetrappers: Farah, Amy, Erin, Darcy, Dylan, Krystal, Hodan, Jesmine, Nelly, Tilly and so many more). An important thank you to our childcare providers too, especially Sharon and her team, because 'the revolution cannot happen without childcare' (Hot Brown Honey).

To Katie Webber Tsang a particularly major thank you for so much but most especially for the hike along the Dragon's Back in Hong Kong which started it all. You are the kindest and best of writers and friends.

Thank you to all my own aunts, none of whom is Merlyn-level bananas but all amazing: Vicki, Caroline, Andrea, Lesley and Sue.

And to all my cousins, especially Prue and Fliss for being so generous with the outright theft of their names. And to the next generation of cousins: Kit, Ziggy, Zeffie and Clem (an excellent name), a cousin's cuddle for you all.

And to my own nieces and nephew: Margot, Sidney, Madelief, Elise and Thomas (like Arthur, the token boy). You are all extraordinary little people and I love watching you grow.

To my Dutch family: Oma Yvonne, Opa Wim, Roos and Bimmer, dankjewel. It is an honour to be your 'cold' sister/ daughter. Thank you for your patience as I repeatedly fail to learn Dutch.

To my beloved grandparents, Grandad Tony and Nanna Thelma, who always had faith I would write stories. And Nanny Paddy and Grandpa Colin – your warmth, humour, generosity and storytelling have inspired me more than you could ever know. I tried to pull out the big puns. (And used old puns instead of current puns!)

Thank you to my mum, Jo, and dad, Martin, for absolutely everything but especially for instilling in me from an early age the power of a family coven and that words were the way forward for me. To my favourite sister Kate (and Pete too). Sisters are something special and you are an actual angel. I'm still sorry for stabbing you with a pencil that time.

To Maarten, who is patient when I am not, sensible when I'm silly and kind when I'm cross, thank you for the life we've made together. There aren't really enough words but I love you and I know how lucky I am.

And finally thank you to my own young hags – Matilde, who was so tiny when I sprinted through the first draft of this story and is now the most outrageous toddler. And Lyra, who was not even dreamed of but has cackled her way through edits on my lap. My girls, you make me believe in magic.

© Jack Barnes

IF YOU LIKE THIS
YOU'LL LOVE . . .

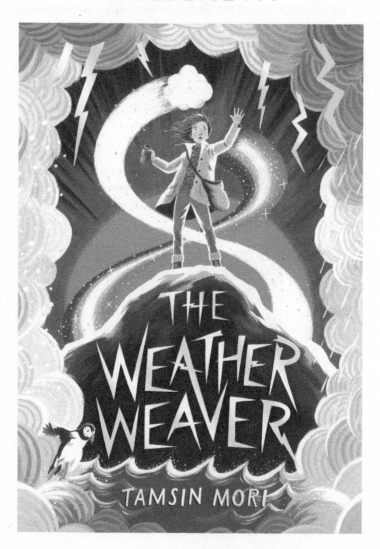

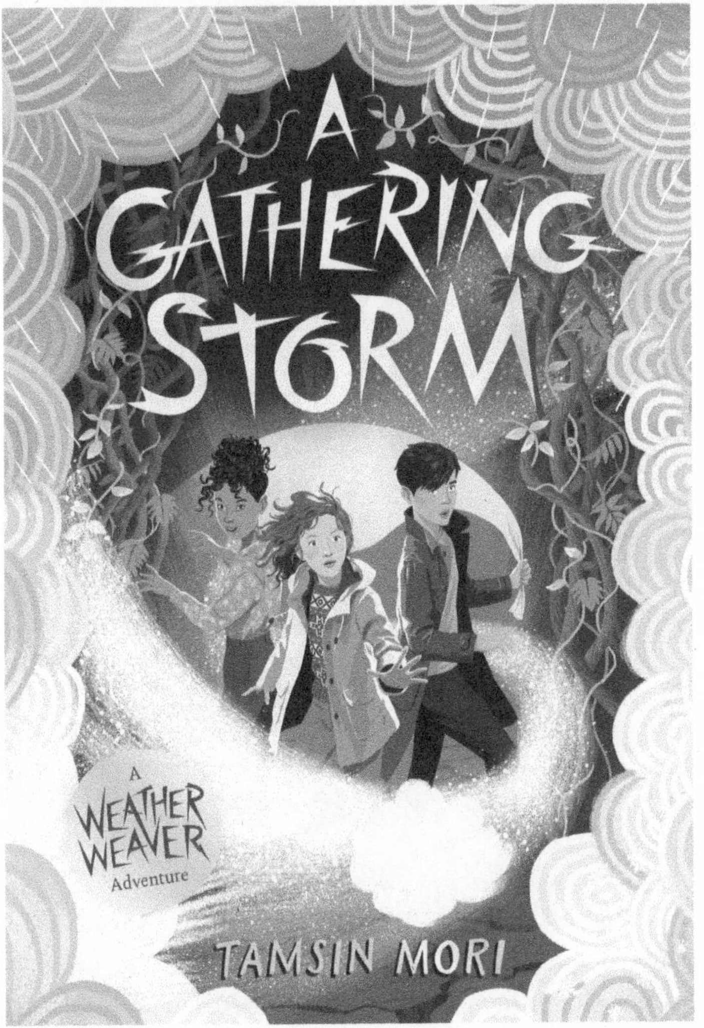
A GATHERING STORM
A WEATHER WEAVER Adventure
TAMSIN MORI

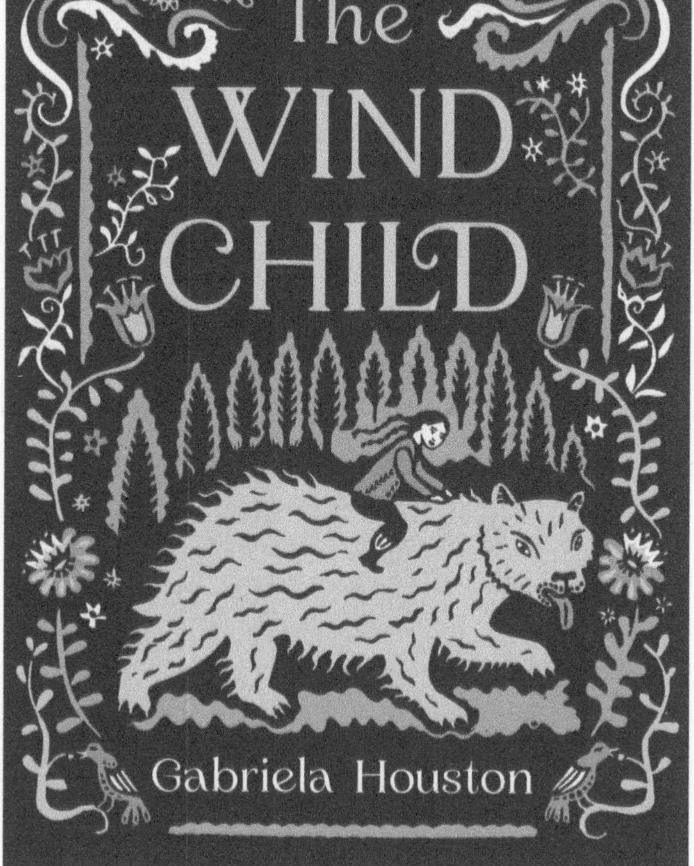
How far would you go to
save someone you love?
The
WIND
CHILD
Gabriela Houston

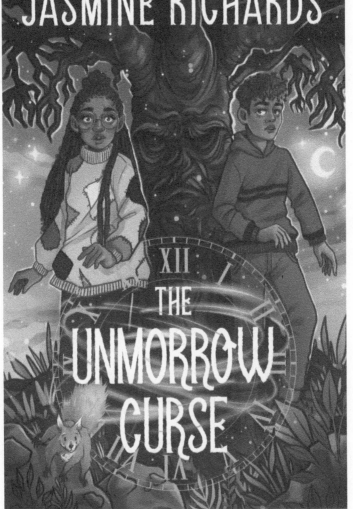

HAVE YOU EVER WONDERED
HOW BOOKS ARE MADE?

UCLan Publishing is an award winning independent publisher specialising in Children's and Young Adult books. Based at The University of Central Lancashire, this Preston-based publisher teaches MA Publishing students how to become industry professionals using the content and resources from its business; students are included at every stage of the publishing process and credited for the work that they contribute.

The business doesn't just help publishing students though. UCLan Publishing has supported the employability and real-life work skills for the University's Illustration, Acting, Translation, Animation, Photography, Film & TV students and many more. This is the beauty of books and stories; they fuel many other creative industries! The MA Publishing students are able to get involved from day one with the business and they acquire a behind the scenes experience of what it is like to work for a such a reputable independent.

The MA course was awarded a Times Higher Award (2018) for Innovation in the Arts and the business, UCLan Publishing, was awarded Best Newcomer at the Independent Publishing Guild (2019) for the ethos of teaching publishing using a commercial publishing house. As the business continues to grow, so too does the student experience upon entering this dynamic Masters course.

www.uclanpublishing.com
www.uclanpublishing.com/courses/
uclanpublishing@uclan.ac.uk